MURDER ON

SUGAR ISLAND

KILL OR DIE QUICKLY
AT THIS MYSTERIOUS
NORTHERN HIDEAWAY

BY MICHAEL CARRIER

Selected as a Notable Publication

You will note that there has been a change to the cover of this book—
a golden emblematic seal indicating that this book has been selected by the
Upper Peninsula Publishers and Authors Association as a
Notable Publication.
We thank them for this recognition.

A number of very wonderful people helped me prepare this book for
publication. Each of them contributed significantly. Thank you Steve W., Evie,
Meredith, and Charity. And special thanks to George and Gay.

MURDER

ON

SUGAR ISLAND

BY
MICHAEL CARRIER

GREENWICH VILLAGE INK

An imprint of Alistair Rapids Publishing

Grand Rapids, MI

MURDER ON SUGAR ISLAND

Published 2013 by Greenwich Village Ink, an Imprint of Alistair Rapids Publishing, Grand Rapids, MI.

For additional information (and sometimes puzzles) visit the JACK website at http://www.greenwichvillageink.com

Author can be emailed at mike.jon.carrier@gmail.com.

ISBN: 978-1-936092-19-2(trade pbk) 1-936092-19-0
Printed in the United States of America

Library of Congress Cataloging-in-Publication Data

Carrier, Michael.
MURDER ON SUGAR ISLAND / by Michael Carrier. 1st ed.
ISBN: 978-1-936092-19-2 (trade pbk. : alk. paper)
1. Art Heist 2. Thriller 3.Murder 4. Burglary 5. Detective. 6. Michigan's Upper Peninsula. 7. New York

Preface

MURDER ON SUGAR ISLAND (SUGAR) is part two of the "Getting to Know Jack" series. The first part of the series is entitled JACK AND THE NEW YORK DEATH MASK (JACK). Two of the three main characters of SUGAR (Jack and Kate Handler) were introduced in JACK.

In short, Jack is a retired Chicago homicide detective and former Army Ranger. Currently he works in private security, often operating on the fringes of the law. His wife (Beth) was murdered when their daughter (Kate) was a baby.

Kate presently works in New York City as a homicide detective. Whenever Kate has a situation that stumps her, she enlists her father's help.

Other JACK characters that re-emerge in SUGAR are Roger Minsk (AKA Roger Burnside), an active Secret Service agent with whom Jack occasionally works; former First Lady Allison Fulbright; and Reginald (Reg) Black. In JACK, Reg was shot during a successful rescue attempt to free Kate from the hands of abductors.

DISCLAIMER: MURDER ON SUGAR ISLAND is not a true story. It is work of fiction. All characters, names, situations, and occurrences are purely the product of my imagination. Any resemblance to actual events, or persons (living or dead), is totally coincidental.

Michael Carrier holds a Master of Arts degree from New York University, and has worked in private security for over two decades.

Chapter 1—The Murder

Alex heard him coming. He thought at first it was Red.

But when Alex detected that the strides were too long and too loud to be those of a fourteen-year-old boy, he waited until his visitor emerged through the stand of evergreens that separated the resort from the fishing pier, and then casually glanced back over his shoulder to see who was approaching.

Recognizing his visitor, he disgustedly muttered, "Now that's the last person I wanted to see tonight."

Alex chose not to face or greet his visitor. His innate old-country stubbornness dictated that he avoid acknowledging the man's presence for as long as possible.

Maybe he'll just go away if I ignore him, he reasoned.

Alex breathed in deeply, relishing the cool breeze blowing in from the St. Mary's River. He recalled the many times throughout the years when he'd walk along the riverbank, or out onto the pier where he tied his fishing boats, and there absorb the nuanced scents of life on Sugar Island.

It seemed the older he got, and the larger his resort grew, the greater the pressures he bore. On warm nights such as this, he would often carry a small aluminum rocking chair out to his favorite spot. There he would allow the lights of Sault Ste. Marie to put into perspective all the problems of his day.

That's what he had intended for this evening—to sit at the end of the pier, while his mind drifted gently downstream with the river.

Alex had no idea why this man was coming to visit him. He just wished it weren't happening.

The man was taller than most, and much taller than Alex. So when he walked up beside him and put his left hand firmly on his shoulder, Alex felt dwarfed.

"Alex, my friend," the man said, "this is *not* how I wanted it to turn out."

Surprised by the visitor's harsh comment, Alex turned his head toward him and exclaimed in an inquiring fashion, "Excuse me?"

"You've not been very helpful to my friends," the man said. "If it were up to me, I would let it pass. But I don't have a choice about it now."

The man then quickly stepped behind Alex but kept a vise-like grip on his shoulder. Using his free hand, he cocked the hammer of a .22 caliber revolver, with a four-inch barrel plus a suppressor, and pressed it against the back of Alex's neck.

A chill seized Alex as he suddenly realized his last sensation on earth would be that of cold steel tingling the nerve endings right beneath his graying hairline.

His mind raced at fast-forward speed: *My God! I'm going to die! Why didn't I marry? Why didn't I at least bring some relatives over from Greece—people to help run the resort I built? What will become of it? And Red—what about Red?*

"Why are you doing this? Surely we can …" he began to plead.

But the tall man said nothing.

Instead, a small flash of light and a muted "pop" shattered the stillness of the autumn evening. Alex's head jerked back slightly when the Long Rifle hollow-point round exploded his brain stem. His fingers stiffened and quivered as he fell face forward to the moist earth of the river's bank—his locked knees not bending as he dropped.

But while Alex couldn't process the sound of the shot that was killing him—Red did hear it.

And Red also heard the second pop a few seconds later, when the shooter put a round through the right temple of the dying man as he lay twitching on the ground.

The fourteen-year-old freckle-faced boy had stopped by to clean the boats and to hang out with his friend—Alex. Red did this almost every night during the resort season.

This time, however, he had arrived just in time to see a familiar figure approach his friend from behind and shoot him.

Red was neither large nor small for his age. He was, however, in amazing physical shape. That might seem surprising, given that he survived entirely on what food he could scrounge up.

Most of the time Red lived in a lean-to he had constructed from scavenged pieces of abandoned nearby hunting and fishing cabins. But when the weather turned cold, he would leave his unheated home and take up residence in various summer cottages on the island. It was not yet that time of year.

Red was regarded by many as a legend. Cottage owners knew that he might be moving in while they were gone, but most didn't mind. Some would even leave food for him.

As repayment, Red would stockpile wood for their stove or fireplace and make sure that he left a cottage cleaner than he found it. Because he was very handy, Red would make small repairs, such as adjusting mal-fitting doors and patching leaky roofs. Sometimes a cottage owner would even leave a list of tasks for him. In a sense, Red served as their unpaid caretaker.

Red had bonded with Alex. He would show up at night to make certain that all refuse was removed from the fishing boats, and would then wash them all down on the inside.

And every night, on Alex's orders, the resort's cook would wrap up some food and place it in a small red and white cooler. The cook would then tuck the cooler under the back seat of the boat nearest the riverbank.

When Red had finished his tasks he would remove the food and set the cooler on the pier. It was the signal that the boats were ready for the next day. Now, with the season virtually over, Alex would be storing the boats. And Red would be out of a job. That fact weighed on Alex right up to the point the pea-sized projectile paralyzed his brain.

The flash of light in the darkness and the sound of suppressed gunfire startled the boy, who was crouching with his dog in the underbrush only thirty feet away.

Red was adept at slipping around undetected, so it was not surprising that neither Alex nor the shooter suspected he was hiding close by.

Red didn't talk. Actually, the boy couldn't talk. A few years earlier he had so severely damaged his voice box that all he could do was squeeze out indiscernible sounds. While his dog was able to understand him, other people could not.

When visiting with Alex, Red relied on a simple set of signs and sounds they had developed to communicate with each other. Alex was fond of both Red and his dog, a large golden retriever whom Alex addressed simply as "Dog."

The smell of spent gunpowder wafted over to where Red was hiding. He hugged his dog tightly to calm him. Red knew the shooter would kill them as well, were Dog to give their location away.

Shock blocked Red's tears—for now.

Red watched the killer look out into the darkness, checking to see if his deed had been detected.

Once reasonably convinced no one had seen him shoot Alex, the tall man set the gun down on a picnic table next to the body, peeled off the latex gloves he had worn, and tossed them on top of the pistol. He then turned away from the body and *long-strode* his way toward a tool shed, which was located halfway up the hill toward the rear deck of the resort. Alex had ordered the shed to be left unlocked at night for Red's benefit. The killer was looking for a trash bag to transport the murder weapon.

As soon as the killer disappeared into the shed, Red bolted toward the now still body of his friend. He dropped to his knees beside Alex. Thrusting his hands under the dead man's head to turn it, he felt the sticky warmth of wet blood. Red realized Alex was dead. He pulled his hands back quickly, and for a long moment he stared at them in the moonlight. He was shocked to see how brown blood looked under a full moon. And the smell. The pungent ferrous odor of wet blood—those two sensations gripped his emotions as he knelt silently beside his fallen friend.

Suddenly Red realized that he had very little time. He would mourn later. Right now he had to escape.

As he jumped to his feet he spotted the gun on the picnic table. Perhaps thinking that if he took the gun he would prevent the tall man from shooting him, he grabbed it.

Bolting back into the brush, Red headed toward his shelter deep in the woods. Dog followed close behind. It began to sink in. His tears mixed with snot as he ran faster and faster through the forest.

He was familiar with eluding capture. Ever since his parents died he had been forced to spend much of his life running and hiding. The authorities had attempted numerous times to place him in foster care, but he would always escape to his Sugar Island hideaway.

Even in the darkness, Red had no problem finding his way. When he reached the small spring-fed stream that passed between the resort and his destination, instead of merely jumping across it, he and Dog jumped into the water and ran upstream fifty yards.

They emerged from the creek on a lengthy patch of rock and then continued their getaway through the woods. Experience had taught Red that this could slow down any effort to follow him.

As he passed through the secret passageway that led into his mini-compound, he carefully brushed out the tracks behind him. Once inside his shelter, he quickly secured the door, snatched his sleeping bag, and pulled it into a dark corner. Sliding down the wall, he drew Dog into his arms, covered them both up, and convulsed in tears.

He then realized that he was still tightly gripping the gun that had killed his friend. With an angry flip of his wrist, he flung it across the floor. The weapon slammed forcefully against the far wall, dragging with it a hitchhiker—one of the killer's latex gloves glued to it by blowback blood.

After a few moments, Dog slid out from under the sleeping bag and assumed a defensive posture between Red and the shelter's entrance.

For several hours Red sat weeping. Frequently startled by forest sounds, he would snap his head up. A single shaft of mid-October moonlight cast an eerie streak across his floor, but it provided enough light to confirm that Dog still stood guard.

Sometime before sunrise, but after Red had finally succumbed to his fatigue, a loud voice pierced the calm.

"Hey, Red!"

Dog sounded a discreet warning growl. Red awoke and lunged forward to silence him before he could bark.

"Red! I know you can hear me. You've got something that belongs to me. That's *all* I'm after. Eventually, you'll have to give it up … might as well do it now. You know me—we're old buddies. Right? I promise not to hurt you, Red. I just want what's mine."

Chapter 2—Old memories come alive

"Dad, you'll never guess what happened."

Jack, not used to Kate expressing such exuberance over the phone, replied, "So, tell me, who's the lucky guy?"

Kate thought for a moment and then replied, "I guess that would be you."

"Hold on here—what's *that* mean?"

"Well, you are now the father of a bona fide resort mogul," Kate replied. "So, if there is a lucky guy in my life, it would have to be you. Right?"

"OK," Jack said. "Maybe you'd better slow down a bit and do some 'splainin.'"

"Uncle Alex, Mom's brother. He left me that resort. The one on Sugar Island."

"He died?"

"He did," Kate said. "Today, this afternoon, five hours ago, a courier, or some court officer. Actually I think he was just representing Uncle Alex's attorney. Anyway, he came to my precinct and handed me an envelope. He asked me to open and read it in his presence. It stated that I was the sole beneficiary of Uncle Alex's estate. Apparently I am his only living blood relative, at least in this country."

Jack reflected for a moment. Beth, Jack's wife, was very close to her brother Alex. And, as far as Jack could recall, Beth and Alex were the sole members of the Garos family living in America. Jack recalled the wonderful times he enjoyed at the northern Michigan resort. He and

Beth spent their summer vacations with Alex during their two-year marriage.

After Beth's funeral, Jack never heard from Alex again. Beth's brother had made it clear that he would always hold her death against Jack.

That seemed only reasonable to Jack, because he too blamed himself for his wife's death. After all, the bullet that struck her down was intended for him. And had he done a better job, Beth would not have been killed—or so Jack reasoned.

"My God," Jack finally said. "After all these years. …You know, I have struggled with Alex … it's been tough. I've always wanted you to get to know him. But he never wanted to forgive me. And I couldn't blame him. But he certainly loved that sister of his. And now it looks like he has transferred that love to you. I only wish I had tried harder to communicate with him. But he was *so* bullheaded …"

"And, of course, you're *not* bullheaded? Right?"

"You know what I mean," Jack said, obviously searching for the right words. "He was old-country. As far as he was concerned, I was the usurper who stole his sister—and then got her killed. And, he was mostly right to feel that way. I could not have been more responsible for her death than if I had pulled the trigger myself."

"Stop punishing yourself. We both know that's not true."

"Oh, my sweet daughter, it is true. It was my job to look out for her. That night … had I just been a little more careful … I knew I had enemies out there. Cops make enemies—and I had more than my share. Alex tolerated me, but he never really accepted me. Then, when your mother passed, his resentment turned to hate. And I could never blame him for that. He was a good man—a *hard-working* man. He built that resort up into quite a place—even back then. You went there as a baby, you know."

"I did?" Kate asked. "I don't remember it. And I don't remember him, either."

"You wouldn't," Jack said. "You would have been … just shy of two. I remember how excited Alex was about having a niece. At first it looked like he was about to accept me into his world—because of you. But that all ended when your mother died."

"Tell me, how should I do this? The lawyer handling the estate wants to meet with me as soon as possible to discuss the details. Is this normal?"

"I'm sure it is," Jack said. "You've got to find out exactly what it is you've inherited. You should be careful. You know, there could be back taxes, or all sorts of other problems. You need to consult a lawyer yourself, before you accept any responsibility for the property."

"Would you go with me?"

"Sure," Jack said. "You know I will do anything to spend some time with my daughter. Can you get off work?"

"I've got some vacation time coming."

"When are you planning to go up there?"

"I need to get some business in order here, but I think I can be ready by Friday," Kate replied. "I could fly into Chicago Friday evening, spend the night at your house, and we could drive up on Saturday. Would that work for you?"

"Sure," Jack said. "Do you have any idea just how long a drive that will be?"

"I Googled it," Kate chuckled. "Four hundred miles from your house."

"At least," Jack said. "But it's fairly straight up, once you hit I-75."

"I'll help you drive."

"Maybe," Jack chuckled.

Kate was well aware that her father would be unlikely to allow anyone but himself behind the steering wheel of his vehicle. She knew exactly how this would play out. She would arrive on Friday evening— probably between eight and nine. Her dad would pick her up at O'Hare, and drive her back to his condo. There they would talk until two a.m. Finally, they would go to bed.

The next morning, at seven o'clock, she would be awakened by the racket of her father's coffee grinder. She would begin the process of getting up, and around seven-thirty she would join him at his small breakfast table for a cup of very strong coffee. He would be on his second cup. He would be seated so that he could look out over Lake Michigan. His condo was on the twenty-fourth floor, so the view was incredible.

And then, between eight-thirty and nine o'clock, they would begin their journey. Of course, she would sleep until they were just about to cross the Mackinac Bridge—at which time she would make some comment about how beautiful the Great Lakes were.

"How did Alex die?" Jack asked. "Accident, or medical? Do you have any info on that?"

"He was murdered," Kate responded matter-of-factly.

Chapter 3—Murder she said

"Murdered!" Jack snarled. "You're kidding, of course?"

Kate genuinely enjoyed shocking her father. "No, I'm quite serious."

"Why did it take you so long to dump *that* on me?"

"I wanted you to make up your mind to go with me without that little detail influencing your decision. I knew if I told you your brother-in-law was shot in the head, twice, behind the resort, and that his body was unceremoniously deposited in the channel off his own pier, that you would cancel all your plans, no matter what, and help me solve the case. … Am I right?"

The introduction of intrigue totally captivated Jack's attention. "Is that what you have in mind—solving the murder?" he asked.

"Not necessarily, but do you have any idea how law enforcement functions up there?"

"Sugar Island, that's right off Sault St. Marie," Jack said. "Would it be City or County?"

Had Jack been given the luxury of time for research, he would have found that Sugar Island had never been annexed into the city limits. He did recall that during the period of time he had frequented the island, it was not part of the city proper. But he knew that things have a way of changing with time. Therefore, he posed the leading question, allowing his daughter to elucidate.

"Technically, Sugar Island falls under Chippewa County's jurisdiction," Kate replied. "But, the truth is that there is not actually any established police presence on the island.

"Get this. Ever since 9/11 Homeland Security has patrolled nearly twenty-four-seven. The primary reason for this is that there is nothing physically separating the Island from Canada except for a shallow channel—probably no more than a couple hundred feet wide. I've read that you can nearly walk across it with waders."

"Sounds like you've been doing some homework."

"A little Wikipedia," Kate said. "And, as soon as I heard that Uncle Alex was murdered, I made contact with the county sheriff up there to find out how the investigation was going. And then I did some Googling."

"And just how is the investigation going?" Jack asked.

"Here's the deal," Kate explained. "Like I said, Homeland Security does patrol the island, but it has no real authority in a situation like this. Unless someone reports a strange boat, or a swimmer in a wetsuit, they don't get involved. They do drive around in marked cars, which seems to provide a bit of a deterrent. But they really can't do much, aside from reporting something suspicious to the county.

"Then, if the county decides to send a deputy over to the island, the officers have to get in line for the ferry, just like everyone else. And rumor has it, as soon as the ferry operators spot a marked car headed for Sugar Island, they make a few calls to a network of people on the island, and those folks make a few more calls. By the time the patrol car reaches land, everyone on the island knows that cops are patrolling.

"The sheriff told me that about the only time they send a car over there is when someone dies. And when they do have to go there, they always return with a car full … sometimes they have to call for backup. He said that lately he's had a patrol car over there on a daily basis. But that's not the way it used to be."

"That must make for a bit of a Wild West scenario," Jack said.

"That's the impression I get," Kate replied.

"So, how's it going—the investigation? What's your gut telling you?"

"The sheriff said that it was ongoing. No real information. Not yet."

"But what sort of feeling did he leave you with? They are actively investigating. Right?"

"Oh yeah—without a doubt. I'd say they're giving it their best. But Sugar Island presents a challenge. Especially if the killer isn't a resident."

"How many people live there—on the island?"

"Six hundred, give or take," Kate answered.

"Good night! More than that reside in my building. Are you talking total residents, or just adults?"

"I'm not sure, but I think that's the total year-round population—six hundred people on a fifty-square-mile piece of real estate."

"Well," Jack said, after thinking for few moments. "If it was a local, then it shouldn't be too hard to get a handle on who might have wanted Alex dead—that population would make for an incredibly small suspect pool."

"That's where I planned to start," Kate said. "See who stood to profit."

"The money trail—follow the money. That's always a good place to look first."

"Alex was a fairly wealthy man—I think. Whoever wanted him dead might have engaged a professional ... if enough money were involved."

That comment gave Jack pause. If it was a professional hit, then he might be able to put out some feelers and see what he could find out. The connections he had made through the years as a shadowy private detective provided many channels for information.

Plus, it would not be common knowledge that Jack was related to the victim, so he might be able to get people to talk.

Kate knew that her father, himself a retired Chicago homicide detective, now contracted in the private sector, but she was not aware of the depths of his darker side.

"How long will you be able to spend up there?" Jack asked.

"I talked to my captain about it, and he said to do whatever I had to—take as much time off as I needed. Just as long as I would let him visit whenever he wanted. He was really good about it."

"Good old Captain Spencer. I thought he would have gone fishing by now—wasn't that the rumor?"

"It's actually more than rumor," Kate replied. "He's officially announced that he is going to take an early retirement. That's probably why he is so easy to work with these days. But, truthfully, he's always been pretty cool."

Jack knew and liked Captain Spencer. And he also appreciated the way Kate's boss looked out for her.

"Nothing wrong with a boss who likes you," Jack said. "I've had a couple of those myself.

"When your mother was killed, there were a couple of my superiors that helped me cope. I wouldn't have survived without them. You need people like that—people who have your back."

"That's Captain Spencer. He supports his people. I would not have moved up through the ranks without his help. There was even talk that we were sleeping together. That really annoyed me. But it didn't seem to bother him so much.

"Actually, I think he relished people thinking that about him. But the truth is he never acted inappropriately toward me—not one time."

"I heard that he viewed you as his protégée. But, I'm sure that your work warrants his good favor."

"I'd like to think I do a good job," Kate agreed. "And how long can you spare?"

"Well, let's see how it goes. Right now I'm a free man."

Just then Kate's phone signaled an incoming call.

"I've got to take this. It's from the UP. Maybe they've made an arrest. How cool would that be? I'll call you right back."

Chapter 4—The sheriff surprises Kate

"Hello. ... Yes, this is Kate."

Kate recognized the voice of the caller. It was that of Chippewa County Sheriff Conrad Northrup. While she had not yet met the man, she had already grown fond of him—probably because he seemed genuinely eager to help her. And, his deep cigarette-honed voice reminded her of her boss, Captain Spencer.

"Well, Miss Handler, are you still planning to head up this way?"

"I am. I was just on the phone with my father, and he's coming with me."

"Let's see," Sheriff Northrup said. "Your father would be the brother, or brother-in-law, of the deceased? Brother-in-law, I imagine. Right?"

"That's correct. Uncle Alex was my mother's brother."

"And your mother passed on twenty-six, twenty-seven years ago?"

"Twenty-eight. My mother passed away twenty-eight years ago—when I was just a baby."

"Well, I certainly look forward to meeting you ... and your father. Now, just what is it that your father does? Retired, I believe? I know *you* are a homicide detective—from New York City, no less. That's really impressive. I'm serious ... I talked to your captain, Captain Spencer, and he could not stop bragging you up. And he told me that you've got police work in your blood. Your father also is in law enforcement—homicide. I'm going to have to polish up on my techniques and procedures if I'm going to be entertaining a couple New York detectives."

"We don't look to be entertained," Kate told the sheriff.

While she suspected that he was spreading it on in order to reduce expectations, she also realized that the sheriff probably never ran into big-city homicide detectives, except over beers at a Vegas convention.

"Well, I understand that. But I'm sure you know that we are just simple country folk up here. And I do not want to disappoint you. Now, tell me a little bit about your father. Is he, or *was* he, a New York detective too?"

"Actually, my father is a retired Chicago homicide detective."

"Oh my God … then it's true!" Sheriff Northrup exclaimed. "Two big-city detectives—right here in the Soo. Well, wouldn't surprise me a bit if you two don't solve this murder before you get your bags unpacked."

"I'm sure that's not gonna happen," Kate replied. "But when it does get solved, I'm equally sure it will be your people who solve it. Dad and I are headed there to tie up some family matters. My uncle left the resort to me—in his will. I have to meet with the attorney to get that squared away. I have no idea what this will involve, or if I even want to accept the inheritance. I know nothing about running a resort."

"Oh, I think you'll want to check out your uncle's estate before you make any decisions like that. Your uncle was a very successful man, and that resort is quite the spread. Everyone in the area knows about it."

"Really?" Kate responded. "Did you know Uncle Alex?"

"I knew him—but not well. We had met on several occasions. It's just the nature of my job. I eventually get to know people like your uncle. Now don't get me wrong—your uncle was an upstanding member of the community … well respected. But he did serve alcohol at his establishment. And when a man sells booze, law enforcement always gets to know him—eventually."

"I understand," Kate replied. "But what about the resort. Who's running it right now?"

"No, no. I'm afraid it's not open. In fact, it might be some time before it can reopen. After all, it is a murder scene."

"That's news to me," Kate said. "I thought Uncle Alex was killed on his pier, and his body dumped into the river. That's not the case?"

"That's partly so," the sheriff replied. "But the actual confrontation may have begun inside the bar—after closing. And your uncle was then forced to walk under his own power to the river, and there shot to death. He fell to the ground, bled extensively from his head wounds, and then was dragged out on the pier and dumped into the water.

"It is likely that the killer, or killers, thought his body would be swept away by the current, but the water in the river is so low these days that he merely got tangled up in the pier's undergirding and stayed there. That's where we recovered his body—from right beneath the pier. It appeared the killer might have been distracted by something, because he pushed your uncle's body off the pier on the upstream side. If he'd used his head, he could have put the body in one of the fishing boats and shoved it off."

"You're thinking it might've started in the resort? Maybe a robbery gone bad?"

"That's one angle we're pursuing. After all, in cases like this, that's how it usually turns out—money or sex."

"So, when Dad and I arrive, are we going to be able to inspect the scene of the crime?"

"It'll be fine with my office. But I am starting to hear rumblings that I might lose this case. It seems Homeland Security wants the FBI involved. And if that happens, they're not gonna be putting up with this old-country sheriff. ... or even big-city homicide detectives. But we'll just have to wait and see what happens in that regard."

"Homeland Security?" Kate muttered. That was not what she wanted to hear. "Why would they be interested? And what could this possibly have to do with the FBI?"

"Beats me. But DHS is all over the island, and they get just as bored as me. Maybe they want to look like they're doing something besides fishing."

"Sounds to me like they might be fishing, all right. But the FBI?"

"Yeah, I know. But it'll be good for the local restaurants. When do you and your father plan to get up here?"

"We're leaving from Chicago on Saturday. After we get settled in, I'll give you a call."

"Well, even if I've been relieved of my responsibilities with respect to your uncle's case, I'll still be happy to meet with you and bring you up to speed as to what I know. … Unless, of course, the Feds stick a gag order on me. No matter what, I look forward to meeting you and your father, and we'll go on from there. I'm sure I can be of some assistance to you. If nothing more than helping you get acclimated to the environment.

"You know, this Sugar Island, it is a totally unique place. I guarantee that you have never experienced anything quite like it before."

"That's what I've heard. I'll call when we arrive."

* * *

"… Dad, tell me I didn't miss the big bridge."

"You got some good rest. I'm sure you needed it. But I did get a surprise for you."

Chapter 5—Kate misses bridge, but not the fudge

"How long did I sleep?"

"You nodded off in Gaylord, and never made a peep until now."

"Where are we?"

"We're just outside Sault Ste. Marie."

"I must have been really tired. Can't believe I slept through it—I was looking forward to crossing the Mackinac Bridge … and chatting with you, of course."

Kate was embarrassed and disappointed. She had planned to stay awake the whole trip this time. "At least I didn't drool," she consoled herself, as she swiped across her mouth with the back of her right hand.

"I'm pretty sure you enjoyed your nap."

"You're right—I must've needed the rest. Tell me I didn't snore. And, what's this? Is this the surprise?" Kate asked, picking up and unwrapping a block of Mackinac Fudge. "When did you get this?"

"While you were dozing, I stopped in Mackinaw City and picked it up."

"And I never woke up?"

"Not until just now."

"I guess it just felt good not to be working. And, thanks for the fudge—it's the best. And so are you."

"Your mom loved it too—it was like a tradition. And she always fell asleep when I was driving … you must take after her."

"You never get sleepy, do you—not while you're behind the wheel? And I'll bet you've never received a traffic ticket?"

"Of course I have."

"I don't believe it. Maybe a parking ticket."

"Speeding … but it has been a while. How do you want to handle this? Do you want to go straight to the sheriff's office? How did you leave it with him?"

"He's looking for us today. What time is it?

"It is exactly two-thirty Chicago time."

"Now what is that in real time?"

"Three-thirty Michigan time."

"I'll give him a call," Kate said, retrieving her cell phone from her purse and turning it on.

"You didn't want to have your captain wake you up?"

"He wouldn't be calling me when I'm on vacation."

"So, this is a vacation, is it?"

"You know what I mean. I'm spending some special time with my father. I didn't want to get it interrupted."

"It does feel good to get away from it all for a while."

"Where's the county seat? Is it around here?"

"Downtown Sault Ste. Marie, I think."

"That's handy," Kate said as she called the sheriff's office.

"Sheriff Northrup—this is Kate Handler. … Hi. My father and I are just arriving. Would this be a good or bad time? … Great. We would like to hit the ground running. So that would be wonderful. See you in … let me check with my father. He might want to get a cup of coffee first or check in the hotel. Hang on just a sec.

"What do you think? Shall we run over now, or would you like to get a bite to eat first?"

"If the sheriff is in right now, and if he will see us, let's go for it."

"That's what I think too," Kate said, removing her hand from over her phone.

"Sheriff, Dad and I would like to run over right now, if that works for you. … Okay, we'll see you in … what do you think?" Kate asked, looking at her father.

Jack flashed a hand of fingers twice.

"Ten minutes, or so. We'll be there in about ten minutes."

Kate then hesitated. The sheriff was trying to say something to her without anyone in his office overhearing.

Chapter 6—Hello, Jack, meet the Department of Homeland Security

"I'm sorry," Kate said. "Could you repeat that? … Okay, I see. … Would it still be appropriate for my father and me to stop in? … Great, we'll be discreet. … And we do appreciate this courtesy. … See you in ten."

"What was that all about?" Jack asked.

"The sheriff's got company—*lots* of it."

"What sort of company?"

"DHS."

"You said that they might get involved," Jack replied. "Is that what's happening?"

"The sheriff couldn't talk, but that would be my guess."

"And he's still okay with our stopping by?"

"Said he was. I don't think that he much likes those guys. They act like they own Sugar Island, but they don't seem to do much. Anyway, that's his opinion."

"I get the picture. Could be he's just a little bit jealous. I would guess that most DHS officers are half his age, and make more … plus a hefty pension. I'm looking forward to meeting this sheriff of yours."

"I don't know much about him. Except that he probably smokes too much—he's got one of those voices. Do you really think these DHS guys are overpaid?"

"No one who puts his life on the line is ever overpaid," Jack said. "Not when a guy who strikes out half the time makes twenty million. Actually, I'm just guessing at how much one of these fellows makes. I suppose it would depend on education, experience, and type of assignment. At any rate, they are federal employees, and guys like a county sheriff have a natural aversion to federal employees. This has all the markings of a classic turf war."

"That's how I see it," Kate said. "If DHS takes this sort of interest in it, the FBI can't be far behind. I'm a little surprised that the sheriff would allow us to stop in with all this going on."

"He probably welcomes the distraction. If we're there, he might think it'll make them back off a bit."

"Holy cow! Look at all those white cars. One, two, three, four."

"Five and six," Jack chimed in, pointing to the rear of the sheriff's office.

"I wonder how fuel-efficient those Tahoes are?" Kate chuckled.

"I would prefer a Tahoe to those golf carts they use in Europe—you need a dozen of them to set up a decent roadblock."

"Yeah, but there the streets are about two feet wide, with lots of hills and buildings."

"You be sure to ask one of those DHS officers about his gas mileage," Jack said smiling, as he got out of the vehicle. "I'm sure they're not very concerned about it."

"I'll bet you're Kate Handler," Sheriff Northrup said, stepping through the door to welcome his guests even before they entered the building. "And you're Jack, this lovely young lady's father. C'mon in. I'm hoping you can help me make some sense of this."

Chapter 7—Sheriff Northrup
plays his games

The sheriff had stationed one of his deputies at the door and instructed him to flash a signal when he spotted Jack's vehicle because he did not want the DHS to intercept his guests.

"Nice to meet you, Sheriff," Jack said, reaching out to shake the sheriff's hand.

"Glad to make your acquaintance, Jack. I understand that you're a retired Chicago homicide detective."

Jack was stunned by the sheriff's imposing stature. *This guy looks like Will Pope, only much, much larger,* he thought. *And, as Kate suggested, I can certainly detect cigarettes in his past.*

Will Pope was Brenda's boss on "The Closer," one of the television programs Kate had coaxed her father into watching when he visited her in New York.

"Mostly I'm Kate's proud father," Jack replied, ushering his daughter through the door ahead of him.

He couldn't help but wonder how difficult it would be for a guy this big to find uniforms that fit.

The sheriff was the tallest man in memory to have entered the Chippewa County Courthouse. While in his mid-sixties, he was still in amazing condition for a man of any age.

A consummate outdoorsman who was particularly fond of fishing, the sheriff had physically and numerically exhausted his list of potential fishing buddies, largely because he would always insist on hiking miles on every trip—forever in search of the perfect fishing spot.

"And proud you must be," Sheriff Northrup said. Jack observed that all the while the sheriff was talking to him, his eyes focused on Kate. "Her boss, Captain Spencer, could not say enough good things about this daughter of yours. I'm expecting her to become New York's next commissioner."

"Not gonna happen," Kate said. "But it's real nice of you to say that."

"Well, I certainly think it could, with a man like Captain Spencer running interference for you. You are obviously doing everything right. It is so refreshing to have the two of you visiting our humble city. I just wish it was under different circumstances. Your father and I might do some fishing. If things were different ..."

"Perhaps another time," Jack interrupted. "I would love to go fishing up here again. But right now we need to get some answers about the inheritance ... and then there is the matter of Alex's death."

"We will certainly have to deal with that nasty matter before planning any fishing trips," the sheriff agreed.

"That's what brought all these fellows up here as well," Sheriff Northrup added, pointing through the glass door toward all the DHS vehicles. "Your Uncle Alex has become quite the center of attention."

"Do they really think that his murder is a matter of interest for Homeland Security?" Jack asked.

"Hard to say," the sheriff said, holding the door to his inner office open, and gesturing for Jack and Kate to enter. "Sometimes I think they just like to hear themselves talk, ... and to get in my way. Why don't we retire to my little office? We can talk better in here."

Jack and Kate did as the sheriff suggested and walked through the glass-paneled wood doorway, while the sheriff held it open for them. Once all three were inside, the sheriff closed and latched the door, responding to an officious DHS officer with an equally officious smile that could easily have been mistaken for a smirk.

"I've never seen anything quite like this before," the sheriff said, as he pulled an uncomfortable-looking wooden chair up for Kate, followed by an identical one for Jack. "Well, these just might be the worst chairs you've ever sat in, but they beat anything on the other side of the door," he said chuckling, as he glared out at the DHS officers buzzing about. "At least we can have a little peace and quiet in here.

"Forgive me if I don't introduce you to these rodents. That way we can pretend like we're doing something significant, and maybe they will leave us alone for a little while. If nothing else, we'll drive them a little more nuts."

Jack was busy trying to size the sheriff up. *He sure seems like my kind of guy. Or, maybe he's just a very good actor*, Jack concluded.

* * *

"Okay, Kate, fire away," the sheriff said. "What can I do for you?"

Chapter 8—Sheriff Northrup shares info

"Sheriff Northrup, …" Kate began.

The sheriff dipped his head to peer over his slightly dirty glasses and began talking to her. Even sitting, the sheriff was almost as tall as most men standing.

"Kate, I apologize for interrupting, but I want to be sure it's okay if I call you two by your first names—Kate, and Jack? I'm hoping that's not too informal."

Both Jack and Kate smiled.

"I think we need to relax protocol here," the sheriff continued. "My first name is Conrad, but everyone who knows me calls me Sheriff. I would like you folks to call me Sheriff. We'll skip the first and last name—just Sheriff. Is that okay if we skip the formalities? Is that good?"

"Sheriff," Kate then said, completing the question she had begun to ask. "Are they serious about my uncle's murder? That it is somehow a matter for Homeland Security?"

"Well, if you ask any of these happy little fellows," the sheriff said, gesturing in the direction of the DHS officers but not looking at them, "they will certainly make you think it is. But I doubt any one of them ever investigated a murder before. Fresh outta college, if you know what I mean. This is all new to them. They're more at home chasing little kids back across the channel to Canada. They don't have any idea what they're doing—at least, that's this old lawman's considered opinion. Now I'm not saying I've investigated a lot of similar crimes … and certainly not any as problematic as this one."

The sheriff then paused for a few seconds. "But, to be perfectly honest, I can't really blame these fellows. Had my investigation progressed a little better than it did, perhaps they would not have been so quick to pounce on it."

Jack was always suspicious of a person who used that figure of speech: "to be perfectly honest." It made him wonder where imperfection left off and perfection kicked in.

"What have you got so far?" Jack asked, glancing out of the glass in the door at three DHS officers who were obviously trying to size up the sheriff's two new guests. "Anyone—or anything—shouting at you?"

"No, not really. For a time we thought we might have something. The victim had fired one of his assistant managers a few months earlier—accused him of theft and doing drugs. But he never filed charges. For a while, it looked like he was going to court for wrongful termination. But, it turned out that the manager had actually been stealing … and his drug use had become obvious. So, eventually it all just went away."

"Revenge? That's usually a pretty good motive," Kate interjected.

"Yeah, on the surface it did sound plausible. But you would have to have seen this fellow—the druggie. Then the way your uncle was murdered—and dragged out onto the pier. Not this fellow's style—nor within his physical capabilities," the sheriff said, chuckling just a bit. "Besides, he had an airtight alibi—he was busy being buried at the time of the murder. He died from an overdose just before Alex was killed."

"Really? Could it be his friends did it seeking revenge?" Jack asked.

"I considered that … at first. But this drug addict had spent the previous month, after he got himself fired, higher than a kite. He lived with his mom, and she says he seldom even got out of bed. He was a real mess. Besides, it appears the poor fellow didn't have any friends. That theory still has some appeal, but it really looks like a dead end to me. I'll be happy to let you take a look at my file, and you can judge for yourself."

"That would be great," Jack said. "I'm wondering what it is that makes the DHS think that they should get involved? Is there anything *specific* that they're looking at?"

"Well, I suppose you could say that there are elements of this case that are somewhat suspicious."

"Such as?" Kate asked.

"Well, for one thing, when we went through the resort's records, we found that there was indeed a number of questionable guests who registered from time to time. One group would arrive at the resort, without a car. And there's nothing to suggest that they ever rented one. That got my attention. The thing is, usually anyone visiting Sugar Island arrives in a vehicle, and gets it transported by the ferry. But that was not the case with these guests. They checked in, three or four of them, stayed a week, and then checked out. In fact, this last time the group checked out the same day the victim, your uncle, was murdered."

"This time?" Jack asked. "You mean there was a pattern?"

"Might have been. Every few months, for some time, a similar group registered at the resort. Each time they stayed for a few days, never longer than a week, and then left together. No women—always just the men."

"And how long has this been going on?" Kate asked.

"Well, it's not easy to tell—not for certain. The resort's records were not always the best kept. However, about eighteen months ago, the pattern I described seems to have evolved. The first time there were three men—no women or vehicles. They registered together, and then they all checked out together, within the week. They made three such visits. The last one, like I said, just before Garos was killed."

"How'd they get around? And what'd they do while they were here?"

"Each morning they'd have breakfast in the restaurant and then seemed to hang out at the resort all day. Didn't go fishing, as far as we know. They'd get picked up by a van in the evening, and then dropped back off a few hours later. But, for the most part, they would stick around the resort during the day."

"Do you have names?" Jack asked. "Did you run them through the FBI, or Interpol?"

"We have names, all right, but they all appear to be fictitious. That's why I've got all this company running around here. There certainly did appear to have been something unusual going on at the resort, but we really don't know what that something unusual was."

Just then one of the two DHS officers (who were standing and talking outside the sheriff's door) knocked. And then knocked again, only louder.

The sheriff smiled and winked at Jack and then got up and opened the door.

Chapter 9—DHS throws its weight around

"Sheriff," the taller of the officers voiced, intending to interrupt if necessary. "May we have a word with you ... in private?"

"Sure, I'll be with you in a few moments," the sheriff said, beginning to close the door.

"My boss wants to know who these people are, and if they're associated in any way with our case."

"Sonny, right now you are a guest in my house. And as a guest, you will respect me, and my other guests. I will talk to you when I'm ready ... and it's none of your business who these nice people are. Now, you and your little friend here, take two steps back. I'll talk to you later. And, as it stands right now, you don't have a case."

With that the sheriff closed the door in their faces and locked it again.

As was usually the situation, the sheriff was the tallest man in the building. He stood six feet six inches. So although he referenced the officer's "little friend," from his vantage point, almost everyone was little.

"Probably should not have opened the door to start with," he said. He was agitated but not angry—still able to manage a sincere smile as he walked back to his seat. "Fortunate for me that maggot ..." The sheriff paused for a moment, choosing his words carefully so as not to be offensive. "I suppose you could say that it's fortunate for me these fellows don't vote in my county. Now, where were we?" the sheriff said, returning to his seat behind his desk. He took a deep breath to slow his heart rate.

"Sheriff," Kate said, "if we're making this awkward for you, we'd be happy to come back another time."

"Darlin', you and your father are not making anything awkward. It might seem like I'm making it a little difficult for them. But they have no authority over me. And they are guests in my house—the good people of Chippewa County placed me in charge here. Now, it does seem likely that the Feds will eventually wrestle this case away from me. But that's the extent of it—they might take this case, but they can't take my house away from me. I'm sorry, but I seem to have lost my train of thought. What was I talking about when we were interrupted?"

"You were explaining that Uncle Alex had some unorthodox guests staying at the resort."

"Right. Now they were unorthodox all right … and the names and addresses they gave were untraceable. But there was something else that was even more interesting."

The sheriff then walked over to a media player and slid a thumb drive into it.

"Check these guys out, and tell this old lawman what you think. Here, this is the first video. Okay, we're talking about these three fellows, the ones checking in here. From left to right, we are looking at a Bill White, John Jones, and Larry Smith."

The sheriff then paused the recorder and turned to face Jack and Kate.

"Now, tell me, do those names seem to fit the faces? Here, I'll move it in for you."

The sheriff zoomed in on the three men and played the video in slow motion.

"What do you think, Jack? If one of your officers brought this fellow in for questioning, and he told you his name was Bill White, what would your reaction be?"

"I would ask for a driver's license," Jack responded. "Actually, I might ask to see his passport.

"Can I get a closer look at that one?" Jack continued, pointing to the man on the left.

"Well, I'll see what I can do. We might loose a little focus, but here goes."

Jack studied the first face, and then said, "My guess would be Middle Eastern. What do you think, Sheriff?"

"That's what I thought. And that's what these DHS fellows are thinking. Now, if we go through all the video, we see it repeated—same faces, different shirts."

"What are you suggesting?" Kate asked. "Do you suspect that Uncle Alex was running something on the side? Possibly involving some activity that might include illegals?"

"Good questions, Kate. I knew your uncle. Can't say that we socialized, but I have known him for a decade. He was a businessman, and a good one. I can't imagine him getting involved with anything like that. It just wasn't his nature. I'd be the most surprised person in the county if he got his fingers stuck into something illegal. Just wasn't like him.

"But, I have to admit—I can't explain it. And I can't really blame DHS for wanting to get involved. I just don't think they have the ability to investigate this case the way it needs to be investigated. I think these guys might be pretty good at running down someone they might catch swimming the river. But beyond that, they're just not detectives."

"Wouldn't they bring in the FBI?" Jack asked.

The sheriff looked Jack in the eye without saying anything for a long moment, and then responded, "I'm suspecting that's just what's gonna happen. But they're not here yet. If you wanna get a jump on this, you should do it now. Because when the suits arrive, I'm out of the picture."

"When is that likely to happen?" Kate asked.

"Well, that'd be hard to say. But I wouldn't be surprised if something happened as early as tomorrow. Today, if DHS gets its way."

"Do you have copies of the video that you could loan me?" Jack asked.

With that the sheriff pulled the thumb drive out of the DVR and slid it into Jack's hand, along with a large white envelope.

Thud, thud, thud.

All three of them stared over at the office door.

Chapter 10—Hello—I'm the FBI, and you're not

Suit number one stood at the door, banging his shield on the glass and glaring at the sheriff. Behind him were two more equally grim faces protruding from cheaper dark gray suits, which appeared to have been purchased at a two-for-one sale.

"Well, would you look at that. Wonder who they might be. Where're you staying?" the sheriff asked, smiling at his new visitors through the door. He then stood facing Jack and Kate.

"Holiday Inn Express," Kate replied.

"Well, here's my card. Give me a call in the morning, after you've had a chance to go through some of this stuff. See what you think. I might not be in charge anymore, but I can still answer some of your questions."

"And maybe we will get a chance to go fishing," the sheriff scoffed, looking over at Jack with a scornful smile. "It's getting a little chilly around here, but there's still some good fishing to be had."

Jack and Kate thanked the sheriff as they walked toward the office door.

"Excuse us, please," the sheriff said as he pushed past the FBI agents, forcing his new visitors back a step with a stiff forearm to make way for Jack and Kate behind him. After seeing them out of the building, the sheriff returned to face the suits.

"Gentlemen," the sheriff said. "What can I do for you?"

Jack and Kate did not say anything until they were well outside the County Building. They could not help but feel all the eyes that followed them through the doors.

"I would love to hear what is going on inside the sheriff's office right now," Kate said with a chuckle in her voice.

"I know what you mean," Jack replied. "But if anyone can handle himself in a situation like this, it would be Sheriff Northrup. He is one crusty old dude. It does puzzle me just a bit that the sheriff was so willing to give up information. I would think he'd not be so liberal with what he knows. It was almost like he was trying to win us over … or steer us."

"I noticed that too. I think he sensed he was about to lose the case to the FBI, and he wanted to win us over. But, for whatever reason, it's still nice having him on our side—regardless. Actually, he might be more of a help to us as an observer than as the lead detective."

"You might be right. FBI's going to need him, practically speaking. He can open a lot of doors for them. They might not be sharing much of what they find, but he will know what they're up to nevertheless. He's not a stupid man. And I get the sense that he knows how to work with people. Maybe even work them."

Once in the car, Kate turned to her father before fastening her seat-belt, and asked, "What do you know about Uncle Alex? Does it make any sense to you that he would get involved with harboring illegal aliens? Or anything illegal, for that matter? That seems to be the direction this case is going. Could that be?"

"I haven't seen Alex in over twenty-five years. But I would agree with the sheriff. From what I knew about him through your mom, and from my own experience, he was a straight shooter. However, people do change. We all know that. We need to look beyond the obvious. I'm not ready to buy into that theory—not yet. Now put your belt on. It's the law, you know."

But just as Jack started to back out, two white Tahoes pulled in behind him, blocking his way.

"What's this about?" Jack muttered, sliding his SUV into drive and pulling back into the parking place.

Chapter 11—Jack and Kate questioned

Jack tried to control his annoyance.

"Looks like DHS wants to talk to us," he said. "What could they possibly think we could know? We just got here!"

"I'd say we're about to find out."

"Sir, please step out of the car. You too, ma'am."

Besides the agent who had approached Jack's SUV, three other DHS agents had taken a position behind Jack's vehicle.

"Don't give them any reason to hassle us," Kate instructed her father.

"Like they need a reason," Jack voiced, clearly irritated.

"Sir, could we please see some identification—your passport would be good."

"Passport? Where are we? Why do I need a passport to drive around Sault Ste. Marie?"

"Sir, would you prefer to discuss this in our office?"

"No, not really. But I would like to know what this is all about. What is it you think I've done that warrants this sort of attention?"

The agent did not respond to Jack's question.

Jack, anticipating that his investigation might take him and Kate into Canada, had made sure they both did bring their passports.

"With your permission, sir, I will reach back and get my passport."

"Where is it?"

"Right there," Jack said, pointing to a briefcase lying on the back seat."

"Are you carrying a weapon, or is there one in your briefcase?"

"I'm not … and there is not."

The agent looked inside the car. "Go ahead and get the briefcase, and step out of the vehicle. Then place the briefcase on the hood."

Jack lifted the standard-sized black leather briefcase over the seat and exited his vehicle. With the agent peering over his shoulder, he removed his passport and handed it to the agent.

At the same time, a second agent approached the passenger side of the vehicle. "Ma'am, could we see your passport as well?" he asked.

"Sure. It's in my bag," Kate replied, pointing to a large black leather purse on the floor.

"Do you have a firearm in your purse?"

"No."

"Go ahead and get it. Then step out of the vehicle and put it on the hood."

Kate did as told.

"Isn't this just a bit unusual? After all, I haven't traveled to Canada in over a year," Jack complained.

The agent again did not respond. He simply took Jack's passport back to his vehicle and talked to someone on the radio.

"Ma'am, if you could unzip your purse … and then just hold it open. No, don't step back … just hold your purse open."

The agent, seeing a passport tucked into one of the inner pockets of Kate's purse, told her to reach inside and remove it.

The agent then took Kate's passport back and handed it to the agent who was calling in on Jack's. Two other agents remained standing beside Jack's vehicle, looking eager to pounce if given the opportunity.

After a few tense moments, the first agent returned to where Jack and Kate were standing.

"How long did you say it's been since you've traveled to Canada?"

"Sir, you already know that. You know that it's been a year, over a year, I believe. I don't recall exactly how long ago it's been."

"And what was the nature of your visit at that time?"

"Fishing."

"How long were you in Canada … fishing?"

"Less than a week. Five days, I believe."

"And where in Canada did you go fishing?"

"Dryden area, in Ontario."

"How'd you do? Catch any?"

"It was a successful trip."

"What did you catch up there in Dryden?"

"Members of my group caught some walleye, smallmouth, some northern. I guess that's about it."

"You're from Chicago. What do you do there?"

"I'm retired."

"And before you retired, what did you do?"

"I was a homicide detective for the City of Chicago."

"What brings you to northern Michigan?"

"As you already know, my brother-in-law was recently murdered on Sugar Island. And my daughter, Kate, was named in her uncle's will. We're up here seeing what this is all about and to meet with the attorney to discuss the particulars of the will."

"I see. Are you intending to do some detective work while you're here?"

"I don't know. Do you fellows need some help?"

The agent glared at Jack but said nothing.

"Well, it is certainly not our intention to interfere with any investigation. Of course, we would like to find out what happened. But principally, we're here to figure out exactly what is entailed with the inheritance."

"How long do you intend to stay?"

"I'm retired. Someday you will discover that when you retire you don't have to get back to anything. We'll stay as long as we need to. Is that a problem?"

The agent took a deep breath—he was visibly annoyed. Jack, however, was beginning to enjoy himself.

"Sir, are you having a problem answering my questions?"

"Not at all. I'm loving every moment of it. I like to see how my tax dollars are spent."

Jack leaned against his car and pulled a stale pack of cigarettes from his pocket. "Care for a cig?" he asked.

Jack knew that the agent could not smoke on the job, and that the smoke would be irritating.

"Nothing like a good cigarette, is there sir?" Jack sneered, taking a deep drag and blowing part of the smoke in the agent's direction.

"And the lady traveling with you?"

"That's my daughter, Kate. She is the one who was named in the will."

"You're traveling together? Same vehicle?"

"Yes, we are."

"Do you have any firearms or alcohol in your vehicle?"

"We do not. But I fail to understand how that is any of your business. We have not crossed any borders."

"Are you intending to enter into Canada on this trip?"

"I wouldn't rule it out. But we have no immediate plans to do so."

"Do you intend to do any fishing on this trip—perhaps in Canada, that is?"

"If I decide to go to Canada, then I might go fishing in Canada. But, again, we have no immediate plans to enter Canada."

"Very well, Mr. Handler. I thank you for your cooperation. And, Ms. Handler, thank you. I hope both of you enjoy your stay."

Neither Kate nor Jack responded until the agents had begun to return to their vehicles.

"Aren't you forgetting something?" Jack said, following right behind them. "You never returned my passport. Kate, did they return yours?"

"Yeah, I put mine back in my purse."

The agent turned to face Jack and said, "I didn't give it back? Let me check in my vehicle."

The agent turned and walked over to the driver's side window.

"Well, I'll be darned. You're right. There it is, right on my seat."

He opened the door and retrieved it.

"Here you go, Mr. Handler," the agent said, handing Jack his passport. "Sorry about the confusion."

Jack did not respond. He considered extinguishing his cigarette on the pavement but instead squashed it out in the clean ashtray of his SUV. *Might be some obscure federal law*, he thought. *Don't need a hassle with this fellow; he already doesn't like me.*

"Since when did you start up smoking?" Kate asked as she seated herself and closed the door. Jack noted she was smiling broadly, so he didn't reply.

Before she had a chance to click her seatbelt, her cell phone began vibrating.

Chapter 12—Sheriff Northrup has advice

"Sheriff," Kate said, a little surprised to hear the sheriff's voice. She remained silent for several moments, listening intently to what he had to say. Finally, she asked the sheriff to hold on while she explained to her father what he was telling her.

"Just as he anticipated, Sheriff Northrup has been forced to turn the case over to the FBI. That part is not surprising. But something else has occurred that was not expected. Hang on a second, Sheriff, I'm going to hand you over to my dad, and let you explain it to him. Is that okay?"

After obtaining the sheriff's permission, she handed her cell phone to her father.

"Sheriff, Jack here."

"Jack, I didn't think I'd be calling you so soon. But I thought I should give you a heads-up. The FBI agents assigned to this case expressed a considerable amount of interest in your presence in the Soo. Seems they know something about you. If I read them right, it was a reaction mixed with respect and disdain—if that's even possible. I'm not sure how those two words go together, but I don't know how else to express it. It was as though they respected your reputation, and feared it at the same time. While at the same time they were not at all pleased that you were taking a personal interest in the case.

"I explained that you were related to the deceased, but that didn't mollify them much."

"Did they get specific?" Jack asked.

"Well, not really. But I would say this. You would be wise to tread lightly. I don't think it would take much for them to strike out at you. You know, find some technicality to charge you with. That's just the feeling I got. Maybe it's just an old man's intuition, but it was uncomfortable when the conversation focused on you."

"I can understand that," Jack said. "I've been known to poke my nose where it doesn't belong. And sometimes I get it punched. Did they give up anything of significance about the case?"

"Nothing that they wanted to share with me. But they did want my help. That means I might be in the loop, at least from time to time."

"I appreciate the heads-up. I will watch myself. I think that we are going to find our hotel, get a bite to eat, and then take a look at the file you gave us."

"Good idea. Give me a call in the morning."

Jack handed the phone back to Kate, and she disconnected the call.

"What do you think? About our reputation beating us here?"

"Looks like it. But you know the FBI. They're afraid we might get in their way."

Kate reached into the space between her seat and the middle console and pulled out the envelope containing the file the sheriff had given them. In it she found a number of digitally enhanced printed images of men's faces. All of them appeared to range in age from late twenties to mid-forties. And all of them seemed to be of Middle Eastern descent.

"I see what the sheriff means," she said. "Call it profiling, but to me, all of these guys look to be from someplace other than Sault Ste. Marie. Even their clothes are different. And their haircuts. All but one has facial hair—most have significant facial hair."

"How many are there?" Jack asked as he looked into his rearview before backing out.

Kate fingered through the images.

"There's eight. Eight different individuals. About twenty images in all, but it looks like there are eight separate individuals. I think."

"Eight?" Jack asked. "I thought the sheriff said there were four. Must be there were more than one group that frequented the resort. Show them to me."

Kate held each of them up for a second, so her father could see them.

Jack observed that some images were sharper than others. *A couple of them appear to have been reworked*, he thought.

"I wonder how much is on the thumb drive the sheriff gave you?" Kate asked.

"Good question. That was a sixteen-gig drive. Depending on the compression software, there could be a whole lot. Let's take it back and get a better look at it. Who knows what we might find?"

"Where's the hotel from here?" Kate asked.

"It's on Easterday, just before the bridge to Canada. Should be easy to find."

"Where shall we eat?" Kate asked. "I hear there are some really good Italian restaurants on the Canadian side."

"I don't need that adventure today," Jack replied with a smile. "We'll find something on this side, even if it's a Big Mac and a Coke."

As Jack pulled away from the County Building and headed for the hotel, he looked in his mirror and saw a white Tahoe pull out right behind him. It followed him at a distance.

Chapter 13—Dinner and a movie

"What're you watching?" Kate asked. "Do we have company?"

"We do. Looks like it might be some of the same fellows who questioned us. I sort of anticipated this."

Jack turned left on Ashmun St. and headed for Easterday Ave.

"They're not gonna do anything, right?"

"They've already done it. They just want to confirm where we're staying ... and to get under my skin a bit."

After a few moments, Kate asked, "Is it true that you're not carrying a firearm?"

"You couldn't call it a firearm—not in its current state."

"It's in pieces?"

"Right."

"A Walther .380?"

"And a Smith & Wesson .38 Airweight.

"You switched?"

"Not really. The Walther breaks down better for transporting on flights. But, given a choice, I've always favored a revolver ... that is, when I don't have to get it past security."

"Ammo?"

"I've got some rounds, but not in my luggage. They're in a waterproof magnetic container inside the engine compartment. It might be a while before I will want to retrieve them," Jack said with a chuckle in his voice.

"Why we pulling in here? The hotel is straight up the hill."

"I'm buying you dinner, my darling daughter. Do you want fries with that burger?"

"You were serious."

"Aren't you eager to get into that video, *and* the file? Besides, I wanted to see how that Tahoe handles itself. It'd be interesting to find out if he knows how to conduct a discreet tail."

"Are you going in, or driving through?"

"I'm going to park and go in. You keep your eye on that white Tahoe and see what he does."

Jack pulled his vehicle around to the side and parked so that Kate could view the approach into the restaurant, as well as the drive up the hill to the hotel.

"Make sure my soda's diet," she said as her father closed the vehicle's door.

Immediately Kate's sunglass-covered eyes located the white Tahoe. It had slowed down near the restaurant but did not enter the parking lot. It then continued up the hill toward the hotel and parked overlooking McDonald's. As far as Kate could determine, no one got out of the Tahoe. Its running lights remained on.

Several minutes later her father re-emerged from the restaurant carrying a couple white paper bags and a beverage carrier.

"Here, set these down. And, how about our friends—what happened to them?"

"They're sitting on top of the hill. I am betting that they are watching us right now."

"That would strongly suggest that they know we have reservations at that particular hotel."

"Does that bother you?"

"No point—it's just good to know when you're being watched. And by whom."

"Who'd we tell?"

"Just the sheriff," Jack replied. "And he wouldn't have told them. They must have done some homework. Let's just get checked in and un-pack. And you can get us rigged up to view that video."

As they drove into the hotel parking lot, they observed that the white Tahoe appeared empty; however, the headlights remained on.

"I guess you could say that they forgot about the running lights—not too swift," Jack chuckled.

As soon as they entered their room, Kate unpacked her MacBook and plugged in the thumb drive.

"What have we got here?" Jack asked.

"This is interesting," Kate said. "The drive is full—all sixteen gig. And there is a lot more on it than just what the sheriff played in his of-fice. Look, that is from a different camera, and it shows what appears to be three of the men, but from behind, with a shot of the desk clerk at the counter. It must not have been busy that night—it appears only one person is working.

"Hey, you can hand me that burger now."

Chapter 14—Information overload

Jack began unpacking, while Kate devoured her hamburger and drank her shake. She intently scrutinized the video at the same time.

"Let me take a look at that," Kate said, wanting to examine the Walther .380 that her father had just assembled.

"I don't see a serial number on that piece," she commented. "Same one you had when I was a girl?"

"Kitty, you've got a memory like an … like a New York City homicide detective."

"You were going to say I had a memory like an elephant. Good thing you caught yourself. And didn't I ask for a *Diet* Coke?"

"You don't like the strawberry shake?"

"Yeah, of course. I love strawberry shakes. But I *requested* a diet soda."

"You know, when I asked for a diet soda, they suggested the drug store on Ashmun. They said they didn't carry *soda*—that I had to go to a drug store for soda."

"Okay, I'm glad you got me that shake—you made my day. But I still would never order one of those for myself.

"Why don't you turn on the local news—I want to see the weather forecast. I need to know what to wear tomorrow."

Jack turned the TV on with the remote and pushed buttons until he found the local news.

"There's a new twist in the Alex Garos murder case. Garos was the resort owner who was gunned down on Sugar Island. This afternoon a team of investigators from the FBI flew into the Soo, and they have announced that they are taking over the Garos case. You may recall that nearly a month ago the body of Garos was found shot to death at his Sugar Island resort and dumped into the St. Mary's River. As of one hour ago the FBI met with Chippewa County Sheriff Conrad Northrup and informed him they would now be heading up the investigation.

"Special Agent Fred Lamar has been placed in charge. Special Agent Lamar, could you explain what it is about this case that warrants the FBI stepping in to lead the investigation?"

"I am not at liberty to talk about that at this time. Suffice it to say that the DHS believed that there was sufficient cause to enlist our involvement. When we have something more concrete to say, we will explain further."

"Are there any new leads in the case that you *can* talk about? Do you have any suspects?"

"We are just beginning our investigation. That's about all I can tell you right now. As the events warrant, I will be more forthcoming."

"Is Sheriff Northrup totally out of the picture?"

"Not at all. Sheriff Northrup is a very knowledgeable law enforcement officer and a fine detective. We need his expertise. No one knows what goes on around here better than he does. He will be instrumental in solving this murder."

"Right," Jack said. "They will probably take his keys away and not even let him in his own office. That's how they work. They've got the case, and as far as they're concerned, no one who is not FBI means anything. The sheriff might as well go fishing."

"But we hope he doesn't. Right? The more he stays engaged in the case, the better for us."

"Exactly. While they totally disrespect the old sheriff, they are smart enough to know that he has accumulated a lot of information that might be useful to them. So they will tolerate him. And from time to time, they will use him to open some doors. But in the end, the only thing that really matters to them is what they think—not what the sheriff thinks."

Kate then interjected, "Don't you think that throughout this process the sheriff will glean some things from the FBI—just by virtue of the types of questions they ask him? And that he might then share some of that information with us. At least we hope he will."

"I'm sure he will be talking to us again," Jack said. "They would have to impose a total gag order to silence him. And, even then, he's gonna do pretty much what he wants to do anyway. ... And I can tell he likes you."

"You pickin' on me?"

Suddenly Kate paused the video. "Hold it! Take a look at this."

She then hit the reverse button and backed the video up a minute or two.

"Check this out. See anything that grabs your attention?" she said, hitting the play button.

Jack had walked around behind her and was examining the screen from over her right shoulder.

"Run it again."

The reason both Jack and Kate found this particular portion of the recording interesting was that it revealed a dark-skinned man, with a thick mustache, pushing a two-wheel aluminum cart past the front desk and toward the front doors. An earlier clip depicted this same man checking into the resort, without the cart.

After viewing the video clip a second time, Jack said, "Yeah, I see what you mean."

Kate turned around and faced her father. "I'd like to find out how often that fellow showed up. It'd be real nice to see if the sheriff recognizes him. Do you suppose he was a resort employee?"

"I wonder. We've watched two clips, and he appears on both."

"Be nice to have all the video. You know, the out-takes—if that's what they'd be called. I imagine that the sheriff made the selections. Be nice to know if he did his editing strictly on the basis of his illegal alien theory. Or if he saw what we did. Or maybe he even wanted to influence our thinking."

"I brought a printer," Kate said. "It's still in the car. How about I go down and get it, and we can print some snapshots off the video?"

"I'll get it for you. That way I can check my engine while I'm there."

"Retrieve your ammo, you mean."

"Maybe that too. See you in a bit."

Before the door closed behind her father, Kate was again shocked by what she saw on the video.

"Oh my God!"

Chapter 15—Jack checks his oil, and more

Jack briskly walked to his vehicle, intentionally ignoring the white Tahoe that was still parked in the lot—now with all its lights off.

First he opened the rear hatch and removed Kate's printer.

He carried it around to the driver's side door and put the printer on the front seat. He then pulled the hood latch.

As he was reaching in to disengage the secondary hood latch, he casually glanced to his right in the direction of the white Tahoe. He observed that the Tahoe appeared to be empty. *I wonder what they're up to now?* he thought.

Jack then stretched to reach the small watertight box that was secured by a magnet to the firewall. He popped it open with his left hand and removed a small Ziploc snack-sized plastic bag containing ten rounds of Federal 125 grain +P, and an equal number of .38 special hollow-point. He slipped it into his left jacket pocket and re-engaged the magnetic latch on the ammo box. At the same time he pulled out the dipstick with his right hand and checked his oil. Sliding the dipstick back firmly into its place, he then feigned checking other engine components.

Never know who might be watching, he reasoned.

Jack wanted to get one more look at the white Tahoe that had been following him, so he walked around to the rear hatch of his SUV and removed a red shop towel from the back, and wiped his hands on it. Before he tossed the rag back into his vehicle, he fixed his eyes on the white Tahoe.

"Heavily tinted rear glass," he observed. "Could actually be someone in that vehicle. Or even more likely a camera."

Jack went back around and dropped the hood.

"Time to go," he whispered aloud.

Grabbing Kate's printer from the front seat, he then closed the door and locked it, and headed back.

But before he reached the hotel entrance, his cell phone rang. He checked the display and then answered it.

"Kate, what's up?"

Chapter 16—Jack meets
Special Agent Lamar

"Yeah," Jack said. "I'm on my way. Everything okay?"

"I'm fine. I just think I spotted Uncle Alex on one of the video clips. All I remember about what Uncle Alex looked like was from Mom's photo album—and most of those pictures were all thirty years old, or more. But if I'm right, I'm looking at some video of him behind the counter, talking to a couple of our questionable characters. You should come up and take a look."

"I'll be right there," Jack said, using his remote to be sure he had properly secured his vehicle.

Kate's comments triggered old memories as Jack headed toward the hotel entrance. He recalled how nervous he was the first time he met his wife's brother, and how important it was to her that the two men should grow to like each other. Alex was, after all, her only family in America. And after she learned she was pregnant, she wanted to strengthen that family tie.

Family—her old-country sense of family was so important to her, Jack recalled. *I was so pigheaded back then, and Alex was just as bad. But we did have one thing in common—Beth.*

Initially, Beth had wanted to spend Christmas at her brother's resort on Sugar Island. Despite serious reservations about driving that far north during that time of year, Jack agreed.

Alex, however, rejected the plan.

"Crazy idea!" Alex told her. "The ferry might be iced in on Christmas. Thanksgiving would be a better bet."

Thanksgiving, 1982. Jack smiled as he thought about it. *Beth's eyes were as big as saucers when we crossed the Mackinac Bridge. And then, when we reached the ferry … it was unbelievable. I'd never seen her so excited.*

Jack had stopped in Mackinaw City for lunch, and to pick up a present for Alex—a sizeable slab of his favorite Mackinac fudge—black walnut. Before they resumed their journey, Beth called her brother to report their progress.

"Alex wants to know how long before we reach the ferry," Beth said, turning to Jack. "He wants to meet us there—at the ferry. Got any idea about the time?"

Jack looked at his watch and thought for a moment. *It's two p.m. Chicago time—three p.m. Michigan time. We'll leave here at three-thirty, make Sault Ste. Marie at about four thirty.*

"Should be at the ferry between four-fifteen and four forty-five," Jack replied loud enough for Alex to hear.

"… Alex wants to meet us at the ferry, on the mainland side. He said he has to pick up supplies in the Soo. … He'll be watching for us at four-thirty. He's driving a black Jeep. He wants us to *not* get in line when we first get there … just look for his Jeep and pull alongside. … Then he will get in the line, and we can follow. … This is so exciting. I can't believe it—we'll soon be there."

Jack was relieved that Alex was going to meet them at the ferry. "That will make it much easier," he said. "I wasn't looking forward to that last part of the trip."

Jack knew very little about Sugar Island, aside from the stories Beth had shared with him, which were based on communications with her brother. Fortunately, Alex had managed to obtain telephone service at his resort earlier that year. And since that time, Beth and her brother conversed regularly.

Seemed to me at the time, Jack recalled, *that it would have made more sense for Alex to have spent Thanksgiving or Christmas with us. But Beth really wanted to visit her brother's resort. I think it was important to her that she honor him by having us drive up there. And, I had a feeling that he might have been strapped for cash … that he simply couldn't afford to make the trip to Chicago.*

"Might be best," Jack said, "just to park on the mainland side, and ride with your brother to the resort. We don't have four-wheel drive."

"Don't be silly," Beth said. "It's not snowing."

"This time of year the big storms come up in a hurry. Remember the Edmund Fitzgerald—it went down early in November. That storm produced ninety-mile-per-hour winds at Sault Ste. Marie—with lots of ice and snow. And that's where the ferry is—in Sault Ste. Marie.

"When the Big Fitz left Minnesota, the weather was fine. But before it could reach Whitefish Bay, it sank. …The weather might be fine now, but who knows what it'll be like in a day or two."

"Really? The Edmund Fitzgerald went down around here?"

"West of Sault Ste. Marie … about sixty miles."

Just as Jack reached the hotel's front entrance someone grabbed him by his left bicep.

"Handler. You're Jack Handler—right?"

Jack had not noticed this person in the parking lot. And no new vehicles had pulled in. So he had no notion of where this person might have come from.

"Who's asking?" Jack snarled, before turning to face the man who had violated his space.

The neatly dressed middle-aged man produced a badge and said, "Special Agent Lamar, FBI. Please step inside. I have some questions I want to ask you."

Jack quickly recognized him from the sheriff's office. "Look—I'm totally exhausted. I've driven all the way from Chicago. Can't we do this tomorrow?"

Jack had been caught off guard and did not like it. Plus, this stranger had the nerve to physically touch him. That, he detested.

No matter what this jerk does, I've got to keep my cool, he kept telling himself..

"It'll only take a moment or two," Special Agent Lamar persisted.

Jack begrudgingly acquiesced to the agent's wishes. The two men entered the hotel, proceeded through to the lobby's eating area and sat down at a small round table. Immediately Special Agent Lamar leaned forward until again he violated Jack's space—that posture fostered further irritation for Jack.

I'm really beginning to dislike this guy, Jack thought.

"I know you talked with Sheriff Northrup earlier today," the agent said. "I saw you there. Would you tell me the nature of your meeting?"

"It was a private conversation. I don't see how it is FBI business."

"The Bureau has taken over the lead of the Alex Garos murder case. The sheriff is no longer involved. So I'm going to have to talk to you … the sooner the better."

"Alex Garos was my brother-in-law. I merely asked the sheriff how the investigation was going, and if my daughter would be able to visit the resort. She was, after all, named in her uncle's will."

"Did the sheriff give you anything?"

"He gave me some free advice, and invited me to go fishing with him. Maybe you would like to join us."

"A witness said he handed an envelope off to you. Is that true?"

"I think we're done talking for now. If you want to ask me more questions, it'll have to be tomorrow. I've had a long drive. Give me your card, and I'll call you in the morning," Jack said as he stood to his feet.

"I'll see you at nine a.m. at the County Building. Ask for Special Agent Lamar."

"This meeting's done. Right?"

"Until tomorrow morning. You should be there on time. And bring with you everything the sheriff handed you."

Jack turned and walked toward the elevator without responding to the special agent's order.

He must have been waiting for me in the parking lot. Strange that he didn't follow me up to the room, Jack thought as he got on the elevator. *Maybe he's as tired as I am.*

Jack continued to ponder what had just happened. Had the agent come up to their room, he probably would have confiscated the contents of the envelope. *Could it be that he wants to give me a chance to copy what the sheriff handed off to us?* Jack was almost talking to himself as he went up to his room.

"Hey, Dad, come over here. Isn't that Uncle Alex?" Kate asked, pointing to an image she had paused on her screen.

Jack slipped his glasses on in order to get a good look at the video. The camera was on the opposite side of the lobby from where the person in question was standing, so the quality was not the best.

"Go ahead and run it," Jack said. "I'd like to see him move around a bit. You know, I haven't seen Alex for nearly three decades."

Kate hit the "play" button, and Jack immediately responded.

"That's him. That's the way he gestured, and that is his smile. It's definitely your Uncle Alex."

"Just what I thought," Kate responded with a smile. "He strikes me as a nice person—not just friendly, but nice."

"Back it up and run it again," Jack said.

Kate stopped it and ran it back to the point just before the man they determined was Alex walked across the screen.

"Okay, that's good. Now play it again," Jack said.

The two of them watched intently as Alex walked directly behind one of the mustached persons of interest. As he passed, both Jack and Kate observed that neither of the men turned to acknowledge, much less greet, the owner of the resort at which they were staying.

Instead, once they had spotted Alex in the mirror behind the counter, the two men made it a point *not* to greet Alex. In fact, it appeared as though once they saw Alex approaching, they tried not to look at him at all.

That was not the case for the employee manning the counter. As Alex walked past, the employee greeted his boss, but in a most curious fashion—almost as though Alex's presence made him uncomfortable.

"Okay," Jack said, "back it up and run it one more time. Do you observe anything unusual about the reaction of the employee?"

"Definitely. It is almost as though Uncle Alex surprised him. The clerk appears to have been caught off guard—like it's awkward for him."

"And Alex seems to be sizing up the situation. Look at the time stamped on that video: 3:47 a.m. And it's from less than a week before the murder. What would Alex be doing up at that time? Doesn't make sense. It almost looks like he was checking out what was going on—as though he suspected something. Do we have the video for the rest of this night? I wonder if Alex makes another appearance."

"It doesn't appear that the sheriff included additional video for that night. Seems all he was interested in here was trying to ID the suspected aliens."

"Most of those security DVRs automatically loop the video, and erase the oldest video after a period of time—two weeks, maybe a month, depending on the size of the hard drive. And type of compression software."

"But that's only if they remain powered up and turned on," Jack said. "Most likely the sheriff removed the units and stored them as evidence—right after the murder."

"That means that the FBI has them by now," Kate said. "Cinch we're not gonna get to play with them."

"You know, I would not put it past the sheriff to have copied all the video, or as much as he could, onto a different hard drive, and have it stored offsite. He strikes me as a very thorough cop. I'll bet he's got a lot more than what's on this thumb drive."

"Think he'll let us see it?"

"He might ... I'm sure the FBI has already confiscated his office computers."

"We're going back in the morning?" Kate asked, assuming a positive reply.

"We are," Jack replied. "At least I am, for sure. I ran into Special Agent Lamar outside the hotel, and he invited me to return the envelope the sheriff gave us. He wants to see me at the County Building in the morning. But he really didn't stipulate that he needed to see you."

"I'll scan and save the contents of the folder," Kate said. "I've already copied the thumb drive onto my desktop."

Jack walked over to the window to take a look at his vehicle in the hotel parking lot.

"What's *this* all about!" he grumbled. "The dome light is on. ... Someone's in our car!"

Chapter 17—The freckle-faced boy

Jack did not take the time to excuse himself. He shot through the door, turning right toward the stairs, instead of left for the elevator, and bolted down the corridor. He allowed the mechanical closer to shut the door behind him.

Even though he had not used the staircase on his previous trip to his vehicle, he had spotted from the parking lot where it emptied. He thought that if he ran to where he was parked, he might possibly catch whoever had broken into his SUV.

His room was on the third floor, so he had two flights to conquer.

Not bad for an old man, he thought, taking the steps three at a time, while steadying himself by sliding his right hand along the railing.

Flying through the door leading onto the parking lot, he quickly spotted his vehicle about ninety feet away. The dome light was on, and the horn still blasted from the alarm.

The thief, spotting Jack, opened the passenger door and summoned his golden retriever to follow him out. The dog had been in the vehicle with him. As he coolly closed the door behind him, he looked back at Jack and smiled. He then casually slipped out into the darkness.

"I can't believe it!" Jack exclaimed out loud. "It's just a boy—a freckle-faced boy."

Jack marveled at the boy's demeanor. *The way he ran off … he did not seem concerned at all about the alarm, or that I might go after him. It was as though he sensed he was in total control—very relaxed.*

For a brief moment, Jack considered giving chase, but he quickly discarded that idea.

Futile, he surmised, given the confidence the young boy demonstrated, and his own lack of familiarity with the terrain. Besides, Jack fully understood the perils of pursuing anyone with a dog.

What is this all about? Jack wondered, as he slowed to a walk and continued toward his car.

At least he didn't break a window. That kid must have used something to get the door open. I didn't think Slim-Jims worked on these newer models.

For a moment, Jack questioned himself: *Could I have left a door unlocked? ... No! I locked them—I'm positive about that. This kid is pretty good, to get in a new, locked vehicle without doing damage. Wonder what he stole?*

Jack then jumped in his SUV and closed the door behind him. As the dome light dimmed, he hit the switch to turn it back on.

The only things he noticed out of place were an empty bag of pretzels and a candy wrapper.

"Nothing is missing," Jack said aloud. "Just the pretzels and a candy bar. The kid was hungry—he broke into my car for food."

"I wonder how many other cars he got into tonight?" Jack muttered. And then, detecting the scent of dirty hair, continued, "or when he took his last shower?"

Jack remained in his vehicle for a few moments, further scrutinizing what had just occurred. He wanted to convince himself that this freckle-faced redhead was acting on his own, and not in some strange way connected with the murder case. He glanced around the parking lot to see if there were other vehicles burgled.

While you can never be totally sure about anything when it comes to murder, Jack reasoned, *it does look as though I'm the only lucky guy tonight ... must be my number just came up.*

After he convinced himself that the boy and his dog were not in any way responsible for the death of his brother-in-law, Jack decided to gather up some evidence—he felt it might prove useful down the road.

Jack slipped on some latex gloves, a supply of which he always carried with him in his center console, and slid the empty wrapper and pretzel bag into a one-gallon Ziploc bag, which he had also removed from the console.

He took one more minute to look around his vehicle for additional evidence. It was then that he spotted an unusual item on the floor of the passenger side—almost hidden under the seat. He reached down and picked it up.

"What's this?" he muttered, as he picked up a very bulky implement. "I doubt that Kate would be carrying a pocket knife, and certainly not one like this. It must have been dropped by the freckle-faced boy."

It was not just a pocketknife. The utensil he held in his gloved hand was a very expensive-looking camping style knife containing not only a carefully sharpened cutting blade but also a fork and spoon.

This is not a weapon, Jack determined. *No, it is a tool of necessity.*

"My freckle-faced friend is a survivalist."

Jack placed the knife in the bag as well and took one last look around his SUV before exiting and locking it.

He closed the bag and slid it into his pocket.

Wonder what the front desk knows about this kid? Jack was thinking, as he entered the front lobby.

An attractive woman in her thirties was working behind the counter. She was on the phone.

"Gotta go," she said as soon as she noticed Jack approaching.

"Hi. What can I do for you?" she asked.

"The strangest thing just happened. I was in my room, on the third floor," he said pointing up. "And I spotted someone in my car. When I got down there I found this kid. He looked to be about thirteen or fourteen years old. Maybe five feet three. Skinny. Red curly hair..."

"Did he have a dog?" the woman asked.

"I see you're familiar with him."

"Yeah, sort of," she said. "He's harmless. A few times a year he shows up here. I suppose he's about due. He looks for unlocked vehicles, and steals food. Never takes anything but food. We first spotted him here two years ago. I think he has hit most of the hotels in the area. He used to rummage through our dumpster—for food. But then we put lights and cameras in back. Lately, he has been stealing food out of cars."

"My vehicle was locked," Jack said. "But it didn't stop him."

"He's actually quite good with cars—and quick. I'm sure we have him on video. Would you like to see it?"

"I would, if it's not too much trouble."

"Not at all," she said, turning back toward the video recorder behind her. "Are you going to call the police?"

"He didn't do any damage," Jack replied. "I don't want to waste their time."

"There he is," the woman said, pausing the recorder at the point the skinny kid first approached Jack's vehicle. "He must have seen something in your car he liked."

"Can you zoom in a little?" Jack asked.

"I can. Our new system is very cool. ... We will lose a little clarity, but it will still be amazingly good."

"Is that the kid you're talking about?" Jack asked.

"That's him. When he's been here before, we usually don't find out until after he has disappeared into the night."

"The police ever question him?"

"They know about him," she said. "But they've never apprehended him. They think they might have had him in the system for a while, several years ago. A child matching his description was placed in foster care, but he kept running off. Originally he's from Sugar Island. Probably still lives there."

"Sugar Island?" Jack questioned. "The only way to get to Sugar Island is on the ferry, right? So how could that be?"

"Oh, it could be, all right. This kid is sneaky. Once he was spotted getting on the ferry. When they approached him, he ran. But then, when the ferry docked on the island, there he was. Somehow he managed to sneak back on and hide. And when the cars started pulling off, he popped up and ran off the ramp. He must have somehow hidden in the back of a pickup truck. No one can catch him."

"How about his dog? Did he leave the dog on the island?"

"Nope, story has it the dog was hiding in the back of a different pickup truck, but on the same ferry. When the boat docked, the dog ran off with the kid."

"This happen often?"

"I really don't think so. Most of the time the kid stays on the island. There are a lot of empty cabins, most of them with food stored, and we think he resides in some of them too."

"Being this is the off season, wouldn't it seem likely that he would have better luck on the island than in the city?" Jack asked.

"That's what I would think. But, that's definitely him in the video, breaking into your car. So, what can I say? For some reason, known only to him, tonight he's off the island and right here in the Soo."

"From your experience," Jack asked, "what are the chances of his coming back to this parking lot, and hitting my car again?"

"He's not going to hit any more cars tonight—at least not here. He might visit our dumpster later. But, to answer your question, there's zero chance he hits you again tonight."

"So, you think that he might be in the system, from a few years ago?"

Jack knew that if the kid had ever been picked up, there might be information in it that could help him find the boy. And Jack wanted to talk to him.

"Nothing recent, I would guess. Actually, I don't think the sheriff or the local police *want* to catch him—at least as long as he doesn't do anything really serious. If they busted him, he would only end up in foster care, and at his first opportunity he'd be back on his own, and back on the island.

"He's an orphan, you know. Lives totally on his own. His parents were both killed a few years ago in a gas explosion.

"… One more thing about him," she continued. "He can't talk. I don't know why, but I think it is physical."

"Really?" Jack said. "Does he have a name?"

"I'm sure he does," the woman said. "But I don't know what it is. Some know him as 'Freckleface,' and others just refer to him as 'Red'. If you talk to any local on the island, and you mention either one of those names, they will immediately know who you're talking about."

"And how about you?" Jack asked. "What's your name?"

"Me? My name is Donna," the woman said. "And you, you're Mr. Handler. I already know your name."

"My name is Jack. Please just call me Jack."

"Okay, Jack. How long are you planning to stay here?"

"My daughter and I will be in town for a week—at least. Maybe longer. We're registered at the hotel for the next six nights."

"Well, then, you'll have to stop in again and talk to me. Most of our guests are in and out. None, or very few, are here for a full week. You do know about our breakfast? We set it out at six. And it lasts until nine. It's really pretty good. And, best of all, it's free to our guests. You and your daughter should try it."

"We'll do that, thanks."

"It's best if you get down early. We almost always have some peewee hockey teams staying here. By eight the place is hopping with ten-year-old Phil Kessels. I think they're cuter than heck, but some of our guests get irritated by all the commotion."

"Thanks for the warning, but kids won't bother us a bit."

"You're sweet," Donna said.

"I don't get called *that* very often," Jack chuckled, taking half a step backward. "... Donna, you've been very helpful. I'm sure I'll talk to you again."

"I hope so. And don't forget about the breakfast. We're kinda famous for our continental."

"We'll keep that in mind. I think as long as you have good coffee in the morning, I just might come down. ... My daughter, on the other hand, most likely will choose to sleep in."

"If I can help in any way just look me up—I'm usually down here from two to ten."

"Thanks," Jack replied.

But just as he prepared to head up to his room, he stepped back toward the counter and asked, "I do have one more question. This one might seem a little strange, but it involves the recent murder on Sugar Island. The victim was my brother-in-law ..."

"Oh, I'm so sorry," Donna said consolingly. "I did not know Mr. Garos personally. But from what I've heard he was an okay guy. Paid his help well. Was a good boss. I once applied to work there—I liked the idea of having winters off. Unfortunately, I didn't get the job. But everything I ever heard about Mr. Garos was good."

"Do you know anything about the way he died? Or if there is any talk about why he was murdered? Or maybe even who people think might be responsible?"

"Oh my," Donna said. "People don't talk to me about stuff like that."

"But you might have overheard something. Or, maybe just have a little bit of what they call 'woman's intuition.'"

"Funny you would bring that up. I did hear a couple of our guests talking about it. And it was the day after that poor man was killed."

"Really?" Jack responded. "And what were they saying?"

Chapter 18—Two men talking

"They were sitting over there," Donna said, pointing toward two comfortable-looking brown leather armchairs off in a corner of the lobby.

A row of large, well-groomed potted plants partially obscured the front desk from the chairs. Jack estimated the actual distance between the front desk and the place where the men were sitting to be only fifteen to eighteen feet.

"I'm not sure why," Donna said, "might have something to do with the acoustics, but when I'm standing right here, where I always stand, I can hear everything that is said over there."

"Then I guess I'll watch what I say if I'm sitting in your lobby," Jack said, chuckling as he glanced over toward the two chairs. "Little Sis might be listening."

"That's right," Donna replied. "I just might be."

"Tell me, what was it that got your attention?"

"I heard them say the name 'Garos' several times, and they were quite agitated."

"Was this before or after you had learned of the murder?"

"It was before I saw the news on TV," Donna said. "But apparently soon after he was killed. I wouldn't have thought much about it, but the two men were almost yelling at each other. They were trying to whisper, but it was clear they were angry—and very animated."

"Did you catch any of their conversation other than the name?"

"They used a lot of profanity. I'm not gonna repeat that part. But I did hear the younger one say that *he got what he deserved.* Can't be sure, but I now think he might have been referring to Mr. Garos."

"Did they actually say that name, Alex?"

"Strictly the last name—Garos. But I don't know of another Garos around here. So I can't imagine who else they could have been talking about, except for that Mr. Garos."

"Besides that, can you remember anything else about their conversation?"

"Well, yeah," Donna said. "I'm not sure how to express it, but the sense I got was that one of them, the older man, was angry at the other one about something."

"But you're not really sure about what? Or did they say something that might suggest what the older one was upset about?"

"I couldn't tell," Donna said. "But after I heard that Mr. Garos was murdered, I got to thinking about what that could have been—what the older man might have been angry about. Unfortunately, I didn't understand everything they said. They were speaking in very broken English. … And sometimes in a foreign language."

"Really? Could you tell what language they used?"

"Mr. Handler. This is the UP. In case you haven't noticed, there aren't many foreigners around here—just Canadians, and they speak English or French. All I know is that these two men had short black hair, and mustaches. And they both wore sunglasses—in the evening."

"Both of them? They both had mustaches?"

"That's right," Donna replied.

"If you were going to pick three countries—you know, if you were going to guess three countries, where these fellows might be from, which would you choose?"

"Pure guess?"

"Right. Just name three possible countries. It's okay to guess."

"Saudi Arabia," she replied. "That would be my first thought."

"For someone who doesn't know accents, you came up with that pretty quick," Jack teased her. "Any particular city in Saudi Arabia?"

"C'mon, Mr. Handler. You're mocking me. I don't know one country from another, but I remember a Saudi prince I saw on TV one time, and these men reminded me of that fellow. That's all I know."

"I'm just kiddin' with you, darlin'," Jack said. "Tell me, did Sheriff Northrup take a statement from you? Did he ask you to come in for questioning?"

"He did—earlier today, in fact. He's a very sweet man. My father actually used to work for the department—he was the sheriff of Chippewa County before Northrup got elected."

"So, your father was a cop. That explains your attention to detail. But about the sheriff—I doubt that a crusty old lawman like Sheriff Northrup gets called 'sweet' very often either."

"He is sweet," she insisted. "And he did ask me to come in and talk to him."

"Did he show you pictures?"

"He had some video from Mr. Garos's resort. And we spent almost an hour looking at it."

"Were you able to spot either of those two men in that video?" Jack asked.

"I couldn't be certain," Donna said. "I saw a couple men that resembled the two men I heard talking, but I couldn't say for sure it was them. And they weren't together on the video."

"Have those two men ever been back to this hotel?"

"Not while I was working."

"Is there anything else you can remember about them?" Jack asked, getting ready to head up to his room.

"There was one thing, but I'm not sure about that either. It's just a gut feeling."

"What's that?"

"On their way out, as they walked past me, the older one asked the younger one if he was *sure there was a witness*. That's it. At least, that's what I *think* I heard. The young man seemed to nod his head yes. But I'm not sure about that either. I just know they were both very serious. They looked worried."

"One man asked the other if he was sure that there was a witness to … to something? Is that what you're suggesting?"

"Yes. That's what I heard. But I really didn't understand them very well."

Jack and Donna continued their conversation for another ten minutes, she excusing herself periodically to wait on other guests. She shared additional details about her father and the death of Red's parents.

"Young lady, you've been very helpful," Jack finally said. "Do you work tomorrow? I'd like my daughter to meet you."

"Five evenings a week. I'll be here. And I'd love to meet your daughter. What's her name?"

"Kate," Jack said, slipping a twenty-dollar bill into her hand as he turned to leave. "Oh, Donna, did Sheriff Northrup run against your father?"

"No, my dad was retiring, and he actually asked Northrup to run for the office. They got to be pretty good friends."

Jack smiled and nodded a goodnight. He was anxious to rejoin Kate in their room and find out what she had learned from the video clips.

As he walked through the lobby, he glanced over at the two chairs where the men overheard by Donna had been sitting. For a moment, he considered taking a seat there himself, just to get a feel for what she was talking about. But there was a balding man in a tan windbreaker sitting in one of the chairs. He was looking down at a folded newspaper.

I'll check that out later, Jack thought, as he continued toward the elevator.

But just before he turned the corner, he glanced back at the two chairs. The man was intently watching him. Their eyes met briefly before Jack disappeared into the elevator.

Chapter 19—First night lasts forever

"So, who was in your car? Did you catch 'em?" Kate asked her father before he was able to close the door.

"Red."

"Red? You know his name? Who's Red? You were gone a long time. Whadjado, buy him a beer?"

"Red's a fourteen-year-old freckle-faced boy. From what I learned, he's sort of a legend around here."

"You're kidding? A kid? What was he after?"

"Apparently only food. All that I could confirm missing were some pretzels, and a candy bar."

"Any damage."

"Nope. None. Clean as can be."

"Did we leave it unlocked? How about the alarm?"

"No. I locked it. I guess the kid's pretty good at this. I figure he used a couple doorstops and a clothes hanger. He was very cool—he wasn't the least bit fazed by the horn going off. I talked to a gal downstairs—at the front desk—and she knew all about him. He enters locked cars, and all he ever takes is food … for himself and his dog. … Can you beat that? The kid has a dog."

"Okay. This is too good to be true," Kate chuckled. "A red-headed kid—with a dog—who breaks into cars and only steals food? And they can't catch him?"

"It's not so much that they can't catch him, but they don't have a place for him if they do. … They've stuck him in foster care before, and he simply walks away. But—get this—the police think the boy mostly lives on Sugar Island."

"Really? And how'd he get into the city—swim?"

"According to Donna, the girl at the desk …"

"First names? You're on a first-name basis with this girl? Is she cute?"

"Actually, daughter, she is. And you're going to get a chance to meet her tomorrow. I want you to show her some of the video clips the sheriff gave us. She might have a clue."

"How's that?"

"She might know something. Apparently she overheard two Middle Eastern men talking right here in the lobby, less than a day after Alex was killed. Sheriff Northrup took her statement earlier today. She said that she saw a couple of men that resembled the fellows she overheard. I'm thinking that she might be able to pick the men out again if she saw the video we had. Might not be the same as what the sheriff showed her."

"Why don't you have her take a look right now?"

"She's just about finished for the night. And I didn't feel comfortable inviting her up to our room. I told her I would introduce her to you tomorrow, and then maybe we can set something up. You might even just take your laptop down to the lobby, and let her view it over a cup of coffee. I think that would make her more comfortable."

"So, the sheriff took her statement today? Wonder why he didn't mention it."

"He had the FBI stalking him. Besides, it would not have been appropriate."

Before Kate could acknowledge her father's comment, the whole hotel quaked from a powerful blast.

"What was that!" Kate exclaimed as Jack ran to the window.

Their room faced north, and the explosion seemed to have originated more to the western part of the parking lot.

"Look at that," Jack said, pointing to orange reflections dancing on car windows that were parked below their window to the left.

"There's been an explosion over there," he said, pressing his head against the glass to see if he could get a better view.

"Got your key card?"

"I do."

"Let's go check it out."

Chapter 20—Fire lights up the sky

"What do you suppose it was?" Kate asked as they ran down the hall toward the stairs.

"Sounded like something blew up. From the direction, and proximity, I'd guess a car."

"A car bomb?"

"No. More like a bomb in a car."

"That's what I meant. Can we get out this way?"

"Yes," Jack assured her. "This is the fastest route to the west parking area."

The two detectives ran down the stairs and out the door.

"Oh my God!" Kate screamed. "Half the roof is blown off!"

The heat was so intense it halted them at fifty feet. Kate stood in horror, but Jack bolted toward his vehicle, fingering his remote to open the rear hatch as he ran. He was after the commercial-grade fire extinguisher he always carried in the back of his SUV. Quickly as possible he freed up the steel latches that secured it and yanked it out. He sprinted back to the burning automobile, leaving his own rear hatch open.

"Dad, the driver is still in it!" Kate screamed. "But she isn't moving."

Jack sprayed the smothering fog into the driver's side. By then most of the readily flammable material had already been consumed, so the extinguisher was significantly effective in snuffing out the remaining flames. His goal was to prevent the fire from igniting the fuel tank.

"This is taking care of the fire," Jack yelled to his daughter, who had now joined him at the burning car. "But we've got to cool her down until the paramedics arrive. Go back in the hotel and grab some wet towels. And make sure someone's called 911. Hurry!"

That last command was not necessary. Kate was already running at full speed toward the main entrance.

Once inside she yelled in the direction of the front desk, "Do you have an ambulance on the way? Get an ambulance here now! A woman in the lot has massive third-degree burns."

And give me all the towels you've got back there. Now!

"NOW!"

The young man she was addressing reached under the counter and grabbed half a dozen white folded bath towels. He slid them along the counter toward Kate. By the time he had brought up a second bundle for her, she had already disappeared into the family restroom and was soaking them with water.

Only seconds after she had burst into the restroom did she fly back out. She darted down the hall toward the same west exit door as she and her father had used minutes earlier, leaving the second stack of towels on the counter.

By the time she reached the smoking car, Jack was examining the undercarriage to be sure there were no flames threatening the fuel tank.

"Here's the wet towels, I'll go back for another extinguisher."

"No need," Jack said. "Help me to gently cover her with the towels. We've got to cool her down."

"Is she gonna be okay?"

Jack looked into Kate's eyes and shook his head no.

"She'll be fine," he said for the woman's benefit. "We just have to get her cooled down until help gets here."

Jack then addressed the woman.

"Donna. Don't try to talk. But nod your head if you can hear me."

Kate realized that the dying woman was the same one her father had told her about.

Ever so slightly, Donna nodded her head in the affirmative.

"Did you see anyone around your car before it exploded?"

Again she nodded yes.

"Was it one of those men you told me about earlier?"

It took her a moment to think, and then she signaled no.

Then Jack remembered the balding man with the tan jacket who had been sitting in one of the leather chairs in the lobby.

"Was it a shorter, balding man … wearing a tan jacket?"

Donna slowly nodded her head yes.

"Shall I get some more wet towels?" Kate asked.

"No, we're good," Jack said, realizing that Donna was struggling for her last breath.

Jack bent over the dying woman and kissed her gently on the top of her charred head, which was so hot that it burned Jack's lips. But he completed the kiss.

"Donna, darlin', we've got the paramedics on the way. They will have some medicine that will take away your pain."

Jack knew that Donna was no longer feeling any pain. He could tell that her lungs were seared and unable to function. She had slipped into shock, and her entire body was now shutting down. He also realized that even though she was no longer able to respond to him, there was a great likelihood that she could still hear him and process his words.

"Don't try to talk anymore, darlin'. But I promised to introduce you to my daughter. Well, she's the one who got the wet towels for you. Kate, this is that sweet girl I told you about. This is Donna."

Just then the paramedics arrived, and one of them came running up to the car.

"Make room! Let me through!" he commanded.

As Jack and Kate both stepped back, Jack continued speaking in Donna's direction.

"Okay, darlin'. Kate and I are going to get out of their way. But we'll be right over here if you need us."

Jack then put his arm around Kate and pulled her close. Without looking at his daughter, he could sense that she was crying.

"Is she gone?" Kate finally whispered, looking up at her father through her tears.

Jack nodded but did not take his eyes off the young woman he had just met. He too was fighting back the tears.

It was then he noticed dozens of shattered dog treats scattered outside around Donna's car.

Chapter 21—The world is going to the dogs

"Kate," Jack said, pushing one, and then another, of the dog treats toward Kate with his foot. "What do you make of these?"

"I don't know," she said, looking around. "They're not crushed by car tires."

"That's right. Yet they are concentrated around Donna's car. I'd say they were in the car with Donna when it exploded."

Jack then bent down and picked a few of them up.

"Why would Donna have had these in her car?" Kate asked.

"I think that she was a little more familiar with our freckle-faced kid than she let on. I think she brought the dog treats out here for the kid's dog. And when she didn't immediately find him, brought them into the car with her. Could be he is around here someplace, watching us right now."

"Do you think he might have been injured by the explosion?"

"That's a real possibility," Jack agreed. "In a few minutes, the cops are going to be crawling all over this place. Their first objective will be to block the scene off and take statements. I'm gonna take a quick look around, and then we should get out of here. Run interference for me for a few minutes if need be."

Jack assumed that if Red had been walking up to Donna's car, he very well might have been cut by flying glass. It was obvious that the young woman had rolled down the driver's side window. That could suggest that she was attempting to attract Red's attention with treats for his dog. And, because almost all of the treats were scattered near the driver's side, it appeared as though she might have been holding a plastic bag trying to signal her intentions.

If Red were waiting for Donna, he would most likely be lying in the tall grass watching, Jack reasoned.

Jack then walked toward the area where he had earlier seen the boy disappear. It was there, about a hundred feet from the car, just before the paved area ended, that he first spotted blood.

"Red did get cut," Jack said out loud. "I wonder how badly?"

Jack pulled a small LED flashlight out of his pocket and began looking for a trail of blood. He would not be disappointed.

"Here we go," he whispered, as the bluish beam from his flashlight reflected off two more elongated droplets of blood. "Looks like he was running."

Jack glanced around for the presence of police. He really had no desire to share this discovery with the FBI, particularly if they were to draw a connection between the bombing and the murder of his brother-in-law.

Jack observed that the first officer on scene was a city cop, but he then spotted a second car pull up, and it was county. He knew that their main concern would be aiding the paramedics with the victim. He also realized that soon they would be cordoning off the area. Quickly he took several steps leading into the tall grass where he suspected the freckle-faced boy had been waiting for Donna. Again, he was right.

"Well, whaddaya know," he said out loud. "Somebody's been hiding here."

Actually, two somebodies had been there recently—and one of them was a dog.

Realizing that he was right—that Donna had been providing food for Red and his dog, Jack headed back to where Kate was waiting.

"Be nice to get out of here before we draw some unwanted attention," Jack whispered to his daughter.

But it was too late.

"Excuse me, sir," one of the uniformed officers barked in Jack's direction. "I want to ask you a few questions."

Jack tipped his head backward and donned an irritated smile. He knew he and Kate would be interrogated.

"Can you show me some identification?" the officer asked.

"Sure," Jack said, pulling his wallet out of his pocket and handing the officer his driver's license.

"Do you need to see mine as well?" Kate asked. "My name is Kate Handler—I'm this man's daughter."

The officer was studying Jack's Illinois driver's license and did not respond to Kate's question.

"My name is Mark Restin, Deputy Mark Restin. And I see you are Jack Handler. Is that right?"

"Yes."

"And what would you be doing in Sault Ste. Marie? Are you on vacation?"

"Not exactly. My daughter and I are here to meet with an attorney regarding an inheritance."

The officer then looked at Kate and then back at Jack.

"Are you staying at this hotel?"

"That's right. We were in our room, and we heard an explosion. So we came down to see what was going on."

"And, Mr. Handler, what do you do for a living?"

"I'm retired."

"And before you retired?"

"Thirty years for the City of Chicago—I was a city employee."

"Congratulations. Chicago is one of my favorite cities. Wrigley Field—has to be the coolest ballpark in the world."

"It's terrific."

"And when you were working for the City of Chicago, what did you do?"

"I was a homicide detective."

The questioning officer took a long hard look at Jack, and then said, "A big-city detective. How fortunate for me. What can you tell me about this? Any ideas?"

"None, I got here after it blew up. I did not see a thing."

"You didn't see anyone fleeing the scene? Or anything else that looked suspicious?"

"When we got here, the car was still burning. I got my fire extinguisher out of my car and put it out. Actually, it had pretty much burned itself out before I got down here—not a whole lot left that was flammable."

"Are you the one who put the wet towels on the victim?"

"My daughter got them from the front desk, and we applied them. The girl was obviously already dying, but we thought the cool towels might relieve the pain a little. She was in deep shock. She didn't have a chance."

"Do you know who she is?"

"I think she is one of the women who works at the front desk. But it would be hard to make a positive ID at this point."

The officer then turned to Kate.

"What is your first name?"

"My name is Kate, Kate Handler."

"And you are here in the Soo with your father to see an attorney about an inheritance?"

"That's correct."

"There's been a death of someone close to you?"

"My uncle was Alex Garos."

The officer, who had been staring at his notepad while asking his questions, suddenly looked up at Kate: "Alex Garos? The owner of the resort on Sugar Island?"

"That's right."

The officer thought for just a moment and then said, "You two wait here. I'll be right back."

He then turned and walked toward his patrol car—but he did not get in it. Instead, he pulled his cell phone from its holder and made a call. Jack surmised that the officer was calling his superior.

"This is not going to turn out well," Jack said to Kate. "We're about to visit the inside of the County Building—again."

"My boss wants me to bring you in and get a statement," the officer said as he returned to where Jack and Kate were waiting. "Deputy Jordan will escort you to my car."

"Can't we do this in the morning?" Jack asked. "I'm already meeting with a Special Agent Lamar at that time."

"Is that so? Well, it looks like you're gonna get a chance to talk to the Special Agent a little bit sooner. Now, please follow Deputy Jordan and get in my car."

Chapter 22—Adversity, or good fortune?

Both Jack and Kate knew that they had no choice in the matter and that the surest way to make this night last still longer would be to protest.

"How about we drive and follow you? That way we will have our vehicle at the station and you won't have to bring us back to the hotel?"

The officer glanced over at his partner, who shrugged his shoulders.

"I was thinking more along the lines of a holding cell," the officer said not smiling. "But, that's fine—if you want to drive. Where's your car?"

"Right over there," Jack said, pointing at his SUV. "We'll just follow you in."

"That works for us."

With that, the two officers got in their patrol car and headed over to the County Building. Jack pulled into traffic behind them.

"Does this surprise you?" Kate asked. "That they want to question us yet tonight?"

"Not at all. I'd be more surprised if they didn't."

"I know."

"This will actually be more beneficial to us than it is to them. We're already aware that we don't know much. Undoubtedly they have more information than we do. If we pay attention to their line of questioning, we can probably learn something."

"Do you suppose they will question us separately?" Kate asked.

"This is the FBI. I have no doubt that they will conduct a very professional interrogation. They will try to get us to differ on our stories.

The only problem we could have would be if they ask us about the freckle-faced boy. On that, we should plead ignorance."

"Well, we are, aren't we?" Kate asked.

"Yes. But don't you think we would be well served if we coaxed some comments out of them along that line? I think that it would be good to state that I saw a freckle-faced boy in my car earlier. That I must have left it unlocked, and he got in and found some junk food. Then just let them take it from there."

"What do we tell them about the girl behind the counter—Donna?"

"Nothing. We heard a blast, came downstairs, saw the car on fire, and you ran back in and got some wet towels."

"That's it?"

"I would think so. We wouldn't want to offer up more than we know. And that's really all we know."

"Where could we screw up?"

"We should not deny that the sheriff gave us some tapes. They already know that. I trust you've copied them onto your notebook."

"I have."

"They're going to want them back."

"They're in my purse. Do I tell them that I made copies?"

"If they ask. Don't lie."

"I wouldn't lie. But I do not intend to be totally forthcoming, either."

"Think and listen. Then listen some more."

"Exactly."

Both Kate and Jack were silent for an extended period of time. They were contemplating the best way to gain information without giving much away. And then Jack's phone rang.

"Yes," Jack said. He immediately recognized the voice on his phone. It was that of Sheriff Northrup.

"Jack," the sheriff said. "What are you up to right now?"

"Coming down to see you. Actually, I'm coming down to the station to talk to Special Agent Lamar. What do you know about him?"

"You're going to the County Building?"

"Yes, we are. Right now we are following two officers in a patrol car, and we're headed there as we speak."

"I left over an hour ago. I'm out on Sugar Island right now. At your brother-in-law's place. I was hoping you could come out. I would give you the Island Tour.

"I think that my evening has already been planned for me. Actually, it's already been planned for us—Kate's with me."

"Really? What does Lamar want with you?"

"Did you hear anything about the bombing over here at the hotel?"

"*Bombing?* What're you talking about?"

"You know that young lady, Donna? The one who overheard a conversation between two men in the lobby of the hotel? Well, she's dead. Someone placed an explosive device in her car."

"Well, if that just doesn't beat all. When did this happen? I met with her earlier today."

Jack glanced down at his watch and replied, "Forty-eight minutes ago."

"Big explosion?"

"Not really. It appears to have been designed to kill only the girl. I don't think it even peeled the paint on any other vehicle. Just hot and violent in the driver's seat."

"She's dead?"

"Right."

"Did she tell you anything?"

"Not exactly, but she responded affirmatively when I asked her if she had seen a short, balding man in a tan jacket. She nodded her head yes."

"Really. And what made you ask that?"

"Earlier the girl and I had a long talk. She told me about the conversation she had overheard. And she told me that you brought her down for questioning and showed her some video."

"That's all true."

"When I left to go to my room, I took a look over at the chairs where she said the men had been sitting, the ones she had overheard, and I saw a man sitting there—tan jacket, balding. It was almost as though he was trying to listen in on what she and I were talking about."

"Look, Jack. I might not be the seasoned homicide detective you're used to working with, but I'm beginning to think that there is something very different about this murder case. This is getting to be pretty bizarre. What do you make of it?"

"I sure wish I could meet up with you out on the island. But I know that is not going to happen tonight. What do you know about this Lamar fellow?"

"Pretty typical FBI, I suppose—almost stereotypical. Of course, I don't know *that* much about the FBI. But this guy seems to fit the bill, from everything I've ever heard. He's by the book. Seems to me he's smart enough. One thing I know for sure, he does not want me poking around. He made that clear. That's why I'm out here tonight. By tomorrow, I'm sure he will make this off limits to me."

"Any suggestions?"

Sheriff Northrup thought for a moment and then replied, "Yeah. I'm fairly sure he's been given a significant amount of info that he did not get from me. From what I gathered, the DHS has had his ear. If I were you, I think I might listen more than I talked. He just might give you some indication of what he knows by the nature of his questions … you know what I mean. That's how I handled it earlier today."

"I understand. What do you think I should tell him about the fellow in the tan jacket?"

"I can't advise you on that. You know you can't withhold evidence from a federal officer. But I'm not sure that they need to know about that fellow. Who's to say he has anything to do with the case?"

"Have you ever heard anything about this bald guy?"

"No. He's a new one. Maybe tomorrow I can show you some books. You might be able to pick him out, if he's a local."

"Didn't appear to be local to me," Jack quickly replied. "If I were to guess, I would make him to be fifty-six years, five feet seven or eight, one hundred seventy pounds. He looked fit enough, for his age. And I would guess him to be from the East Coast. Just something about him. He looked like New England to me. I would like to have heard him talk a little. Maybe someone around the hotel has talked to him. His prints would be on that chair. Maybe I'll get the chance to lift them."

"Along with a thousand others," the sheriff quickly added.

"It's still worth a shot. When the FBI finishes with me, I'll do some poking around. The hotel would have him on camera."

"They might," the sheriff agreed. "I'll have a deputy check into that."

"Will that upset the FBI?"

"Probably will," the sheriff chuckled. "Maybe I'll give them a copy. … I just want to make sure it don't get erased."

Just as Jack was preparing to disconnect, he overheard the sheriff talking to another man.

"And who might you be?" Sheriff Northrup asked.

As those words left the sheriff's mouth, Jack heard the distinctive muffled double 'pop' of a suppressed .22 caliber Long Rifle. And then he heard Sheriff Northrup groan, and groan again.

"Sheriff! You okay?" Jack asked. But the sheriff did not reply. It sounded like the sheriff's cell phone bounced off something hard. And then a third 'pop', followed by virtual silence.

Finally, Jack heard what sounded like a man picking up the sheriff's phone.

Chapter 23—No interview tonight

Jack jerked his car to the side and parked crooked. He placed his hand tightly across the mouthpiece of his cell phone to muffle it. And then he waited, listening intently for anything helpful.

After a few moments, he heard a second voice.

"Whatcha got? The sheriff's phone? Let me see that."

There then was a pause.

"Josh. You idiot—he was talking to someone."

"How do you know that?"

"Look at the display. See that number? Write it down. Can you see it? Have you got it? All right, now smash it on the pier."

Five seconds later the call dropped.

"I heard part of that," Kate said. "The sheriff is dead, isn't he?"

"It would seem so. At least that's what it sounded like. I need to get my hands on that phone."

"What's the problem, Handler?" the officer said, tapping his flashlight on Jack's window. He had observed Jack stop, and he made two rapid U-turns, pulling in behind Jack and Kate. He appeared very irritated.

"I think Sheriff Northrup has been shot," Jack told him. "He called my cell. I was talking to him, and I heard what sounded like suppressed gunfire. I'm pretty sure he's been shot."

"Where was he? Did he tell you where he was calling from?"

"Sugar Island. He said he was at the resort, out by the pier where Alex was killed. There were two men with him."

"Interview's off," the officer shouted as he headed back to his patrol car.

"Let's go," Jack said, glancing over at Kate.

Jack was careful to allow the patrol car to pass him before he pulled out to follow.

"We better not get to the ferry before he does," Jack said, ducking in behind him. "I'm sure he wouldn't think much of that."

"Is he going to get hold of the FBI about that interview? Or did he just come up with that on his own?"

"You can bet that Special Agent Lamar will be headed to the island too," Jack said. "And he's not gonna be so keen on seeing us there."

"I'm sure that won't make him happy," Kate said. "We need to get one of those ticket books for the ferry. Like the ones the residents use. Huge discount."

"How did you learn about that?"

"Online—before I left New York."

"Why didn't you buy one online?"

"You're right—I should have. But I'm not sure they're even available like that. I think you might have to buy them at the boat. …Whoa, Dad. Coming up fast."

One patrol passed them at double their speed, and another was close behind.

"I see them," Jack said, pulling over to the side of the road to let the second car by.

"I think we might have to catch the second ferry," Kate quipped. "The first one appears to be filling quickly."

"They might shut it down."

"Seriously?"

"They might," Jack said. "In fact, they should … to everything except emergency vehicles. That would be the best way to keep whoever is on the island right now, on the island."

"Let's see if we can sneak on."

"It won't be a matter of sneaking," Jack said. "If they do what they should, they will load the ferry up with police and pull out. Then search it thoroughly on the trip to the island and hold it over there. I'll bet they call in every on-duty officer and dispatch them to positions along the river."

"Do you think that's where the killer or killers are? Trying to escape to the mainland?"

"I doubt it," Jack replied. "If they haven't fled to Canada by now, they're holed up on the island—hiding. Probably blending in pretty well."

"Look, the ferry is about to dock," Kate said. "And we're fifth in line. We should make it, don't you think?"

"If they allow us on."

"Take a look down the river," Kate said, pointing at the two cars that had just passed them. "Those two cars are taking up positions down-river. Or is that upriver?"

"The St. Mary's River flows out of Lake Superior, and into Lake Nicolet, and then into Huron."

Jack was right about the river, but that had not always been the case. Until the late nineteenth century, the St. Mary's flowed north out of Sault Ste. Marie, and then curved around to the east side of Sugar Island. There was a smaller channel of the river that did flow along the west side of the island, but its treacherous rapids posed a problem for vessels drawing more than three or four feet of water.

So, even though the distance around to the east of Sugar Island was forty percent greater, the eastern route was chosen because it could handle significantly larger boats.

In 1882 dredging started on the west channel, and in 1894 the new shipping channel was opened. It is an interesting fact that had the principal part of the river originally flowed on the west side of Sugar Island (as it does currently), instead of the east, the possession of the island would most likely have been granted to Canada by the Treaty of Paris in 1783. That is because the main argument the United States offered to support its position was that the St. Mary's River should serve as the national boundary, and therefore Sugar Island should be part of the United States.

Today the east channel has so shrunk that it is a mere fraction of what it was in the early nineteenth century.

"What are the chances the killers are headed this way?"

"Seems unlikely," Jack said. "After all, the channel to the east is so shallow a man could almost walk across to Canada. It would pay, however, to do a thorough search of the ferry after it pulls out. The chances are pretty slim that the perps are headed this direction. But you have to cover all the bases."

"Hey, Dad, they're gonna let us on. Terrific!"

"Looks like."

"They must not have overheard you."

"I wasn't really expecting to get across tonight," Jack said. "That's going to be one big crime scene—the whole island should have a ribbon around it."

"Looks like we're not the last on," Jack continued, observing three more vehicles in his mirror, all of which he had just passed on Portage.

"So, what do you know about the sheriff?" Kate asked. "Is he married? Does he have children?"

"Don't know for sure," Jack replied. "His ring finger was empty. But that doesn't always mean something."

"He could be a widower," Kate said. "He strikes me as someone who would have married—at some point in his life. Maybe he's divorced."

"Funny how we never thought much about that ... until now."

"I know," Kate agreed. "Isn't that a shame? We too often regard the value of a life by those who are left behind. But I really think he had a family, probably eight grandkids—five boys and three girls."

"Now you're speculating—not healthy for a homicide detective."

"I call it profiling," Kate chuckled.

"Pure speculation," Jack responded. "Let's get serious about this."

"I am serious," Kate said. "It's just that I like laughing better than crying."

"If I were to do some speculating," Jack said, dropping his smile, "I would speculate that the sheriff's murder is connected with your uncle's murder."

"How sure are you that the sheriff was murdered?"

"We should know in just a few minutes," Jack replied. "It certainly sounded as though he was shot three times, with the last round placed where it would do the most good."

"Professional?"

"It doesn't seem likely to me that it was a professional hit—not clinical enough."

"Why do you say that?"

"There were two of them. I heard them talking over the sheriff's phone. In a sense, it felt more like a spur of the moment thing—the opportunity presented itself, and they took advantage of it. I will admit that the use of a suppressor reflects some degree of professionalism. But I can't understand why there would be two shooters. It just doesn't feel like a real professional hit."

"Was he lured out there?"

"That could be," Jack said. "I would like to know who else he talked to tonight. I would really like to get hold of his cell."

"Is that possible?" Kate asked, "with all those cops around?"

"I'm not even sure we will get to visit the scene. But I would surmise that our best opportunity would be immediately after we get there. Hard to say how quickly they will rope it off, or if they will even allow us to check it out. If the FBI has anything to say about it, they will see to it we're kept at bay."

"I know," Kate said. "Do you have a plan?"

"Maybe," Jack said. "The patrol car ahead of us will be the lead car. There are only a few roads on the island. So if they drive off the ferry before we do, and they should, then if we stick to their bumper …"

"And when they pull in, we'll scoot past them and drive around to the pier?" Kate finished her father's thought.

"Exactly. Pretend we did not notice their signals, and head right for the pier."

"That could work," Kate agreed. "Won't give us much time, but perhaps enough."

"I'm not sure if the FBI made the boat," Jack said, turning around and carefully scrutinizing all the vehicles behind them.

Chapter 24—The race for evidence

It had been years since Jack had driven out to the resort, but he was confident that he remembered enough about the way the buildings were arranged on the property to make a maneuver to the river and perhaps beat the patrol car to the scene of the crime. Jack stared out of the windshield and into the sky, trying to picture the exact layout of the resort.

Finally, the ferry pulled out into the river and began the fifteen-minute trip across the St. Mary's.

"Only two marked cars on the boat," Kate observed, "At least that's all I spotted. Could be some unmarked. But it doesn't appear to be so."

"That's what I counted," Jack agreed.

"Surprising."

"Small boat," Jack replied. "Small city."

It felt to Jack like a very long fifteen minutes. He was a little surprised that the officers did not perform a search of the ferry before or even after it pulled out. "Could have been someone hiding onboard, waiting for an opportune moment to escape to the mainland," he reasoned.

"Finally," Jack blurted out when the ferry docked and the cars began pulling off.

He was directly behind the second patrol car, so when the chain came down, he was ready. By the time the patrol car's rear wheels hit the dock, Jack was already in motion. The car to Jack's right had been signaled to pull off ahead of him, but Jack would have none of that.

"Careful, Dad. You're gonna get a ticket."

"Right."

As soon as Jack had established his position directly behind the patrol cars, he backed off a bit, following at a safe distance.

"Hilltop Bar," Jack announced as they passed a small building with a large parking lot. "That is the only drinking establishment on the island—now that your resort has been closed. At least as far as I know."

"Really?" Kate responded. "No restaurants?"

"Not right now. Alex's resort had a great restaurant and a bar. But that's it, I think."

"I don't see many houses," Kate observed.

"How many people did I say lived on the island? Six hun—"

"I don't believe it! Did you see that?" Jack said, almost yelling.

"See what?"

"The patrol cars—they shot right past the main road … Brassar Road. The one that heads down toward the resort. The deputy must have been on his cell. That's a break."

Jack slowed his vehicle abruptly and turned right.

The brake lights triggered first on the brightly illuminated lead patrol car, and then on the second car. Both were skidding to a stop two hundred yards past the intersection. Now Jack's became the lead vehicle. Jack hit the gas pedal. That north/south stretch of Brassar Road was straight and virtually flat.

"Looks like our friends figured it out," Jack said, "Just a little bit too late."

"That changes things," Jack continued. "Now we're going to do this differently. When we get there, I'm going to pull right up front and stop. You jump out and walk up to the main entrance—like that's where we're expecting to find the sheriff. And you wait there for the officers. Make sure they see you. I'll leave the lights on and engine running."

"And what are you gonna do?" Kate asked.

"I'm going around to the rear and head out to the pier. Maybe I can locate that cell phone before they do."

"Is that tampering with evidence?"

"I suppose," Jack said. "But whoever killed the sheriff probably killed Alex. If your uncle's case is ever going to get solved, it might be up to us to do it. At least that's how it's beginning to look."

"How far to the resort?" Kate asked.

"One—two miles at most," Jack replied, glancing over at his GPS.

"Shall I enter the location of the resort?"

"No need," Jack said, pointing to the screen. "That's the resort, right there."

He then zoomed in and pointed again.

"Right before that drive ends, that's your Uncle Alex's resort. Or should I say, *your* resort."

"Watch out!" Kate yelled.

Chapter 25—Jack on night watch

Without looking up from the GPS Jack slammed on the brakes.

"That's him?" Kate asked. "Your freckle-faced boy? Right?"

Jack, looking up just as two figures disappeared into the woods, roared, "Sure was … with his golden retriever right behind. Where'd he come from!"

"Could he be headed to the resort?" Kate queried, as Jack rapidly accelerated again.

"How'd he get back here so fast? That's what I'd like to know. He was breaking into my car at the hotel only a couple hours ago. That kid must have contacts. Or else he's just very good at being Tom Sawyer."

"Maybe both," Kate replied. "At some point we're gonna have to talk to him."

"That could be difficult. I understand that he doesn't talk."

"Really? Where'd you hear that?"

"Donna, the girl whose car blew up. She said that Red—that's the name people have given him—that Red spent some time in foster homes. But mostly he survives on his own. … And somewhere along the way he lost his ability to talk."

"No kidding. Is it something physical?"

"Think so, but not sure about that."

"Well," Kate said, "Everyone has to develop some way to communicate with other people. I imagine he has too."

"Here we are," Jack said, "Six Mile Road." He slowed abruptly to maneuver the one-hundred-fifty-degree right turn back toward the resort.

"We've got less than a quarter mile on the patrol cars. And I'm sure they're screaming," he said. "You're going to have to be quick. As soon as this car stops, jump out and head to the main entrance. Make sure the officers can see you when they pull up. Leave your door open. And behave as though I'm right there with you. Hopefully, they will follow your lead."

"Got it," Kate replied. The road they had turned onto angled back, affording them a good view of what was behind. They could see the flashing lights of the patrol cars fast approaching on the main road.

"We've got ten seconds to pull this off," he said. "They're right on us."

Jack struggled to find some landmark that might help him orient himself to the campus.

"What are we looking for?" Kate asked.

"Not sure, but just before the river we turn right. Should be a road here."

"That it?" Kate asked. "South Westshore Drive—does that sound right?"

"I don't remember—if the GPS says we're there, we must be," Jack said as he hit the brakes hard and skidded around the corner. "Maybe a quarter mile ahead, and there should be a marked drive to the west."

"There it is—that's gotta be it."

Jack agreed but did not respond, except for slamming on his brakes again, and making a sharp left onto a well-kept drive.

"Now, if memory serves me, just before we get to the river, we'll have to make one more right, ... and that should lead us right up to the resort."

The two patrol cars had gained some ground, but Jack still had nearly an eight-second lead on them.

"This place has changed dramatically," he said as he pulled in. "And not just cosmetically. Your uncle must have put a million into it since I've been here. But, I should still be able to pull right up to the main building. Then my car will give me cover to hit the river."

Jack cranked the wheel to the right and applied the brakes hard, stopping his SUV inches from the corner of the main building. He left the engine running.

"Now!" Jack shouted. "Run!"

Kate bolted from the vehicle and darted to the front entrance. The headlights of the first approaching patrol car cast her shadow on the darkened building. She turned to face the spotlight that the cops were throwing on the resort's façade.

Jack ran as well, except his form was concealed by his vehicle and the building.

Once he was sure he was out of sight of the officer, he illuminated a small LED flashlight that he had yanked off his keychain as he got out.

The last time Jack had visited the resort, the area between the main building and the river was not developed. But now there was a glass structure containing an indoor swimming pool, a small shed that he did not remember, and another larger structure, the purpose of which he had no clue.

"Well, at least the river's still there," he muttered, slowing down as he approached the pier.

Just as he had suspected, right at the step leading onto the pier, he spotted blood. Jack knelt down and examined it.

"Still red and wet," he said aloud. "Looks like they dragged the sheriff out onto the pier, just like with Alex. This is where they shot him. His cell ought to be around here somewhere. If they attempted to destroy it, they probably didn't take it with them."

When Jack pointed his flashlight onto the pier, he spotted some plastic debris and a scuff mark.

That looks interesting, he thought.

Jack stood and walked over to the spot. It looked to him as though someone had smashed an object with his or her foot and then kicked it into the river.

Judging by the marks, Jack thought, *what is left of the sheriff's cell phone ought to have just about reached the water.*

Jack then walked off the pier and over to the river's edge.

"There," he said aloud. "That's it."

Lying on his stomach, Jack reached into the shallow water and retrieved what he suspected was Sheriff Northrup's cell phone. Still lying by the water, he shone his flashlight into its inner workings to be sure the SIM card was intact.

"Great," he said, determining that the memory card was still in the smashed cell. "That will do it."

Jack stood to his feet and slid the phone into his coat pocket, but not before removing the SIM card and slipping it into his pants pocket.

"Handler!" the officer shouted in his direction. "Whatcha find?"

Jack looked up, holding his hand over his eyes to block the beam of Officer Restin's large five-cell Maglite. Jack was a little surprised that there was only one officer headed back to where he was standing.

"Looks like a crime scene," Jack said, pointing to the blood. "Still fresh. Looks like someone was shot here—I would assume it was Sheriff Northrup—and then dragged out onto the pier."

"You need to back off," the officer commanded. "If you're right. And this is a crime scene. It would be *my* crime scene."

"What if the sheriff is still alive?" Jack asked. "We'll need to try to save him, right?"

"That's true," the office replied, keying his radio. "Hold on," he said.

"Wait right there … don't take another step."

"This is Deputy Restin. I'm at the rear of the resort on Sugar Island, on the river. I have blood. And it appears as though someone was dragged out onto the pier here at the resort. I'm requesting a medical response unit."

"We've got a unit waiting to get on the ferry right now."

"How about Homeland Security. Do they have medical?"

"No. But that unit should be right behind you."

"Ten-four."

"I think we should follow the drag marks and see if the victim is still alive," Jack advised.

Chapter 26—Blood in the water

For a moment, Jack considered handing the sheriff's cell phone over to Deputy Restin but decided to take a chance and hang onto it.

"Right," the officer replied. "But try not to mess up the blood trail."

Deputy Restin pointed his flashlight out onto the pier and removed his Smith and Wesson service revolver from his holster.

Jack observed the relatively small amount of blood, both on the ground where the sheriff was shot and on the pier.

Must have been a small caliber handgun, Jack figured. *Probably the .22 I suspected when I initially heard it going down.*

Jack chose not to share those thoughts with Deputy Restin.

"Looks like they grew impatient," the officer said, shining his flashlight off the right side of the pier, less than twenty feet out. The beam struck the sheriff's body, half in and half out of a small boat that was tied to the pier.

"Point your flashlight down here. I'll check for a pulse," Deputy Restin said, setting his flashlight down and stepping out into the two-foot-deep water.

Jack picked up his pace until he reached the officer, and he illuminated the sheriff's unresponsive body with his own small flashlight.

The boat supported the upper portion of the sheriff's torso, face down. Deputy Restin positioned and repositioned his fingers on the sheriff's neck, searching for a pulse. Finally, he looked up at Jack and announced,

"The sheriff's dead."

"You're going to need help pulling him out," Jack said, dropping to his knees on the edge of the pier. He laid his keychain flashlight down and reached out to grasp the boat to pull it closer to the pier.

"No!" Deputy Resin strongly insisted. "We should leave him right here, right where he was dumped. I suspect the FBI is not going to want anything disturbed."

"Let's see if the killer dropped anything in the water," the deputy said, picking his flashlight back up.

The beam of light reflected off the shiny surface. So Deputy Restin lay down on his stomach and held his flashlight below the surface. The river was running very slowly, and it took a long time for the sediment he had disturbed to dissipate.

Jack seized the opportunity. While the officer was waiting for the water to clear, he removed the sheriff's cell phone from his pocket. Then, after he wiped off his fingerprints and double-checked to be sure the SIM card was not in it, he knelt and silently slipped it into the water on the opposite side of the pier.

After Deputy Restin had satisfied himself that there was nothing of interest on the upstream side of the pier, he turned to the other side.

"Let's see if anything drifted downstream," he said, shining his flashlight into the water. As the light's beam struck the surface, it illuminated a small stream of blood that had been carried off by the water running beneath.

The river was still too muddy for the officer to easily examine the bottom, so he again dropped to his stomach and submerged his flashlight below the surface.

"What's that?" he asked when the light beam reflected off something shiny.

Jack dropped to his knees beside the officer.

"Looks like a cell phone," Jack said. "Possibly the sheriff's."

"Wonder if there's anything else down there," the deputy said, continuing to scour the bottom with his submerged flashlight. The officer knew that once he stepped into the water, he would again stir it up.

Finally, he pulled the flashlight out of the water, stepped down into it, and retrieved what they both thought to be the sheriff's cell phone.

"Okay, Mr. Handler, time for you to go. I'm going to accompany you back to your car now, and I want you to wait there with your daughter until I've given you permission to leave."

Jack replied nonverbally by standing to his feet and turning toward the resort.

But before the two men had taken a dozen steps, they were startled by a thunderous rush of noise exploding from the woods about a thousand feet to the east.

"That sounds like a bird—a big one," Jack observed. "Is it yours?"

The officer peered toward the noise. "You've gotta be kidding. A chopper on our budget? We're lucky to have three-year-old patrol cars."

Chapter 27—The black helicopter

With a deafening burst of twin jet engines compressing the air beneath its rotors, a huge black machine shot straight up out of the trees and quickly disappeared over the island into Canadian airspace. The two men watched intently.

"What is an Apache doing on Sugar Island?" Deputy Restin asked. "Must be DHS."

"I doubt that," Jack retorted. "That was no government bird. Sounded like a Bell 429. Too dark to pick up markings—if it even had markings. And no lights."

"You're right about it having no lights," Deputy Restin agreed. "Is that legal?"

"Only over Nevada," Jack quipped.

"What did you call it? A Bell 429? How can you be so sure about that?"

"Not positive," Jack replied. "But that would be the most likely candidate. The Bell 429 is the most popular twin jet chopper out there—and that was a twin. Could be an earlier model, but most of *them* were prototypes. Best bet is that it was a production model—a Bell 429."

"So, it wasn't military?"

"Doubt it. But it was definitely not an Apache," Jack said. "The Bell 429 is popular for medical evacuation but not for military use. And they're not cheap—easy five million. I doubt there's many of them around, but without markings it would be impossible to identify. Wouldn't want to get caught in one like that—crossing the border with no markings. But with its speed and range, catching it might be difficult."

For nearly a full minute, both men stood silently on the pier. Finally, Deputy Restin broke the silence.

"Okay, Handler. You're a big-city homicide detective—"

"*Retired* homicide detective," Jack interrupted. "I've probably been retired for as long as you've been a deputy. Things change every year."

"Anyway, you seem to know a lot about this business. And you've certainly seen a lot more murders than I have. So what are you making out of this? What do you think we're up against?"

The deputy's question surprised Jack—he anticipated that Deputy Restin would be more reticent in sharing his concerns about the case.

"That's an excellent question," Jack responded. "We just got in today, so I've not even begun to get my head wrapped around it. And already there's been two more murders."

"Do you think they're both related to your relative—Alex?" Deputy Restin asked, starting to walk toward the resort, expecting Jack to follow.

"Anything is possible, I suppose, but I would be surprised if they were *not* somehow related," Jack said, dropping in behind the deputy. "And now we're dealing with unmarked choppers that are darting over the border into Canada. There is definitely something very strange going on.

"Surely the DHS has some theories. Right? What do you know about what they're thinking? They were all over Sheriff Northrup's office earlier today. What do they think about this? And why are they so involved?"

"I've not had personal contact with the DHS," Deputy Restin said. "But I've heard rumors."

"What sort of rumors?"

"Look," Deputy Restin said, stopping in front of Jack. "Up until a few weeks ago the most exciting thing I've been involved with was the Smith case. Jake Smith got drunk and beat his wife to death. The sheriff sent me out to his house, and I found him dead—self-inflicted gunshot wound. That's it. Eighteen years on the road. And that's the biggest thing I've had to deal with around here. And then your uncle gets murdered."

"Actually my brother-in-law—Alex Garos was my brother-in-law."

"Well, your brother-in-law. He turns up dead in the water off this very same pier. Gunshot wound, just like Sheriff Northrup."

"What are they saying about all this?" Jack asked. "When you and your buddies have beers—what's being suggested?"

"Frankly, we really don't know," the officer said.

"Right, none of us knows anything for a fact, not yet. But when you talk about it, where does the conversation take you?"

"Some are suggesting drugs," Deputy Restin said.

"You think that Alex might have been involved with trafficking?"

"Not so much Alex Garos himself—but others. And maybe he learned about it. That's one of the theories."

"There's other theories?"

"Yeah, there's others."

"Such as?"

"Well, did the sheriff share any of those videos with you?"

"He showed us some of the resort's videos," Jack replied. "Seems like there were some shady characters that were frequenting the resort. Is that what you mean?"

"Exactly. Some of the same guys popped up several times over the past year ... and even earlier," Deputy Restin said. "We really cannot pin names on them. We've got names on the register, but the names do not seem to consistently match up with the faces. That is, we've got the same faces, but with different names."

"Is that right?" Jack asked.

"And it's not in one or two instances," Deputy Restin continued. "Two of those fellows seem to appear on the video four separate times, but the names attributed to them on the register are always different."

"So, what do your buddies suspect?" Jack asked, taking advantage of his opportunity with a now accommodating Deputy Restin.

"As far as anyone knows," the deputy continued, "none of these characters actually appear in the video with your brother-in-law—you know, communicating with him. So, some are assuming that he had no direct knowledge of what was going on ... or if he did, he was *very* careful. I have to tell you, the conventional wisdom has your brother-in-law involved, but on the highest level. How else could it be? He owns—rather owned—the resort. He was neither careless nor detached. In fact, he was an old-country, hands-on type boss."

"Really?" Jack asked. "Didn't he have managers? Like a day manager, or a night manager?"

"Sure, but almost any time we'd get called to the resort, it was by him. And it was him that we looked up when we responded. I've probably responded three or four times in the past two years. And it was always at his request."

"What sort of problems did you run on?"

"Once there was an overdose—one of the resorters, a man in his thirties, OD'd on sleeping pills and booze."

"Dead?"

"Sure was. Then there was a domestic dispute—husband and wife. He apparently caught her messing around with one of the other guests. Beat him up and then slapped his wife around."

"You said you've been here three or four times? What were the other instances that you recall?"

"In one case a guest got drunk and fell off the pier. He bumped his head. Nothing very serious, but the emergency responders requested an officer because the fellow got a bit belligerent."

"And the fourth?"

"That could have been more than two years ago—now that I think about it. That time there was an altercation between a guest and a desk clerk. Didn't amount to much more than a shouting match."

"Do you recall what the argument was about?"

"You know, I do remember. The guest wanted to be moved to a different room, and the clerk wouldn't oblige. The guest threw a hairy fit, but the clerk wouldn't budge. By the time my partner and I got across on the ferry, and showed up at the resort, they had it all sorted out. The night manager stepped in and gave the guest the room he wanted. As I recall, the desk clerk was very angry that his boss didn't back him up. When we got there, they were having words. And the guest was nowhere to be found."

"Are they both still employed at the resort—the night manager and his assistant?"

"I haven't seen the assistant around—not after *that* night. He might have quit. Or got fired. Like they say—the customer's always right. The assistant didn't get that rule."

"How about the night manager?"

"He's still here. And he's still the night manager. At least he was until we closed the resort. He's been here for as long as I can remember."

"He's the squirrely looking one in the video?"

"That would be him. Some people think he's one of the owners—but he's just an employee. He strikes me as a cold fish. I didn't really like him much. He was very hard to talk to. But Mr. Garos must have liked him, to keep him around for so long."

"Maybe he did a good job."

"Or worked cheap. I've heard that he never missed a day and that he pulled a lot of double shifts."

"Handy guy to have around if you own a business. Otherwise, you end up filling in."

"But, like I was saying, most of the time, when the cops were called to the resort, it was either by Mr. Garos, or at least Mr. Garos was the one meeting us. He was a hands-on type of guy."

"So, are you suggesting that if there was something illegal going on at the resort, Alex Garos would most likely have known about it?"

"That's just about how most of us feel. We all liked your brother-in-law, and we even sometimes stopped in and had a beer with him—off the clock, of course. But it seems to us that if something was going on, it would have been hard to hide it from him—especially over an extended period of time. It just seems weird that he wouldn't know."

"And if you had to pick the type of illegality—what would it be?"

"Now that's a great question," Deputy Restin said. "In a place like this, you know, on the border, imaginations can run wild—drugs, illegals, human trafficking, terrorism, you name it. We've discussed them all. But no one can produce evidence of any wrongdoing. Except, of course, murder. And we've seen plenty of that lately."

"But if you, or your associates, had to pick a crime—anything that stands out—what would it be?"

"Truthfully, we don't have a clue. A city cop—a good friend of mine—said he has seen some people around town, over the past several months, and that they did not appear to be your typical tourists or fishermen. He thought they might be from the East Coast area."

"You mean like New York, or New Jersey?"

"He suggested New England—Connecticut, Massachusetts. Maybe Boston."

"What made him think that?"

"The way they dressed and the way they talked."

"Does he have any reason to associate them with the business at the resort?"

"Not really. But he thought that these fellows stood out. And when he mentioned that fact to me at the coffee shop, the owner of the coffee shop said that they sounded like some fellows who had stopped in there, and that they had asked him a lot of questions about Sugar Island. Nothing specific, but general stuff."

"What's the name of that coffee shop? Where is it?"

"It's just called 'Joey's.' On Ashmun, just south of the Business Spur. It's not one of those chain shops, like Starbucks. They do make an excellent espresso. You ought to stop by there. Joey, the owner, is a fount of information."

"Looks like we've got company," Jack said, pointing toward a medical emergency vehicle pulling around the corner of the main building and heading down the hill toward the pier.

"They're gonna get that thing stuck down here," Deputy Restin said, stepping off the pier. He started trotting up the hill, waving his hands over his head to signal the unit to stop at the top of the incline.

"I'm sure that the sheriff's not in a hurry," Jack replied, as he followed Deputy Restin.

When they reached the point where the pier met land, Jack spotted his daughter coming around the corner of the main building and walking back to where he and Deputy Restin were standing.

"Dad," Kate shouted in his direction. "Can you come up here for a minute?"

"How about it, Deputy, will tomorrow work out for the interview?"

"Yeah," Deputy Restin said. "Nothing more you can do around here. We'll take your full statement tomorrow morning. I'll let Special Agent Lamar know. If it doesn't work for him, I'll get back to you."

Jack was ready to get out of there.

"Great," he replied. "I'll be at your office at eight a.m."

"Make it ten—and call first," Deputy Restin said.

"That works," Jack said as he headed up the hill to where his daughter was waiting.

"What's up?" he asked, detecting disquiet on her face.

Chapter 28—Kate makes a discovery

"Let's get in the car," she said, opening the passenger door and getting in without waiting for his response.

Jack recognized from her earnestness that something was up.

"Okay," he said. "Are you ready to tell me what's got you so excited?"

"Back up to your left and turn around."

"Will do," he said, sliding the shifter into reverse.

"Now, pull out slowly … very slowly. Put your high beams on."

Jack flipped on the high beams and steered his vehicle in the direction Kate had indicated.

Just as his headlights hit a growth of trees, both his and Kate's eyes caught sight of Red.

"There," Kate said, grabbing the wheel. "Stop."

Jack had seen the boy at the exact moment that Kate did.

When the boy realized that he had been spotted, he jumped up out of the undergrowth and bolted into the woods, with Dog close behind.

"How did you know he would be there?" Jack asked.

"Just had a feeling," she responded. "I heard some rustling around at the edge of the woods and was pretty sure I heard his dog talking to him.

"Anyway, doesn't it just figure that he would turn up in a situation like this?"

"Like what?"

"Like murder," Kate said. "The call goes in, and he shows up. Like an albatross."

"Or a harbinger," Jack interrupted.

"You gonna go after him?" Kate asked.

Jack detected a chuckle in her voice. "You're younger than I am. Maybe you should chase him down."

"What would I do with him if I caught him?"

"What do you do with 'juvies' in New York?" Jack retorted.

"You can't win these. The guys on the street hate dealing with teens."

"And this one's got a dog," Jack said. "You know, we saw him scooting across the road on our way here.

"Let's go back to that spot and see if we can pick him up on his way back."

"Can you do anything with your running lights?" Kate asked, knowing that many private detectives install a cut-off switch.

"Check in here," Jack said, popping open the center console. "There's a couple pair of night vision goggles. See if you can figure out how they work."

"I thought you'd have some."

Kate pulled out the first pair and examined it.

"What language is this?"

"Russian," Jack replied. "But they're pretty self-explanatory. There's an on/off on the right side.

"They should be charged and ready to go."

Kate found the switch and turned it on, turned her head to face the side window and then slid the strap over the back of her head.

"They don't exactly look like those our guys use in New York, but they seem to work fine."

"You guys have a bigger budget than I do. Let me have the ones you're wearing, and you take the second set."

Before putting the goggles on, Jack hit a kill switch, which turned off the dashboard lights and disabled all running lights.

He then quickly slipped the goggles over his head and pulled out of the driveway. Kate found the second pair and put them on.

"What are you thinking?" Kate asked. "Do you think the kid lives around here?"

"It figures that he is at least staying somewhere close by. First we see him running across the road heading toward the resort. ... Then he turns up *at* the resort, probably watching us. Wouldn't surprise me if he was holed up in a nearby cabin, maybe east of here."

"From what I've heard, there's a lot of them—cabins that is," Kate said. "And probably most are stocked with some kind of food—something that won't freeze."

"I would imagine that many of the residents don't much care if he shares their cabins, as long as he doesn't wreck them or take anything except food."

"He's becoming a legend. Everyone knows he exists, but no one's figured out how to deal with him."

"Or cares to," Jack added.

"It's the age-old story of a boy and his dog—how romantic."

"I think this was just about where we saw him cross earlier—about fifty yards up. What do you think?"

Jack then pulled as far off the right side of the road as he could.

"There, Dad. Do you see it? Off in the woods to the left. I see two figures, but they've stopped moving. Do you see them?"

"I do," Jack replied. "Let's wait here and see what they do."

For nearly a minute, Kate and Jack sat motionless, waiting for Red and his dog to cross the road.

Finally, three sources of heat emerged from the woods and crossed the pavement—a mother raccoon and two babies.

"Well, Kate, there's our boy and his dog—they shrunk."

"Hang on," Kate said. "I think the raccoons might have been spooked. It looks to me like there are two more objects moving right behind them."

Chapter 29—Following at a distance

"You're right," Jack agreed. "These look more like our subjects."

Kate and Jack sat still, waiting for Red and his dog to cross in front of them.

"Think he will spot us?" Kate asked.

"He might. For a kid, he sure is pretty savvy."

Jack sensed Kate was chuckling.

"Okay, give with it," he said. "What strikes you as funny now?"

"I was just thinking. If this kid is as savvy as you say, maybe he has night vision too. Wouldn't that be a hoot?"

Jack couldn't help but laugh out loud.

"He's taking his time," he finally said. "Looks like he's making sure that no one's around."

"Can he see the car?" Kate asked. "It's bright enough, I'll bet he can see the car."

"Probably, but he won't see us if we stay still. He will eventually think that it's broke down or out of gas. It's a cinch that he wants to move along. Probably back to where he is staying."

"He's moving," Kate observed. "Looks like he's tired of waiting."

"It's late, he's tired—might have to take a leak."

"He might be tired and cold, but the kid has a fourteen-year-old prostate. Besides, I'm pretty sure he's able to get along without indoor plumbing. At least, he's gotta be more experienced at that than we are."

"Speaking of—" Jack said.

"I wondered about that," Kate said, again chuckling.

"Look at him go!" Jack exclaimed as he watched Red and the dog cross the road and rapidly scamper through the woods. He was still careful not to be heard outside the vehicle.

Without speaking another word, both Jack and Kate exited the vehicle and briskly walked over to the point where the boy and his dog had crossed.

Jack pointed to a path that led into the woods, and then both he and Kate silently disappeared down it.

They had progressed nearly two hundred feet before they stopped for a moment to contemplate their next move.

It was clear that the boy and his dog knew exactly where they were headed and were able to navigate through the woods at a more rapid speed.

Leaning over to whisper in Kate's ear, Jack spoke in a voice only she could hear.

"You head back to the vehicle. There's no need for both of us to follow the boy. We will be less likely to make noise if there's just one of us. I'll see if I can identify where he is staying."

Kate did not say a word. Though not happy with her father's command, she merely nodded in the affirmative and turned back toward their vehicle.

Jack quickly grabbed her by the shoulder and pulled her back. He reached into his pocket and retrieved the SIM card that he had removed from Sheriff Northrup's cell phone and handed it to her. She slid it into her pocket without checking to see what he had given her.

Jack then patted her on the shoulder and gestured for her to head back toward the road.

Before he had taken more than a dozen steps, he again caught a glimpse of the boy. Crouching as low as possible, he followed at what he considered to be a safe distance.

As is the case with much of the terrain on Sugar Island, as soon as you step off the main road, you're unpredictably engulfed in patches of thick undergrowth or knee-deep mud—sometimes worse.

This isn't going to work out well, Jack thought. *The kid is totally familiar with this terrain. I'm going to need some light, or who knows where I'll end up.*

So he took out an infrared illuminator and switched it on.

That should do it, he reasoned.

Jack then stood erect and looked for the ffreckle-faced kid. For a long five seconds he thought he had lost the boy. But finally he spotted Red and his dog moving through the woods about one hundred and fifty feet ahead.

"There they are," he mouthed silently. "Looks almost like they've made a left turn."

Jack reasoned that there must be an intersecting path at that point, or at least a dog leg.

I'd better get a move on, or I'm going to lose them, he thought. So he pressed forward a little more quickly. All the while keeping an eye open for the path that Red had taken.

Finally, he found it. Just as he had suspected there was a trail that led off to the left. But it was a fork in the path, not an intersection.

Okay, that must be it, he determined. But he could no longer see Red and the dog. Either they crested a hill, or entered into some structure that obscured them.

If they entered a heated cabin, I would be able to see its signature. So, maybe they just went over a hill. I suppose I'll soon find out.

Jack then removed his night vision goggles and took out a small LED flashlight, fitted with a hood to make it more directional. He turned it to minimum illumination and proceeded.

Jack had taken only an additional fifty steps before he ran face to face into the unexpected.

Chapter 30—Jack gets more than he bargained for

Standing in front of him was a large figure of a man, dressed from head to toe in an insulated jumpsuit, making him virtually undetectable with night vision goggles.

In one split second, Jack's entire world went dark.

He later deduced that there was a second man—most likely also dressed in a jumpsuit—and that second man had hammered him from behind with a blunt object.

Fortunately for Jack, the blow was not well aimed. Glancing off the right side of his head, the major force of the blow was absorbed by Jack's muscular right shoulder. It caused the entire right arm to go numb and dropped him face first into the moist soil.

For a moment, he struggled to get to his knees. But that effort was in vain, as a second blow, delivered with stunning force to the side of his head, knocked him unconscious.

As soon as Kate had reached their vehicle, she tried to locate her father using the GPS on his phone. "Looks like I'm roaming Canada. My captain's not gonna like this bill," she said to herself.

However, after a few moments she was able to locate Jack's cell.

"Looks like Dad is moving along nicely," she observed.

She followed his progress for about five minutes, and then it stopped.

"Wonder why he's not moving?" Kate asked herself.

For nearly fifteen minutes, Jack's phone did not move.

"That does it," she said, reaching into her purse and slipping her Glock from its holster. "This does not make sense."

Kate no longer sensed the need to use her night vision goggles. For one thing, she had no desire to sneak up on her father. That, she knew, could be dangerous.

Instead, she pulled a large five-cell flashlight from the center console and retraced her steps. She carried the flashlight in her left hand and her Glock in her right.

This trip took much less time.

Once she had passed the point where she had left her father, she took another look at her cell phone to see if she was still moving in the right direction.

Looks like Dad headed off to the left up ahead, she deduced, shining her flashlight up the path to see if there was a trail that veered off the main path.

Must be he spotted Red changing direction. But why'd he stop? According to the GPS, Dad didn't go much more than a couple hundred feet. This does not make sense.

Kate slid her cell into her jacket pocket and proceeded to move forward along the path.

After she had taken another dozen steps, she observed that one part of the trail led off to the right while the GPS had indicated her father was dog-legged off to the left. She pulled her cell out of her pocket and rechecked his location.

"According to this," she inaudibly uttered, "Dad should be right over there. Must be Red had left the main path and Dad followed him."

She shined her flashlight as closely as possible to the location where she believed her father should be.

"He should be right there," she concluded, slowly moving in the direction indicated by the GPS.

"Dad, where are you?" she whispered.

After a few dozen carefully planted steps, her five-cell flashlight illuminated a dark protrusion rising above a thick patch of ferns.

"Dad!"

Before rushing toward him, she used her flashlight to scrutinize the surroundings.

Seeing nothing suspicious, she widened the beam on her flashlight, and held it in her left hand against the side of her face. With her trigger finger snug against the trigger safety, she moved toward her father.

"Dad, you okay?" she asked as she approached his fallen body. But he was not able to respond.

Slowly she scanned the flashlight in a full three-hundred-sixty-degree pattern, searching for anything suspicious. After convincing herself that there was no imminent threat, she lowered her Glock and holstered it.

"Dad!" she exclaimed, placing her finger on his neck to see if she could detect a pulse.

"Thank God," she said, finding a strong throbbing heartbeat.

Carefully she removed Jack's blood-soaked cap and ran her fingers over his head to determine the location and severity of his injuries.

As soon as her fingers hit the open wound on the back of his head, Jack began to moan.

"Dad, it's me. Don't try to get up. Not yet."

Encouraged by his response, Kate continued to probe.

"You've got a gash on the back of your head, but I don't think that's what knocked you out—too glancing. I think your cap helped deflect the blow. Must be something else."

"Here we go," she said as she gently passed her fingers over a bump half the size of a golf ball just above his right temple. "That's what put you out. What happened?"

"Oh, Kate, my head is splitting."

"Literally. I'd say you were in need of at least a dozen stitches."

"What?"

"You've got a goose egg the size of a large walnut above your right temple—and a nice gash back here," she said gently touching the open wound. "I'm guessing you took a glancing blow to the back of your head. And probably got kicked after you hit the ground. Do you remember anything about it?"

"Man, my head aches."

"How'd your attacker get so close—without your hearing him?"

"Attacker?"

"Someone did this to you, Dad. You didn't get that goose egg from a fall. Someone had to have come up from behind and clocked you a good one."

"I don't know how that could have happened. I'm always very careful."

"I wonder if it happened right here. Or if you were dragged?"

"I don't feel so good. I think I'm gonna throw up."

"You've got a concussion. Just sit here for a minute and take it easy. I'm gonna look around a bit."

Kate then stood and reexamined their surroundings. She looked to see if she could catch some reflection, or movement—anything that might suggest her father's attacker was still in the area. But she saw nothing.

She then drew the flashlight's beam in closer, to see if the ground around them would yield some evidence. Almost under Jack's body she saw a shiny metal object. Kate reached down and picked up Jack's LED flashlight. The illuminated end was driven into the ground. She picked it up and turned it off.

"It looks to me like you dropped right where I found you—no sign of your being dragged. I was following you on GPS, and I don't think you changed location for over twenty minutes. You've probably been out about that long."

"Really. That long?"

"I'm pretty sure you were. The blood on the back of your neck is tacky and dark. And you've virtually stopped bleeding. I'd say about twenty minutes."

"Can you tell what hit me? Are there tracks?"

"The ferns are broken down. But I'm not seeing any discernible tracks."

"I don't think I put up a fight … at least I can't recall a struggle. I think I would have heard someone coming up behind me. He would have made *some* noise."

"It would seem so," Kate agreed. "Unless … unless he was waiting for you, maybe behind that tree."

Jack sat up and looked in the direction Kate was pointing.

"That tree, right there. It would have provided excellent cover for an attack like this."

Jack then started looking around from where he was sitting.

"What're you looking for?" Kate asked.

"My goggles. Do you see them?"

"Weren't you wearing them?"

"I don't remember. I might have taken them off—"

"I'll bet you did—that would explain your flashlight. You must have removed the goggles. They should be around here somewhere."

"If I did take them off, I would probably have been carrying them in my left hand. And if so, they should be lying around here."

Kate shined the flashlight in a circular fashion, illuminating the area three to ten feet away from where she had found her father.

"You're right. There they are," she said, locking the light on the camouflaged goggles lying about six feet from where he had fallen. Kate walked over and retrieved them.

"These don't look damaged," she observed. "I don't think you were wearing them."

"Not sure about that … but suspect I wasn't," Jack replied, obviously in a great deal of pain and still substantially disoriented.

"I'd bet that you had removed the goggles, and used the flashlight to get a better look at the terrain. That would explain why you didn't pick up your attacker's body heat as you approached him."

"I don't recall anything. Not after I sent you back to the vehicle. Good thing I did, or I might have got you killed."

"Or I might have prevented this."

"That could be," Jack replied. "I'm just glad you didn't get hurt."

"You don't think Red could have done this?" Kate asked.

"Not on your life," Jack replied. "But I can't understand why his dog didn't catch scent of this guy. Red and his dog must have passed within a few feet of him."

"Not necessarily," Kate said. "I think it is more likely that he slid in right after Red got past."

"Have you heard about these insulated ghillie suits? Combine them with a wetsuit underneath, and not only can you beat thermal imaging, but a dog could walk right past you and not pick up your scent. Maybe that's what this fellow was doing."

"How about his breath?"

"Some of the more sophisticated systems recirculate breathing. I know it sounds like a stretch. But he got past a dog's sensitive nose. So anything is possible. These fellows do seem to be fairly knowledgeable. After all, if they can afford a dual-engine jet helicopter, a simple insulated suit would not be out of the question."

"That's possible," Kate acknowledged. "But why would they go to all that trouble just to hide from a dog?"

"I think he just got lucky," Jack countered. "If he was wearing a thermal suit he would have been doing it to avoid detection by a helicopter's thermal imaging equipment. That same equipment would have insulated him from Red's dog. And with or without my night vision goggles on I could easily have missed him if he was tucked in behind that tree. Tonight it just all worked in his favor. Lucky for him, or I'd have killed him."

"Maybe we're the lucky ones," Kate said. "How'd you like explaining to the FBI that you shot the Michelin man?"

"Yeah, maybe you're right. But right now I think I'd take my chances. It's not much fun on the inside of my skull."

"I think we're done here for the night. I've got to get you in for some X-rays."

"I don't think that's such a good idea. We both know that I've got a concussion. That's a given. All they're gonna do is give me some painkillers—which I won't take. And tell you not to let me sleep for more than a few hours at a time."

"And then the FBI would be on your case," Kate agreed. "Better to let it go and take our chances. Is that what you're thinking?"

"Without a doubt—it's how it's got to be."

"Hey!" Kate whispered. "Did you see that?"

Chapter 31—Jack and Kate have company

"Did I see *what*?" Jack asked, still sitting on the ground.

"Did you see that light? Where'd it come from?"

"I didn't see anything," Jack responded, beginning to climb to his feet.

"There, coming along the path. I see a flashlight."

"Well, I suppose we should have expected that. What you wanna bet it's my buddy—Officer … Ripkin?"

"You mean Deputy Restin?" Kate asked. "I'm thinking you might want to let me do the talking."

"You could be right," Jack agreed. "Take a good look at me. Make sure there's no blood showing."

Jack was now standing.

"Oh, man, have I ever got a headache."

"I can only imagine," Kate said. "Here, let me take a good look at you."

She took the small LED flashlight that Jack had been carrying, and carefully examined his face, and his clothes.

"Your eyes are a little bloodshot, and there is a swelling where you got kicked. But I don't see any blood … except on the back of your head, and a little on your collar. I think your cap absorbed most of it. Here, stick it in your pocket. Unless you turn your back on Deputy Restin, he'll not see anything."

"Let's meet him half way," Jack suggested.

"Good idea," Kate agreed. "What shall we tell him?"

"The truth," Jack said. "That we were abducted by aliens. And they dropped me on my head. How does that sound?"

"Like maybe you've had too much to drink."

"Then what would you suggest?"

"How about this," Kate said. "What if we tell him that we thought we saw someone running into the woods, but when we got out there we scared a couple deer? So, what we saw must have been the deer. How does that sound?"

"Like a story a city girl might come up with," Jack said, chuckling. "You don't ever sneak up on deer, except in a snowstorm."

"Then what would you suggest, Davy Crockett? We don't have much time."

"I was serious about telling him the truth—that we thought we saw the freckle-faced boy, and his dog. But that if we did, we lost them somewhere out here in the woods. I'm sure he knows all about the kid. He might be able to fill us in. But I think we should leave out the part where I run into the baseball bat."

"That should work," Kate said. "It's good to see you feeling better."

Jack and Kate had walked only about eighty yards before they came within shouting distance of the man they correctly presumed to be Deputy Restin.

"Jack," the officer shouted in their direction. "That is you—right?"

"Deputy Restin?"

"Yeah … We spotted your SUV on the road. What are you doing out here?"

"Long story," Jack replied.

It was apparent that Jack was going to do all the talking—Deputy

Restin would have it no other way.

"You're a long way off the beaten path. You looking for a flusher?"

"We thought we saw that kid—the freckle-faced redhead. Not positive about it. But we both thought it was him and his dog."

"Oh, I doubt that," Deputy Restin said. "*Highly* unlikely. He was seen in town earlier this evening. He couldn't have made it back across the river that quickly. We assume he has to sneak across on the ferry. Like a parasite, hiding in the back of someone's truck. At least, that's how we think he does it. Usually, no one actually sees him crossing ... could be he has help. But, like I said, he was spotted in the Soo not that long ago, so he's most likely still there."

"You're probably right. We weren't too sure about it but thought we should check it out anyway."

"What do you know about the kid—the redhead?" Kate interrupted. "When he is on the island, where does he hang out?"

"Cabins. Wherever he finds one vacant. It's a bit tricky for him in the summer time. The island gets quite busy. But there are hunting cabins that are used only in the winter. He's pretty adept at what might be available at any given time. As far as we can tell, he limits himself to the island, year around. At least as far as living accommodations. He does come into the city on occasion, mostly for food. But by nightfall, he gravitates to the island."

"Then what makes you so sure that it wasn't him that we saw tonight?" Kate asked.

"I've got a patrol car watching the ferry. If he'd attempted to hitch a ride, we'd have caught him."

"That makes sense," Jack said. "Must have been a couple of lovebirds—making out in the woods."

"Could have been," Deputy Restin said. "But I doubt it was Red."

"Well, then we must've wasted our time out here—a bit of a wild goose chase," Jack said, attempting to add a note of finality to the matter.

"Is this your first visit to the island?" Restin asked.

"On this trip," Jack said. "I'm still on for the morning? Right?"

"As far as I know," Deputy Restin said.

"Anything new about the sheriff?" Jack asked as the three of them began walking back toward the road, with Deputy Restin leading the way.

"No. I'm hoping they can get to the autopsy in the morning. Sometimes these things take a while around here. I'm thinking that the FBI might expedite it. Sometimes it helps to be a prick."

"So that's what you think of them?" Kate asked.

"For the most part," Deputy Restin said. "Don't get me wrong. I think even the sheriff welcomed their help. We all recognized that this case was going nowhere. If it is going to get solved, we're gonna need them. Especially since it occurred on Sugar Island. This place is basically lawless. Most of the residents don't trust us. It's gonna take an outside agency, like the FBI, to get to the bottom of it."

"An outside entity, with a prick persona," Kate chuckled. "That does sound like the FBI to me."

"I trust you won't quote me on that," Deputy Restin said.

"Your opinion is safe with us," Kate assured him. "I've worked with the FBI on several occasions—some experiences were good—and some not so good. It all depends."

"It all depends on the individual agent assigned to the case in question," Jack added. "Just like it is with any federal agency."

Officer Restin nodded in agreement. "Well, you'd know more about that than I do. But it just seems to me that J. Edgar sent us far more than he needed to. No offense, but this Alex guy, your relative, was no JFK.

And the guy who shot him—no John Dillinger. We could have used one or two agents. But I'll bet they've dispatched half a dozen ... and I've heard that there may be more on the way."

"I think the thing is that some agents have a reputation for not respecting other law enforcement agencies—at least not as they should," Kate added.

Jack and his daughter had Deputy Restin talking again. And Jack was all about encouraging the officer to keep talking. "You never learn anything with your mouth open," Jack was fond of saying.

"Deputy Restin," Kate asked, "given the fact that this time around the freckle-faced kid is not on the island. ... If that *weren't* the case—if we *didn't* know where he was—if we actually thought he was on the island, where would you start looking for him?"

"I wouldn't," the officer immediately retorted with a smirk behind his chuckle. "What would be the point? I don't know why, but we used to waste our time with that kid. Probably because some do-gooder felt sorry for him and his dog and wanted him to have a 'real' home.

"We'd expend dozens of man hours looking for him. Once we even totaled out a patrol car trying to catch him. Not that far from here in fact—just about a quarter mile in that direction," Deputy Restin said, pointing to the northeast.

"We got the warrant, about four years ago, and practically drew straws to determine who was going to go after the kid. None of us wanted that job. But we had the warrant, so we had to give it a shot.

"Well, the kid was spotted on the island, and we got the call.

"Thankfully I was not the lucky one. Officers Henry and Burns drew the short straws. They got on the island—about an hour before dusk. And wouldn't you just know it, they had turned around at the end of the island and were headed back to the ferry.

"And then they spotted them: Red—and, of course, his dog.

"The officers pulled into a drive, fifty yards from where they saw the boy enter the woods. They got a few hundred yards into the woods, and they spotted the kid again—this time sprinting over the top of a hill. The officers were distracted and smacked right into a tree. Bent the frame. Completely ruined a perfectly good patrol car.

"One of the officers gave chase and managed to catch the kid. We sent another car out to pick them up … with a tow truck, of course.

"When we got him down to juvenile detention, they held him for the night and stuck his dog in the pound. That triggered one of the darkest periods in the history of our department, and gave birth to the kid's legend."

Chapter 32—How the legend was born

"The next day the judge put him into a temporary foster home. A lot of good that did. Ten minutes after the foster parents showed him his room, he bolted out the back door and busted his dog out of dog jail. Everyone in town heard about it. It was on the front page of the paper. And overnight the kid became the hero of every teenager in the UP ... while my department became the butt of every joke. ... The craziest thing about it—I sincerely doubt that the kid even knows about his own legend.

"So, as far as I'm concerned—why bother looking for the kid? If I'm ever tempted to go after him again, I think I'll just poke myself in the eye with a sharp pencil. Same thing."

"I see your point," Kate said. "But if he were on the island, and if for some reason you did want to find him, where would you start looking?"

"Same place the other officers found him, I suppose. About a quarter mile to the northeast. He's been known to borrow cabins in that area. From there to Lake George. Some think that he actually boats across the shallow channel to Canada, but no one knows that for sure. At least I don't think so. My guess is that story just might be part of his legend."

"I'm intrigued about the legend you keep referring to," Kate said. "Is there more to it than that one incident?"

"More to it? Is there ever!" Deputy Restin replied. "I'm sure that most of it is just that—legend. But there are dozens of stories about him. Some of them are true. But, like I said, I suspect just as many of them are made up."

"Do you have time to tell us one of the stories?" Kate requested. "Perhaps your favorite?"

"Sure, if you want to listen," Deputy Restin said, stopping in his tracks and turning to face them.

"We've got the time," Jack said.

"Well, my favorite story about Red happened three years ago. And this one is definitely true. We have evidence."

"Red would have been about ten or eleven at that time—probably eleven. We had just picked the kid up, again, and had him held in lock-up. We detained him for about a week, trying to figure out what to do with him. This time we didn't put the dog in the pound. Instead, the sheriff got one of his friends to take care of it.

"According to some people I know, the kid never went to sleep. And when he did, it was during the day, right after breakfast. All night long he stayed awake, in his cell. They had to keep him isolated from the other boys—to protect him. The kid was a little different, even then, and the caseworker was afraid he might get hurt if placed with the other boys."

"We've heard that he couldn't talk," Kate said.

"At that point," Deputy Restin continued, "the boy was still able to talk. He lost his voice shortly after that time … actually, the loss of his voice occurred as a direct result of what followed."

"Really," Jack said. "How'd that happen?"

"Well, the court finally decided what they were going to do with the kid. They found a foster home that was not located on Sugar Island. In fact, it was not even close. It was a little south of Trout Lake, in the far reaches of Chippewa County, way out in the middle of the woods. They thought he might settle in there if he didn't know his way back."

"How'd that work out?" Kate asked, already suspecting that it didn't.

"Red stayed there only long enough for the caseworker to drop him off and introduce him to Lawrence and Molly Klyburn—that's the names of the foster parents.

"As soon as they turned their backs, Red took off. He jumped out of a second-story bedroom window. The caseworker was still sipping her coffee at the foster home. When she went up to Red's room to say goodbye, he was gone."

"Did he head back to the city?" Kate asked.

"He sure did. He hopped the train that passes through Trout Lake. It was in late November—real cold. How he managed to keep from freezing to death I'll never know. Somehow he got himself lodged underneath a car. It should have killed him.

"Apparently he switched from one foot to the other, letting it rest against the axle of the train. That's how he tried to keep his feet warm—using the friction of the turning axle.

"Unfortunately, his left foot grew numb from the cold, and he lost feeling in it. Apparently he fell asleep. Well, the motion eventually ate through his shoe and literally wore off much of his left foot.

"When the train arrived in the Soo, he jumped off and tried to walk. But by then both feet were frostbitten—two of his toes dangled out of the side of his shoe. I actually saw it."

"He had collapsed from shock, right at the station, and I got the call. It was awful. The kid almost died from loss of blood, and shock. Had his feet not frozen, he probably would have bled to death. Three of his toes had to be amputated.

"When he woke up in the hospital, he started calling for his dog—non-stop. Even though he had been drugged up. At that point, he could still talk. This is what happened. We checked him into the hospital. And when he woke up, he went nuts. He had to be restrained to keep him in bed. When he was sedated, he would sleep. But whenever he woke up, he screamed at the top of his voice for his dog.

"We explained to him that his dog was being cared for. But that wasn't good enough. Unfortunately, one of our officers made the mistake of telling the boy where his dog was staying. That only made him scream more. He almost never stopped. They would give him a shot. He would fall asleep for a while. But when he came to, he'd start screaming again.

"Finally, arrangements were made to move him to a psychiatric hospital. On the way there, you probably guessed it, he escaped."

"With his bad foot? How'd *that* turn out?" Kate asked.

"Apparently okay. We found the partial cast by the ferry. So we assumed that he made it across. But not without locating his dog first—of course."

"And his foot healed up okay?" Kate asked.

"Hey, did you get a chance to see him run? No one I know would ever be able to catch him. He can handle this rough terrain better than me or any of the other officers. We can't even detect a limp. The kid is amazing."

"You know what they say about the medicinal benefit of a dog's tongue," Kate said with a smile.

"It's true," Jack added. "Most likely his dog nursed him back to health by licking his open wound."

"That's what I've heard others say. Odds are good that he did not have the benefit of a first-aid kit. So the dog thing might just be what did it."

"Were you ever able to figure out where he was living at the time?"

Kate asked. "Back then?"

"We assumed not far from here. He always seems to end up on the island. But there are so many vacant cabins in the winter—no one knows for sure where he's holed up. And you know, like I said before, we don't really know what to do with him if we do catch him—it's futile.

"We can laugh about it—now. Every law enforcement officer in the surrounding UP communities knows about the kid. And no one in the area wants anything to do with him. I swear, unless that kid kills someone, I'm not running on any calls that involve him."

"I can appreciate it—with that dog of his, it would be really hard to sneak up on him," Jack said, seeking some common ground with the deputy.

Just then there was a large explosion, followed closely by an enormous secondary flash. It appeared to be close to where Jack had parked his vehicle.

Chapter 33—Twice in one night

All three of them snapped their heads in the direction of the blast.

"What was that?!" Jack exclaimed. "Sounds like it might be just down the road from where we parked—less than half a mile!"

The force of the initial blast was substantial—Jack had not experienced anything like it since Vietnam. All three felt the shockwave from even that distance.

But while the first explosion riveted their attention, the explosion of fire that followed a second and a half later was equally impressive. All three could feel the heat of the fireball on their faces.

"I'd better get over there," Deputy Restin declared.

"We'll go with you," Jack said.

"Best if we stay on the path straight back to the road," Deputy Restin added without turning to face the other two. Already his long legs had carried him twenty-five feet toward the road. "Don't know what we'll get into if we wander off."

Neither Jack nor Kate responded verbally to Deputy Restin's words. Kate glanced over at her father in disbelief as he took off behind the deputy. She followed close behind.

"Got any ideas?" Jack asked, as he closed in on Restin's heels. The deputy had intentionally slowed to allow him to catch up.

"Not really, but it appears to have been a substantial explosion—probably of a vehicle."

"Another bomb?" Kate asked.

"I would say so, much like the one earlier tonight, but with a substantially larger initial explosive device. But that secondary explosion, that looked more incendiary. At least that's how it appeared to me."

"I think you're right," Jack said. "Unless that was a fuel truck, it should not be burning like it is. Has to have been a significant accelerant involved to get that type of burn."

Once the trio reached the road, they could get a closer look at the source of the flame.

"That looks like an ambulance," Jack said. "Must be the one that came for the sheriff's body."

Deputy Restin did not comment. He merely picked up his pace and began trotting toward the flaming chassis of a large vehicle.

"That's what it is, all right," Deputy Restin said as he got closer. "They were getting ready to pull out when I left."

"I don't see how anyone could have survived that," Kate said, as she began to catch up to the two men. They all pulled up about a hundred feet from the flame. "I can't believe how intense the heat is, even out here."

"We should check for survivors," Jack said. "Kate, why don't you get in as close as you dare on the east side. And I'll hit the west. The trees will block most of the heat, but don't get hurt. I think the flame is starting to burn itself out. We'll meet at the road on the other side. If anyone was able to get out after the explosion they might have crawled away and into the woods, and then collapsed. They'd most likely be in shock. Look for a blood trail."

Deputy Restin then removed his radio and began calling in.

"This is Deputy Restin. Do you copy?"

"Go ahead, Restin."

"We need another ambulance out here on Sugar Island. *And* a fire truck. The ambulance transporting the sheriff's body has blown up presumably with all occupants still in it. That would include the sheriff's body, and the driver, and a third person. I see nothing moving at the scene. I'm gonna need some help out here."

Jack got in as close as he could but spotted no movement. He then made his way around the scene from the west side, wading through a small drainage ditch to avoid the heat. He scouted that area and emerged back on the road once he was sure it was safe to do so. But still he found no sign of life. After completing a cursory examination of the burned-out ambulance from the front, he made his way over to where Kate was beginning to emerge from the east side of the road.

"I don't know what you're thinking," Kate said to her father, "but I can't imagine anyone surviving that explosion—much less the fire."

"Whoever was in that ambulance when it exploded, is toast," Jack agreed.

"That's for sure," Deputy Restin concurred, after having walked over to join them. "There were probably two of them in there. Plus the sheriff."

Deputy Restin then pulled out his radio a second time. "I need you to hustle up the local fire responders. This thing is still burning."

"I'd grab my extinguisher and hit the hotspots," Jack said, "but I've already used it up earlier tonight. You've got one in your car, right? Maybe we can at least keep this from spreading until the trucks arrive."

"Good idea. I'll get it," Deputy Restin said. The deputy headed toward his car. Jack walked with him, stomping out smoldering patches as he proceeded. Fortunately, the drainage ditches on either side of the road had blocked the fire from creeping.

Just as Deputy Restin returned to the fire with his extinguisher, the second car on scene at the resort pulled up behind the other two vehicles.

"Jeff," Deputy Restin called out. "Grab your extinguisher and let's see what we can do to protect Smokey's trees. This could get really ugly."

Deputy Restin had left Officer Jeff Jordan to secure the crime scene until the detectives arrived. But when he heard the explosion, and then heard Deputy Restin's call for backup, he pulled off and headed toward the fire.

"Let me see that," Jack said, almost yanking the extinguisher from Officer Jordan's hand. "We've got something smoldering over here in the brush."

By the time Deputy Restin and Jack had emptied their fire extinguishers, most of the fire not directly involving parts of the ambulance had been reduced to harmless smoking embers.

In a few cases, sparks had ignited some of the undergrowth beyond the ditches, but those were easily stomped out by Jack and Deputy Restin.

Officer Jordan did not venture into the mud. Instead, he concentrated on locating and extinguishing various pieces of the ambulance that were still smoking and then kicking the debris back toward the middle of the road.

Finally, both extinguishers were exhausted.

"Looks like we've about got it under control," Jack observed. "It's running out of flammable material."

"I wonder if we have to worry about the fuel tank exploding?" Deputy Restin asked.

"That's what was burning," Jack quickly retorted. "The bomb was placed so that it would rupture the fuel tank immediately. It surprises me a little that the tank must have contained a surprisingly small amount of fuel. I would think that emergency vehicles would be kept topped off. At any rate, there's not much left here that will burn."

"It sure went fast," Kate commented. "From the time of the first explosion, until now—twelve minutes. Maybe fourteen. And it's almost going out by itself. That was pretty quick."

"Can you tell what sort of bomb it was?" Deputy Restin asked Jack.

"My guess is plastic—given the ferocity of the initial explosion … and the odor. It smells like plastic. But there's a lot of medical supplies that were consumed as well. Who knows what might have contributed to the overall aroma. I'm sure your crime lab will be able to piece it together."

"My crime lab will never touch this," Deputy Restin retorted sarcastically. "The FBI will have this within the hour."

"Do you hear that?" Kate asked.

"Hear what?" Deputy Restin replied, raising his head to see where Kate was looking.

"Over there," she said, pointing into the woods to the northeast.

All three of the men then turned their attention to the direction Kate was indicating.

Chapter 34—Twice in one night—again

"That! It's the helicopter again." Kate said. "Listen closely. It sounds like one of those Medevac choppers."

"Wouldn't be a Medevac—I'm pretty positive about that," Deputy Restin said.

"I hear it—but don't see it," Jack said, pointing north and west of where they were standing. "No lights. It's got to be the one from earlier tonight, maybe a thousand yards in that direction."

"I hear it too," Deputy Restin said. "Sounds like it's landing."

For nearly a minute, the four of them stood silently staring into the western sky. Finally, the sound of the rotors grew to a roar.

"There, they just gunned it," Jack said. "They must have touched down and now they're back up again. That is *very* strange."

"Sounds like they are heading east," Kate said.

"My guess is that they are just gaining altitude," Jack said. "They probably came in from Canada and are now headed back. But taking a little different route. I would sure like to get a look at that chopper in the daylight."

"I doubt you'll get that chance," Deputy Restin responded. "Not unless DHS or Canada puts a rocket into it."

"They've gotta be tracking it. Right?" Kate asked. "Someone's gotta be following it."

"Not necessarily," Deputy Restin said. "This is Michigan's Upper

Peninsula, not New York or Chicago."

"Are you suggesting that it's stealth?" Kate asked.

"No, wouldn't have to be," Jack said. "If it hugs the treetops, and just jumps up and down, it will generally avoid radar. It's a civilian craft—expensive, but pretty pedestrian."

"There, I can barely hear it anymore," Kate said. "You think it's back in Canada?"

"Yup," Jack said. "You can be pretty certain about that."

"What a great night," Kate chuckled. "This is beginning to remind me of home. That would be the local fire department, I presume."

Her comment was in response to flashing lights and a siren coming from the north.

"That it would," Deputy Restin said. "I suggest we give them room to maneuver."

"Are you going to let them put water on this?" Jack asked. "That might destroy evidence."

"We'll see what the options are. For the most part, we've extinguished it."

"Right," Jack agreed. "It's not going to spread from here. I'd suggest that they hit it with something dry, or CO_2 if need be, and skip the water. Besides, you aren't going to want to wash any of those chemicals off into the drainage ditches. Who knows what kind of pollution that could involve."

"I suppose you're right. … The last thing I want to deal with is the EPA. Bad enough to have the FBI looking over my shoulder. Anyway, they're gonna be giving me lip about something no matter what I do. But it doesn't have to be polluting the environment."

As the truck slowed, three Sugar Island volunteers jumped off and trotted over to the smoldering remains of the ambulance. The driver then crept his vehicle up as close as he could and hit the smoldering ambulance with a floodlight.

"Hey, fellows," Deputy Restin instructed. "I've got the FBI to deal with here. What say we avoid washing this thing out into the woods? Can we just make sure nothing spreads into the water table and let them deal with clean up when they're ready?"

"Sure, Mark, anything you say. Who's injured here? Anyone in the vehicle when it went up?"

"Bud Hughes," Deputy Restin said to his fireman friend. "I suspected I might be seeing you out here tonight."

"Yeah, well, you know what they say about no rest. What've we got here? Is this what it looks like? Is this *your* ambulance?"

"What's left of it," Restin replied. "There were three men in the vehicle—one was dead already, and now I presume the driver and the second paramedic are deceased as well."

"Shouldn't we put some water on it to cool it down so we can check?"

"Jack," Restin said, "what exactly would *you* do in the big city? We obviously need to do somethng to cool it down. But we don't want to pollute the whole island."

"That's pretty strange, Restin," Jack said, but not in reply to the deputy's question. "The whole back end of that vehicle is wide open, and so is the driver's area. But I don't see any bodies. Sheriff Northrup would have been strapped down. But I got a pretty close-up look, and I didn't see a body."

"It'd be burned up," Deputy Restin replied. "Right Bud?"

"I'd expect to see the driver still in the driver's seat ... that is, if he was wearing his seatbelt," Captain Hughes replied. "And the same with the passenger—if there was a passenger. ... Did I hear right? The deceased was Sheriff Northrup?"

"You heard right," Deputy Restin said. "The sheriff was shot and killed earlier this evening. We found his body out back of the resort."

"I don't believe this," Captain Hughes said. "Northrup, dead?

"First I hear a call about a car exploding in the Soo, and now this—the sheriff, murdered. Mark, what's going on?"

"Beats me. But we've now got the FBI investigating."

"I'm not surprised. This stuff has got to stop. This is insane. No offense, Mark—you're probably not that happy to see the FBI. But this stinks," Bud Hughes said.

"We weren't too pleased at first, about the FBI that is, but this situation is getting out of hand. Having the Feds take over will get the pressure off us."

"Dad! Over here! I think I've found something."

Chapter 35—Leaving the scene of an accident

Jack had momentarily lost sight of his daughter. "Kate, where are you?" he called out.

"Over here. See my flashlight."

Kate had walked over a small knoll and had been kneeling on the other side, making her invisible from the area of the smoldering ambulance. When Jack was unable to identify her position, she stood and shined a flashlight in his direction.

"I've got a body over here. Might be the sheriff."

Jack, the two officers, and Captain Hughes all waded through the drainage ditch over to where Kate was standing. Jack reached her first.

"What do you think, Restin?" Jack asked. "Can you identify the body?"

Deputy Restin knelt down beside what was barely discernable as a human corpse. Most of its clothes had been burned off. At first Deputy Restin used his pen to check the left wrist.

"The sheriff always wore a gold wristwatch—a gift for fifteen years on the force out East. It's not here, but neither are most of his clothes—at least none that I can see."

He then dug his pen into the body's midsection. There he hooked onto a wide belt.

"Yep, that's the sheriff's body … at least that's his belt. Quite unique—

only one like it I've ever seen. How'd he get way over here? This has to be … sixty, seventy feet off the road?"

"The explosion must have launched him through the roof of the ambulance," Jack said. "It did appear as though the bomb had been placed right under the vehicle, or maybe there were two devices—one by the fuel tanks and one under the sheriff's body."

"I wonder about the driver," Deputy Restin said, rising to his feet. "Maybe he's out here as well."

"Could be," Jack agreed. "But the large explosion would have been behind him—not beneath. I doubt that he could have survived, but I don't see him flying in the same direction as the sheriff."

"I think we've got the other body," one of the firemen called out. He had been administering CO_2 to the hot spots.

"Looks like a body jammed up under the dash."

"Kate, would you stay here with the sheriff's body?" Jack requested. "We don't want to lose him again."

"Sure."

By the time the three men reached the ambulance, the fireman had cooled off the area around the second body.

"There," the fireman said, pointing under the dash. "His body is jammed right up there. You can see one of his feet hanging down, and part of his back."

Deputy Restin bent down slightly to get a better look. But none of the men got as close as the fireman, because of the intense heat.

"Yeah, you're right," Deputy Restin agreed. "That's a body all right."

"But why is he on the passenger side?" Jack queried.

Jack then shined his flashlight on what was left of the driver's side seatbelt and observed that while the nylon itself had burned off, both ends were visible, but not attached.

Must have been he sensed something, Jack surmised but did not articulate. *He unhooked his seatbelt, turned to look in the back. Maybe smelled something. And then it blew.*

"Get off my crime scene!"

Jack knew immediately what was happening. The Marines had landed—time to make room for the FBI—a lot of room.

"Who are you and what are you doing here!" Special Agent Lamar shouted, this time specifically at Jack, who intentionally kept his back to the special agent.

It was clear to Jack that God was not interested in explanations, so he simply lifted his hands above his head in a pseudo submissive fashion, smiled, and began walking away.

"Restin! Cordon off this whole area—ditch to ditch! I don't want anyone who is not FBI inside it! No one! These other people—what are they doing here?"

"Sir, we have a body in the woods—unidentified, but we think it's Sheriff Northrup."

"Then expand it. Include all debris within it. I don't care if you have to put a ribbon around the whole island. Just get these people, and yourself, out of my crime scene."

"Yes, sir," Deputy Restin replied, in a truly submissive tone.

"This way, Jack," Deputy Restin said, leading Jack to an area outside his intended boundary.

Special Agent Lamar then shouted again. "Restin, don't let anyone leave yet. I'll let them know when they can leave."

"Hey, Kate," Jack called to his daughter. "We're moving back a bit. Come on up here."

Kate knew exactly what was taking place, and complied without question.

As she stood, Kate brushed off her pants and looked one last time into the charred facial remains of the body at her feet.

"Well, Sheriff," she said aloud. "This has been a long day for you. And I'm sure they're not done with you yet."

By the time Kate had reached her father, Deputy Restin had removed the yellow crime scene tape from his car and was beginning to encircle the area with it.

"And get these vehicles back at least a hundred feet," Special Agent Lamar shouted in Restin's direction.

"Yes, sir," Deputy Restin shouted back.

"Even this fire equipment," Special Agent Lamar continued. "The fire is out. Leave an extinguisher, but get it back with all the other vehicles."

Captain Hughes did not respond verbally, but he and his volunteer firemen quickly got in their truck, and he backed it up to where Deputy Restin had parked his patrol car.

"This should do it," Captain Hughes said. And then, handing one of his men a fully charged CO_2 extinguisher, he said, "Here, take this up and set it out in the open, but not too close to Lamar."

But before the fireman could comply with his leader's order, Captain Hughes changed his mind.

"On second thought, let me take care of it."

Captain Hughes then took the extinguisher back and carried it himself toward the smoldering rubble. When he arrived at a place he thought appropriate—which was just outside the cordoned area, but very close to the feet of Special Agent Lamar—he banged the steel container down hard on the pavement. The clang visibly startled the special agent, causing his body to twitch slightly.

When Special Agent Lamar turned toward Captain Hughes, instead of dressing him down, he simply said, "Thanks, that will be fine."

Captain Hughes wore a smirk all the way back to his truck.

Once confident the deputies had secured his crime scene, Special Agent Lamar began marching around the slightly smoldering carcass like a Nazi SS Trooper inspecting a downed American fighter. As he did, it finally sunk in just who Jack was.

"Handler, is that you back there?" Lamar shouted without turning around.

Chapter 36—Kate officially meets Lamar

"Handler! Get up here. I want to talk to you," Special Agent Lamar shouted.

"Jack, maybe you can get your interview over with tonight," Deputy Restin said with a grin as he placed his large hand on Jack's shoulder.

"And Kate, his daughter, send her up too."

Kate smiled at her father and quipped, "I'll bet this is going to be fun."

"Restin's right—we just might be able to do our interview right now," Jack said. "So make nice."

"I'm always nice."

"What I mean is, don't be cute with him. Let's just give him what he wants, and we might be able to get on with our lives in the morning."

"I know what you mean."

"Handler—Jack and Kate," Special Agent Lamar said, affecting his best behavior. "We're scheduled to do an interview tomorrow morning. Right?"

"That's right," Jack replied. "We're planning on being there first thing."

"Well," Lamar said, "this whole business with the sheriff puts a new wrinkle on everything. Now I've got two new bodies to deal with. Tell me, what did the sheriff share with you in your meeting earlier today? Did he give you anything, or tell you anything about the case—the murder of your brother-in-law?"

"The sheriff gave us a thumb drive containing some video from the resort prior to Alex's death," Jack said. "It showed various guests of the resort. All of it was shot by two cameras covering the front desk. I suspect you've already seen it."

"Yes, of course. Have you made copies of that video?"

"Kate copied it on the hard drive of her notebook."

"That's all? Have you shown it to anyone else or made additional copies?"

"No."

"Well, don't. Consider this your personal gag order. Don't discuss anything with the press, or with anyone else. I've heard that you are a retired Chicago homicide detective, and that you, Kate, are currently a homicide detective on leave from New York City."

"That's true," Jack said.

"Then you both know what happens when we take over a case. Everything runs through me. And I mean *everything*.

"I am not giving you permission to conduct any sort of investigation, about anything or anyone, that might even remotely relate to this case. Just leave it alone. You two are nothing more than private citizens visiting Sugar Island.

"In fact, you're less than that—because I've got my eye on you.

"Don't get me wrong—I sympathize with your loss, but you have no authority here—none whatsoever. Have I made myself clear?"

"Yes, you have," Jack replied. "We will not interfere with your investigation."

Special Agent Lamar was not a particularly large man—he stood five feet nine inches and weighed about one eighty.

In stature, he was just about the same size as Jack. While a larger man would use his height to intimidate, Lamar could not. So he did the next best thing.

Taking half a step in Jack's direction, he stuck his nose to within a few inches of Jack's. Jack did not back up.

Then, pushing his finger firmly into Jack's chest, he snarled, "You see to that, Handler. I'm holding you to your word. If I hear anything that sounds like you're poking around on this case, I'll have you both arrested. And that could damage your daughter's career. Is that clear?"

"I understand," Jack replied.

"And how about you, Kate. Do you understand what I'm saying? Or do I have to call your boss and have him explain it to you?"

"I've got it," Kate replied.

"Good. Then is there anything else that you can tell me that might be of interest regarding this case?"

"Not right now, but if something comes to mind, I'll give you a call," Jack said, still not budging.

"I do want to talk to you, but just not in the morning. So don't leave town."

"Sounds good to me," Jack said. "Does that mean that you're finished with us for the night?"

"Do you have anything to say regarding the sheriff's murder?"

"Not that I haven't discussed fully with Restin."

"Then I'll call you tomorrow, or the next day."

"I'll look forward to that," Jack replied. "Can I assume we're done here?"

"I'm done with you for now," Lamar replied, turning his back to Jack.

Jack and Kate then turned and walked toward their vehicle.

As they did, Jack took a handkerchief from his pocket and wiped Lamar's spit from his face.

"You're dead serious about that, aren't you? About looking forward to meeting with Lamar?"

Smiling broadly, Jack replied, "I sure am. We're going to need to know what he knows if we're going to catch Alex's killer."

"Jack, come over here, I've got a question for you," Deputy Restin said, stepping away from Captain Hughes and motioning for Jack and Kate to duck under the ribbon where he was standing.

Chapter 37—Something happens on the way to the hotel

Jack smiled at Deputy Restin and then looked away. He placed his hand on Kate's waist and walked right past the deputy without again making eye contact.

"See you later, Restin," he said without slowing.

Jack knew that the last thing he wanted right now was to re-engage the chatty Deputy Restin in a conversation—the sooner he got to his vehicle, the less time it would give Special Agent Lamar to change his mind.

In fact, Jack did not even talk to Kate again until after he had started the engine.

"Where are we going?" Kate asked. "We can't get past the ambulance. Is there another way off the island?"

"There's only one way across the river, and that's by ferry. But if I turn around here, I can go back toward the resort and take South Westshore up to Six Mile Road, and then back over to Brassar Road. And that will take us to the road where we can catch the ferry—Ferry Road, or Sugar Island Road."

"Restin has your cell number—right?"

"He won't call us," Jack said. "His office might have it worked out with the Canadian towers for roaming charges, but he knows we don't, and so he will assume we won't have our phones on.

"If he really needed to talk to us all he has to do is radio the officer at the ferry and have us detained. That is, if he wants this night to go on forever. But I think that he's got his hands full with Lamar, and Lamar is busy trying to figure out what's going on with his case. They all know that we're not suspects. Lamar will get to us—just not tonight."

"There it is," Jack said. "Six Mile Road. We'll turn right here, and then eventually …"

"You remember all of this from the times you visited the resort—when Mom was alive?"

"Kitty, it's a very small island. Don't give me more credit than I deserve."

"I'm just glad that you're driving."

"There's Brassar. We're almost home now," Jack said, as he turned north. "Do you have any aspirin with you? My head is throbbing."

"I do, but I don't have anything to drink."

"Great. There's bottled water in the back. Can you reach one for me?"

Just as Kate turned to find a bottle of water for her father, he locked the brakes.

Kate screamed her discomfort.

"What's happening!" she complained.

"Red! That kid and his dog just ran in front of us! Again!" Jack replied, pulling to a complete stop right where the boy had crossed.

"There, can you see that?" he asked Kate. "Someone is chasing the boy. Can you see the flashlight in the woods coming up to where Red crossed?"

Chapter 38—Jack has many questions, but few answers

"Yes," Kate replied. "Shall we pursue?"

"The only hot pursuit I'm looking for tonight is for a pillow to rest my pounding head. This will have to wait. See about those two aspirins, and the water. We'll hang around for a while right here to give Red a chance to escape. We'll come back tomorrow."

Jack swallowed the two aspirins and polished off all but about four ounces of the one-liter bottle of water. He then opened his door and walked around to the rear of the vehicle and feigned relieving himself.

"If those guys are still out there, I'll give them something to think about," Jack said, just loud enough for Kate to hear through her open window.

He then walked over to Kate's side and dropped the mostly empty water bottle on the shoulder of the road.

"This will mark Red's point of entry," he said. "I'm sure that he never intended to be in this area. We might be able to locate him in the morning."

Kate had slipped on a pair of night vision goggles and was looking in the direction of the men who were chasing Red.

"I can't see a thing out there. I think they may have given up for the night. Where, exactly, are we?"

"We're back on Brassar, about a mile and a half north of the explosion."

"So, Red must have spotted the men following him, so he circled back?"

"I would guess that's what happened," Jack said. "Whoever it was, they've had to give up for the night. All Red needed was a head start. He'll be fine ... for now."

"Does that mean we can head back into town?" Kate asked. "More specifically, will I soon be able to park my weary body? That bed looked pretty comfortable."

"Sounds right to me," Jack said, putting his hand on the side of his head. "I would still like to get some ice on this lump."

"Probably too late for ice to do much good," Kate said. "And, how is this going to work? Am I going to have to wake you up every hour?"

"You had better not do that unless you want me to shoot you," Jack advised his daughter. "Once I hit the sack, I'm there for the duration."

"I was just teasing," Kate chuckled. "Besides, who would wake me up so I could wake you up?"

Jack and Kate lingered a while longer, to be sure Red had successfully made his escape, and then continued on their way back to the Soo.

Nothing was said for a few minutes—finally Kate broke the silence.

"Hey, what do you make of that explosion launching the sheriff like that? Shouldn't he have been strapped down?"

"Yeah, I was wondering about that too," Jack agreed. "Maybe he was. I'll need to get a look at those buckles. If they were not connected—if he was not strapped in—then something is amiss. I can understand the driver removing his belt to check on the sheriff. Say, if there was something burning back there. But I'm not so settled on the sheriff. My guess is that Special Agent Lamar will have some questions in that regard."

"Maybe we can feel him out when we meet with him, whenever he decides that should be."

"That's what I'm thinking as well," Jack said. "And tell me, was the sheriff's body hot—you know, like he had just been on fire? You should have been able to detect substantial heat emanating from his body."

"He was warm," Kate said. "At least, he wasn't cold. But he wasn't hot either. It was not like he'd just been on fire, if you know what I mean."

"I would think that for a body being that charred," Jack said, "that he should still have been smoking. It's possible that there was a fire in the back, at first. And that is what got the driver's attention, and caused him to unfasten his seatbelt to check."

"And that could account for the sheriff's body being so thoroughly burned," Kate continued the thought. "If there was an incendiary device placed under the sheriff's body, then the flames could have produced the type of charring that he suffered. That flame could also have caused the driver to unbuckle his belt. Then, in the explosion, the blast could have shoved the driver's body up under the dash and sent the sheriff's burning body flying to where I found him."

"So," Kate said, "the big question is whether the sheriff's restraining straps were burned through, or unbuckled."

"That is not the only question, but it's a big one," Jack concurred. "Of course, it is possible that Restin, with his incessant talking, so distracted the driver that he accidently left the straps unbuckled. But it remains important to first find out if the straps on the sheriff's body were secured."

"How are we going to get to the bottom of that?"

"I think that Lamar might be too careful to give us that info, but Restin isn't. If we give it a day or two, and come back to him, he might tell us what we want to know."

"There they are," Kate observed, pointing at two patrol cars strategically positioned at the on-ramp to the ferry. "The last potential hindrances to a good night's sleep."

The ferry had just arrived and permitted the three vehicles it had carried from the Soo to drive off.

"They look serious," Jack observed. "See the uniform behind the car on the left. He's sporting a 12 gauge shotgun. ... Smile big, daughter."

"They'll get my biggest. ... Especially that 12 gauge."

Just before the ferry attendant had a chance to wave the only car ahead of Jack and Kate onto the ferry, two officers began walking toward the short line.

"Side arms not drawn, but unstrapped and ready," Jack said.

"I see that too."

It took only a moment to check out and clear the car ahead. The uniforms then approached Jack, one on either side.

"Good evening, sir. Are you a resident of the island?"

"No, we are not," Jack said.

"And what was the nature of your business tonight?"

"We were meeting with Deputy Restin and Special Agent Lamar, out at the resort."

"Excuse me for a moment," he said while he called Deputy Restin on his radio.

After a short exchange, the officer turned toward Jack, smiled and motioned him through.

Jack nodded his head and smiled back.

"That's hard to believe," Kate chuckled.

"What's that?"

"That our buddy here didn't have to spend half an hour on the radio with Restin."

"Take a look back," Jack said, viewing the officer in his rearview mirror.

Kate glanced back over her shoulder, and then laughed out loud. "He's on his radio again—hazard a guess as to whom he might be speaking?"

The ferry attendant held up two fingers, indicating that Jack should pull into the slot so designated.

"I suspect they would like us to kill the engine," Jack said. "But I don't see any signs to that effect."

"I think they are more interested in not having to peel dead frozen bodies out of stalled cars when they stop. Winters in these parts can be pretty severe.

"Hang on. Did you see that?"

"See what?"

"The pedestrian," Kate replied. "That man just walked onto the ferry— no vehicle. I wonder if that's how Red gets back and forth. Maybe he just walks on. I can't see them kicking him off."

"You're probably right. If Red knew who was working at any given time, and if he struck up a bit of a friendship with him, he could easily get free rides. Wouldn't surprise me a bit."

"After all, what's another ninety pounds?"

"If he even goes that," Jack added. "He's pretty skinny."

"If the cops are watching, Red would stay away. But I'd bet there's a better than good chance they would just let him ride—Red and his dog. Remember what Restin called him? 'A legend?' Who would kick a legend off the boat?"

"Right. Exactly right."

"Okay, *that* mystery is solved," Kate said. "Or at least plausibly solved."

"Besides, it would be a good move on the part of management to let Red ride free," Jack said. "If they kicked him off, and he were to get injured trying to sneak back on, or getting across some other way, there could be big trouble for the ferry's administrators. It would be easier to justify a few lost fares, than a seriously injured child."

"What do you think?" Kate asked. "Do we spend some time tomorrow on the island?"

"Looking for Red, you mean?"

"Yeah."

"I'm up for it," Jack replied. "But first we need to take a closer look at what I handed you in the woods."

"Oh, yes, I had forgotten about that," Kate said as she reached into her pocket to retrieve the object Jack had given her.

"And what is this, exactly?" she asked, handing the thin wafer to her father. "Is that the SIM card from the sheriff's cell?"

Jack smiled his affirmation: "Should be interesting to see who he's been calling—and who's been calling him."

"Dad, are you withholding evidence again?"

Chapter 39—The answers Jack gets only raise more questions

"Yes, Kate, I suppose you could say that," Jack admitted. "But I think it is worth the gamble."

"Shall I put it in my cell and read it?" Kate asked.

"Definitely not," Jack quickly replied. "We have to be very careful with it. If we put it in a regular cell phone, it could get pinged, or it could reach out to a cell tower and be tracked. They have to be wondering where it went by now."

"We're going to have to use a SIM card reader, right?" Kate suggested.

"Back at the hotel," Jack said.

"Great!" Kate replied. "Then what do we do with it?"

"We'll figure that out later," Jack said. "I just know we can't get caught with it."

"I didn't know you did stuff like that," Kate said, pretending to be surprised.

"Daughter of mine, keep in mind that I used to be a detective—a *Chicago* detective."

* * *

As soon as they entered their room, Jack popped the SIM card into his reader.

"Here, see what you can get off of this," he said to Kate. "But don't load anything on your computer. Just write it down. And quickly. I'm half expecting company."

Kate did as her father requested, writing down all the phone numbers she found.

"Typical man," she said. "Actually, I should qualify that statement—he was a typical *older* man."

"And what does that mean?" Jack asked.

"The sheriff never texted on this phone—not even once. I'll bet he didn't even know how to text. Tell me, Dad, how much do you text?"

"I suppose you could say that I am your typical older man, in that regard."

"There," Kate said, "I've got everything off the card."

"That was quick," Jack said.

"The history only went back a few days."

"Really," Jack said. "That's a bit curious, don't you think?"

"It is. But maybe the sheriff just got a new phone."

"Must have," Jack said. "Here, give me the card, and put your notes away."

As soon as Kate handed him the card, Jack walked into the bathroom, cut it into several small pieces with a pair of wire cutters, and flushed the pieces down the toilet. He waited for the tank to fill and flushed a second time.

No sooner had the tank begun filling from the second flush, than there was a loud knock on the door.

"Jack, Jack Handler. FBI. Open up."

"I'll need to see some identification," Jack said, looking over and winking at Kate. He did take a peek through the peephole and then turned back facing Kate, holding up two fingers indicating that there were two suits outside. He then opened the door.

"Gentlemen," Jack said, motioning for the agents to come in. "What can I do for you?"

"My name is Agent Richards," the FBI agent closest to Jack said. "And this is Agent Hendricks. Special Agent Lamar sent us to ask a couple questions before you turn in. Would that be a problem?"

"Well," Jack replied, "You're here, and we're not sleeping. At least not yet. Will this take long?"

"Three short questions, Mr. Handler."

"Fire away," Jack said with a chuckle. "Poor choice of words, I suspect. But how can I help you?"

"First, Special Agent Lamar wanted to know exactly *why* you were on Sugar Island this evening?"

"I had just received a call from Sheriff Northrup, and he suggested that he might have learned something about my brother-in-law's case. While I was on the phone with him, I heard what sounded like three suppressed rounds from a .22. I suspected that he had been shot, so I flagged down Restin and informed him. He and another officer accompanied Kate and me to the island."

"Second question. What do you know about the sheriff's cell phone?"

"I'm not sure what you're getting at," Jack said. "As I mentioned, the sheriff called me from his cell earlier this evening. And while I was out on the pier with Restin, he found what he thought was the sheriff's cell close to where he had found the body. That's about it."

"Then we won't find your fingerprints on it?"

"Not if the cell phone Restin found in the river was the sheriff's. Was it?"

"The third and last question is this. What were you and your daughter doing in the woods near the location where the ambulance exploded?"

"On our way back to Sault Ste. Marie, we thought we saw someone run across the road, and we followed them."

"You followed *them*? There was more than one?"

"Right. There is a boy who lives on Sugar Island. He's known as *Red*. And he has a dog—a large golden retriever. Kate and I thought we saw the boy and his dog dart across ahead of us and disappear into the woods at that point."

"Did you locate the boy? This Red?"

"No. In fact, Restin informed us that the boy was not on the island at that time. So, whoever we were following, he or they were much too quick, and it was much too dark. Kate and I followed something or someone several hundred yards into the woods but then lost 'em out there. That was where Restin found us. We were just about to head back to our vehicle when he came out into the woods.

"So, gentlemen, if that was your last question, do you think you could leave us now? It has been a terribly long day, and we are both tired."

"Absolutely," Agent Richards said, turning toward the door to leave.

"But, if you don't mind, please allow me to rephrase one of my questions.

"You said you had three questions, and we answered three."

"This is not a new question, just a rephrasing of one. Mr. Handler, can we correctly assume that you do not have the SIM card from Sheriff Northrup's cell phone?"

"I do not have it," Jack replied. "Now, please keep your word and leave. We're very tired."

"Say, Mr. Handler, is that blood on your collar? It looks like you've been bleeding."

"Good night, gentlemen," Jack said. "A limb caught me in the woods and scratched my head. Now, it's time to call this a night. Good night, gentlemen."

"Thank you, Mr. Handler, for your cooperation."

"Good night," Jack said, virtually pushing the two men out of his door.

After a few moments, Kate took a look through the peephole. And then she opened the door to confirm that the FBI agents had actually left.

Kate closed the door and engaged the security lock.

"That was totally interesting," she said, leaning her back against the locked door. "What made you suspect that they would be stopping by tonight?"

"The missing SIM card," Jack said. "I'm sure that decision was made directly by Special Agent Lamar. When Restin handed the cell phone off to the FBI, I'm sure that Lamar went ballistic.

"I can almost hear him shouting. I'll bet it went like this: 'Restin, you idiot. Didn't you check to see if the SIM card was in the phone? Was Handler with you when you found it? And did he at any point touch that cell phone? Someone had to have removed the card. Or maybe it fell out when it was damaged. Take me out on the pier and show me exactly where you found the phone'.

"That's when he decided to send the two agents. He isn't quite sure what's become of that SIM card. He suspected that I might have it. But he's not sure that the killers didn't remove it. And it is also possible that it fell out of the phone when it was damaged, in that case, it could be anywhere in the river.

"It would not have floated, but it's light and could easily have drifted downstream."

"Can you imagine how hard it would be to find something that small?" Kate asked rhetorically.

"Not only that, but at that point the bottom of the river has several inches of silt. As soon as one of the agents would step into the river, it would murk up. It's not metallic. It would be a bear to find. One thing for certain. As it stands right now, that SIM card is *impossible* to find."

"That would be true," Kate replied. "Tomorrow we look for Red? Is that right?"

"Unless we get that call from Lamar."

Jack looked at his cell, and then over at Kate, "Restin."

Popping the back off his cell and removing the battery, Jack said, "I forgot to turn my cell off when we got on the ferry. Besides, I don't have the patience for this right now. You should do the same."

* * *

"There it is," Kate said, pointing at the bottle Jack had left to mark the spot where Red had disappeared the night before.

Chapter 40—The hunt for Red (in November)

"Do we dare leave our car parked on the side of the road again? We haven't had much luck doing that lately."

"I don't think that would be a good idea," Jack said. "We need to find a drive that looks unused."

"How about over there?" Kate said, pointing at a two-track on the opposite side of the road. "How would that work?"

"I like it," Jack said. "We can pull in and run it around the bend. At least it will not be visible from the road. Just in case Restin is lurking."

By keeping his left front tire in the center grass of the two-track, he hoped to make his use of the drive less noticeable.

"Are you licensed to carry in Michigan?" Jack asked.

"No, but you are. And after last night, I certainly expect that you're armed."

Jack used his remote to lock his vehicle as the two walked back to the road.

"What'd you do with the info from the sheriff's phone?" Jack asked.

"I stuck it, and the video from the resort, in a Ziploc, and slid it into the large plant in the lobby."

"Perfect," Jack replied. "They're going to toss our room today."

"That's what I'm thinking. Any chance of their finding the SIM card?"

"None. The hotel has municipal sewer services, so what's left of it has probably traveled several blocks already. But I do expect to see your notebook compromised."

"I left the video on it because they already know that the sheriff gave it to us. But there's nothing compromising to be found."

When they reached the plastic bottle, they took a moment to examine the damp gravel on the side of the road where Red and his dog entered the woods.

"Kate, do you believe this?" Jack said. "Looks like size eleven hiking boots—right on top of the dog's paw print. They waited until after we left and then continued their pursuit. Talk about motivation."

"Let's see if we can find them coming back out of the woods."

Remaining on the paved road, Jack and Kate had walked down only a short distance when Kate noticed something.

"Here, looks like he came out right here. Apparently there was only one man."

Jack walked across the road to see if the track entered the woods on the opposite side of the road. Not finding an entry point, Jack concluded that Mr. Size Eleven was picked up by a vehicle.

"He had to have contacted his ride from the woods. Chances are that he didn't use a cell phone—especially with Canadian roaming. Too problematic. Probably just used a simple two-way radio on a standard frequency."

"Whatever the case," Kate said. "Unless Red came out at some other spot, he's probably still in this area. Shall we give it a shot?"

"Let's go," Jack said.

"It's not going to be possible to track him," Kate said. "Got any ideas?"

"Not really. But maybe we'll think of something as we go along."

The two of them followed what appeared to be a relatively straight path for a couple hundred yards. Finally, they reached a clearing overlooking a steep descent.

"I'm betting there's water up ahead," Jack said. "I can smell it."

"That means there are going to be a large number of available cabins for Red to hide out in," Kate said.

"Red must have trained his dog very well," she continued. "Most dogs would be barking when strangers approach. But I've never heard his dog bark."

"Let's hope today's the exception. Listen carefully for a bark, or a whine. That dog of his can't remain silent forever."

"Have you thought about what we're going to do if we find Red?" Kate asked.

"I have. The best we can hope for is to wait him out. This is not his regular haunt. He's here only because he got chased out of his hideout. Eventually, he is going to head back to where he is more comfortable. When he does, we will follow him."

"Would do no good to catch him."

"No, it wouldn't," Jack agreed. "I'd like to find out where he's hiding right now. And when he leaves, I'd like to check it out. If he knows as much about your uncle's case as I suspect he does, we just might find something interesting."

"This could take a while, couldn't it?"

"It might. But I'm thinking that once he is convinced that it's safe for him, he'll venture out. And then he will head back. The critical thing is to listen for his dog."

"He could be in any one of these cabins. Right?"

"He could. But I would look for one that is more run down. One that has the appearance of an abandoned or seldom-used cabin."

"Why would that be?"

"Would be logical for him," Jack said. "He would reason that the nicer the cabin, the more likely the owner might show up. I would also look for one with electrical hookup. He would be more likely to choose one where he might find a toaster or an electric heater. He wouldn't want to burn wood—the aroma is too distinctive. And propane tanks have to be filled on a regular basis. Look for an electrical service—but not necessarily a gas tank."

"And a whining dog?"

"Exactly."

"How about fresh dog dung?"

"That works for me," Jack said. "Just don't step in any—at least not if you're planning to ride back with me."

"I'm serious. Take a look at this," Kate said, pointing to what was most certainly a freshly deposited dog stool.

"Down," Jack commanded, as he dropped to his knees. "That's it—they're nearby."

"Which cabin do you suspect?"

"It's going to be one close to this spot—Red's not going to let his dog wander far. Let's see—we've got that cabin down by the river. Possibly that one," Jack continued, nodding his head in the direction of a small, rundown cabin located off the lake about fifty yards. That would be my best guess. But, if we drop back a bit, to that group of small pines, we can wait there. I'm thinking that Red, or his dog, will be on the move before too long. I'm sure he is not as comfortable here as he would be closer to where he lives.

"You go first," Jack directed. "I'll wait until you get settled. If he spots us, he might take off. Make sure you have a good view of the cabin. When you're satisfied, signal me."

Ducking down as low as she could, Kate scampered to the stand of about twelve smaller pine trees ninety feet away. Shortly after she settled in, she signaled to her father.

Jack waited a few moments and then followed his daughter.

"This works," Jack said, sitting down for what could be a long wait.

"The bathroom is just over that hill," Kate said, smiling as she pointed to another small group of evergreens, the tops of which were visible from their location.

Jack did not verbally respond, but he did glance in the direction she was pointing.

"This could be all day," Kate noted with a knowing smile.

"It could," Jack agreed. "I'm hoping something happens sooner, but we might be here quite a while."

"What will we do when he emerges?" Kate asked.

"Good question. This is what I have in mind. I would like to have you follow him at a distance and see if you can locate his more permanent residence. He's going to be looking ahead for the man who was after him earlier. So he will be less suspecting of having someone coming up from behind.

"If you lose him, it won't be the end of the world. Just try to get us in the ballpark before he discovers that you are following him. When he gets close, he might just surveil his own hideout for a while. Be prepared to wait him out. If you have to, hit me on our two-ways. I've set them for vibrate.

"While you're following Red, I will search the cabin where he is right now."

"How sure are we that we've got the right one?" Kate asked.

"My guess is ninety percent—maybe a little better. It's a cinch that the stool you found was not from last night. It was still very moist. Has to have been from this morning. Maybe better than ninety percent. But we will keep our eyes open just in case. One thing for sure, Red would not have sent his dog out into an area he had not already inspected. So the dog stool you found would have been the direction from which Red entered the cabin. I'm virtually sure that's the cabin he's currently using. The only downside is that he may have spotted us approaching. I don't think he did, but it's possible—"

"Dad!" Kate interrupted. "Check that out. I think I saw the curtain move."

Chapter 41—The hard detective work begins

"I see it too," Jack agreed. "It might have been the dog. But something, or *someone*, is definitely at that window."

A few moments passed, and then Red pulled the curtain over several inches and pressed his face into the dirty glass.

"We found him," Kate announced, as she ducked back so as not to be seen. "Now the waiting game."

"Might not be that long. Red might be checking it out to see if he dares come out," Jack said. "I think that if he were expecting the cops, he would be less concerned. He has a history of escaping from them. Besides, according to Restin, the law doesn't really want to capture him."

"So, whoever it is that is after Red now wants to harm him?" Kate asked.

"That's my bet. Normally the kid just has to try to keep out of everyone's way. But he is overly cautious, much more so than the mere prospect of apprehension ought to elicit."

"Whoa, there he is again."

"Might be he's about to make a move."

"I think you're right … this time he left the curtain wide open. See if I understand how you want to handle this. I'm gonna follow him, but at a safe distance—which means a *substantial* distance—given a dog is involved. You're gonna stay and search the building. When you're finished, you'll hit me on the two-way, and we'll see how we should proceed. Is that about right?"

"Exactly."

"Would you look at that. He's coming out the window."

"That means the door is locked with a deadbolt. Hold very still, and don't talk."

Jack and Kate remained motionless as Red clambered out of the cabin window, followed by his dog. Once they were both outside, Red reached back in and straightened the curtain, and then closed the window.

Red closely scrutinized the landscape and motioned for Dog to head in the direction Jack had suspected. He then turned slightly east and pressed on at a brisk pace.

"Take this," Jack whispered, as he handed Kate a compact thermal imaging device. "It'll come in handy if Red gets too big a lead on you, or if you lose sight in the brush."

Kate took the unit and pointed it in Red's direction.

"Great," she responded. "That should allow me to hang back a bit."

"I just thought of something," Jack said. "You should take this as well."

Jack then handed her his Walther .380 caliber semi-automatic, which he carried in a holster strapped to his calf.

"If you run into the fellows who spooked Red in the first place, you might need it. Keep in mind that this piece could be traced. It should be used only as a last resort."

"Better to be arrested with a smoking gun, than to be buried too young," Kate said with a grin on her face.

"I think it's time for you to go," Jack said, focusing his attention on the cabin. "I'll call you when I finish here."

Jack waited until Kate had disappeared into the forest, and then he made his way up to the window Red had just used to vacate. Sliding the window to the side, he used a planter beneath the window to elevate himself through the small opening.

"Thirty years ago this would have been a piece of cake," Jack muttered after his third attempt to squeeze through.

Just as he had suspected, the temperature in the cabin was at least fifteen degrees warmer than outside. He examined an electric heater and found it to still be warm.

"At least Red turned it off before he left," Jack observed.

Jack then noticed that nothing appeared to be out of place—Red had straightened up before leaving. But one thing did get his attention. Lying on the floor beside the kitchen sink was a large brown trash bag. While it was tied at the top with a red drawstring, it appeared to have a couple pieces of refuse inside.

That's unusual, Jack thought. *I wonder what Red threw away.*

Chapter 42—Jack's startling discovery

Jack removed a pair of latex gloves from his pocket and slipped them on.

"Let's see," he said out loud, carefully untying the plastic drawstring on the top of the trash bag so he could peer inside. He did not believe what he saw.

Jack then carried the bag over to the open window to allow the light from the sun to illuminate the contents.

"That is a lot of blood!" Jack exclaimed. "Red must have been injured ... perhaps shot. What else could produce this much blood?"

Jack then began to piece together what must have happened. If the attacker were close enough to cut Red, the dog would have torn into him. Must have been a bullet. Probably from a distance, or else Red would not have been able to get away.

Jack removed the two-way radio and called his daughter. After the third alert he sent, Kate answered.

"Yeah."

"Kate, is it safe to talk?"

"I can talk."

"There is a bag of trash in the house, I assume left by Red. And it is full of bloody towels. Red must be wounded. I'm pretty sure he's been shot."

"That figures," she replied. "He's favoring his right leg. By the way he's walking, I'd guess he took a flesh wound to his right thigh."

"That poor kid," Jack said. "He never gets a break. I'm surprised we didn't notice it when he scampered out of that window."

"He's tough. And very resourceful—a real survivor."

"Well, Kate. Let that be a warning to you. This kid has got some equally real enemies. It would not surprise me if they were still out there—right now—waiting for him to come back. Quite probably are, in fact."

"I'll be careful. How long you gonna hang out back there?"

"Not long. I'm going to bag up some things and catch up with you. Take care, okay?"

"Sounds good."

Jack sensed that the bloody towels troubled Kate.

"I'll move up as quickly as I can. Have you been able to stay on the same path?"

"Yeah. I'll leave a marker if I venture off it."

Initially, Jack had planned to spend a little more time looking around the cabin for additional clues, but decided quite quickly that he would do well to get out and check up on Kate. The longer he thought about it, the more seriously he took his own warning to her.

Jack checked to see if the door was indeed locked with a double deadbolt, and it was. He was hoping he could exit through the door and have it latch behind him. But that was not going to happen—he would have to leave through the window, just as he had entered.

Eighteen, maybe twenty minutes. That's the lead she has on me, Jack was thinking. *But Red will be moving forward cautiously, so I should be able to catch up by the time they reach the road.*

Jack moved along as quickly as possible, taking care only to stay on the path and to hold down the noise.

As Kate crested a small hill, only about a hundred yards from the road, she momentarily lost track of Red and his dog. So she stopped and pointed the infrared sensing device Jack had given her in the direction she suspected Red to be heading.

And, sure enough, she spotted two sources of heat no more than fifty yards ahead. It looked to her as though they had stopped and were crouching down in some bushes.

I wonder why they've stopped? Could they have seen, or sensed, something?" she wondered. Not wanting to move any further until she figured out why Red had stopped, she began using the device to scrutinize the area to the left and to the right of Red.

At first she detected nothing. But when she repeated her effort for a third time, she picked up another source of heat. It looked to be about one hundred feet away from Red and the dog and was partially obscured behind a tree. She pulled the device down and checked it out with her naked eye.

But before she could do anything she saw a puff of smoke discharging from what she believed to be a semi-automatic rifle.

An assault weapon with a suppressor, she concluded. *My Walther .380 is definitely no match for that. Too bad for me, but that's all I got.*

By the time she was able to get off a shot, Red's attacker had fired half a dozen more times at the boy and his dog. Kate heard the dog yelp, but only one time.

When Kate fired, the gunman turned his weapon in her direction.

Kate immediately hit the ground, as several rounds ripped through the trees above and beside her. She lay totally still, hoping not to draw more fire. The Walther .380 was functionally useless at that distance, particularly when up against an assault weapon. The best she could hope for would be to distract, or perhaps frighten, the shooter.

But that did not happen. Instead, the attacker ran over to where the boy and his dog were hiding, scooped up Red's motionless body, and bolted toward the road.

Kate stood up and started yelling at the man to drop the boy or she would shoot him.

For a moment, the bluff appeared to work. He dropped Red and turned his attention back toward Kate, who was closing ground as quickly as possible, in hopes of getting within range to make her .380 effective.

Unfortunately, Kate was now close enough for him to get off several more rounds, this time taking better aim.

Just as Kate fired, she took a glancing round to the right side of her head.

She dropped immediately—not unconscious, but dazed.

Luckily, her attacker was far more interested in getting Red to his car than he was in finishing off Kate.

Jack, upon hearing the shooting, himself took off like a bullet in her direction. By the time he reached her, she had stood to her feet, and was looking around for the .380. An automobile could be heard accelerating rapidly.

Obviously that's Red's abductor escaping, Jack correctly surmised.

"Kate!" Jack shouted. "How bad are you hurt?"

"I'm not sure," she replied. "I just took one, and it was pretty much just a glancing hit. It stunned me, but didn't do any real damage.

"I didn't go unconscious. I'm pretty sure about that."

"How about Red?" Jack asked.

"Not good. Not sure if he was hit. I didn't see him move. The gunman was by himself. He's a big guy. Tall. He scooped Red up like a sack of potatoes and carried him toward the road. Red could be dead. I'm so sorry, I couldn't get off a good shot. Just too far for a .380."

"Let me check you out," Jack said, examining his daughter's single wound.

"It doesn't look serious," he said. "You were very lucky. It's in your hair, so it won't even leave a scar. No other injuries?"

"I'm fine, I'm sure. But I can't say the same for Red."

"How about his dog? Let's get a look at the scene, and see if his dog is still alive."

As Jack and Kate approached the dog, they could hear his pitiful whines.

"He's still alive!" Kate cried, running ahead of her father to where the dog was lying.

"Oh, Dad, he's been hit," she said. "But he's still alive. We've got to get him some help."

"Where's the entry wound?" Jack asked, bending down beside his daughter.

"All I can see is a graze high on his back—no entry," Kate said.

"Take a look at the upper portion of his right rear leg—in the muscle. It looks like he took a round there as well. Looks like it might have fractured it."

Chapter 43—Red's dog gets a new name

"Be careful, Kate. For sure Red's dog has not had his shots. And it's not likely that he will take to strangers. Not if he's anything like Red."

"We've still got to get him some help," Kate said. "How do we go about it?"

"A gurney would help," Jack quipped, kneeling beside the dog to get a closer look. "We need some way to sedate and restrain the dog. And to secure the fractured leg before more damage is done."

"Look at his eyes," Kate said. "He's pleading with us to help him. I wonder what his name is. We can't just refer to him in the third person."

"I doubt that he has a name. … Red can't talk," Jack said.

"A dog like this needs a name," Kate said. "I think we should call him *Buddy*. After all, that's what he is to Red, his buddy."

"Makes sense to me," Jack agreed. "Now, if we're going to save … Buddy, then we have to get him to a vet. And to do that, we must prevent his going into shock. It's not going to be easy. And, we have to keep him from trying to walk on his busted leg. If he pokes the bone out, it will severely retard healing. And we might have to put him down."

"Do we report Red's kidnapping?" Kate asked.

"Tough question. If we do, then we have to stick around here for who knows how long."

"And Buddy dies, right?"

"My guess is that the authorities will not concern themselves with

Red. After all, they do not hold him in the same esteem as they do other people. To them, he's more like a wolf, or a bear—they will avoid him as long as he doesn't harm anyone or anything. I say we deal with Buddy. And then think about reporting that we found Red's dog in the woods, and that he was wounded. Let them draw their own conclusions. Or, maybe we try to rescue the boy ourselves."

"Okay," Kate said, lying down beside Buddy and pressing her body against his to calm him. She then wrapped her right arm around the large dog, drew herself as close to him as possible, and pressed her face to Buddy's ear.

"I'll stay here and keep Buddy calm," Kate said. "And you can figure out how we get him to a vet."

"He must weight seventy-five pounds—maybe more," Jack muttered. "The only way we can get him out of here is for me to carry him.

"I'm going to my truck and find something to secure that leg. You try to keep him down. If he spooks, you're going to have to let him go free, or he will tear you to pieces."

"He's good with me. He's a smart dog. He knows he's hurt, and he knows we're his friends."

"I hope you're right," Jack added as he headed toward his vehicle.

Just as he reached the road, he heard the now familiar roar of the twin-jet helicopter, and a moment later it launched out over the treetops and headed east into Canada.

Jack stood for a moment watching it disappear.

"Well, Red, good luck escaping this time," he grumbled.

When Jack reached his vehicle, he first opened the rear hatch, and rapidly removed the entire first-aid kit. He then re-locked his vehicle and headed back to where Kate and *Buddy* were waiting.

He found them just as he had left them—still engaged in a full-body contact posture. Except now Kate was gently rubbing Buddy's neck, and whispering close to his ear. The blood from her wound had matted her hair and had run in streaks down her neck. She was crying.

"Hey, Buddy, it's gonna be okay. We're gonna take you in and get you all fixed up. But you can't help your friend right now. If you try to walk, you'll totally screw up your leg. We've got to get it fixed first. Dad and I will help you find Red. And you can get better, and everything will be good again."

"Keep talking to him," Jack said. "He's not used to hearing a human voice. I can see he likes it. I'll get a splint on his leg, and then we can move him."

"Is that gonna hurt him?"

"No, but he's not going to like it much. His leg is still intact. The bone is not protruding. That grazing shot must have stunned him, and he dropped immediately."

As Kate continued to whisper into Buddy's ear, Jack delicately placed a splint beneath the injured leg, and one on top.

Buddy whined and made a slight effort to get up.

"Be still, Buddy," Kate said, comforting the dog. "We'll have you all fixed up in no time."

Chapter 44—Saving Buddy

"That should do it for now," Jack said. "We just have to be sure he doesn't walk on it. This is what we do. You keep talking to Buddy. I can see your voice has a very calming effect on him."

"How are we going to keep him from trying to get away?"

"I'll reach under him, and pick him up. We'll keep his legs in the air. The splint should hold the leg in place as long as he doesn't place any weight on it. As I pick him up, you just keep talking to him."

To this point, Buddy was content with having Kate whisper in his ear. He sensed that Jack had been up to something with his throbbing leg—he just didn't know what. But he was okay, as long as Kate was talking to him in her gentle voice. But things were about to get a little dicey.

Jack reached underneath Buddy and began turning him onto his back. It was immediately obvious to Jack that Buddy was far more trusting of Kate than he was of him. Buddy did not bite Jack, but he did voice his irritation with being removed from Kate's embrace.

"My, what big teeth you have, Buddy," Jack said, trying to encourage Kate to do her magic.

"Hey, Buddy, it's okay," Kate said, taking the dog's large head in her hands and pulling his face to hers. "Buddy, we're gonna get you help … to make you all better. You'd like that, wouldn't you? You get better, and we'll go find Red and bring him home to you. How does that sound?"

"Does he understand you?"

"He understands love. And that's what I'm giving him. Love."

"Well, whatever you're doing, keep it up. Otherwise, he might take my face off."

"My Buddy wouldn't do that. Would you, Buddy? At least not without a warning."

"I think when he showed me his teeth … I think that was the only warning I'm gonna get."

While on one knee, Jack rolled Buddy onto his back and cradled him in his arms.

"That works," Jack said, standing to his feet. "Just keep talking to him, and maybe we can get him to the truck. When we get there, you get in the back seat with him and make sure as best you can that he doesn't put any pressure on that broken leg. I'm pretty sure that I've got it taped up enough to protect it, but if he were to put a lot of pressure on it—like trying to jump—it could be very damaging, not to mention painful."

"When we get to your truck, I'll hold him on my lap, and talk to him. … Too bad we don't have anything to sedate him with."

"That would be useful," Jack said.

After a few dozen steps, Kate asked her father, "What were you suggesting back there? That we were going to rescue Red? What did you have in mind?"

"You saw the helicopter," Jack said. "We both know that they took Red to Canada. Who knows what for? But they are after something. Maybe they think he has some information. I think we can be sure that once they get what they're after, they're going to kill him."

"I'm not so certain that you need to go. You've got a career to protect. I'm just an old retired cop—all I could lose is my pension. You could lose your job."

"So, what do you think I'm gonna be doing while you find Red? I'm a detective—a good one. I can be useful to you. And I can't allow Red to be murdered by these guys. The odds are great that Red's abduction is somehow connected with Uncle Alex's murder—I think we agree on that. If we're gonna solve that crime, we just might have to learn what it is that Red is holding back."

"You're right about everything except for the part where you need to put your future on the line. I can handle this by myself. Granted, you're a great detective, and you would certainly be an asset. I just don't think the rewards merit the risk. I'm not going to tell you that you can't go with me. But I would strongly recommend against it."

"I know how you think. If you didn't want me to come with you, you would flat out tell me to back off. You know I can be helpful, and you are just trying to protect me. Am I right?"

Jack paused for a moment and then answered his daughter—albeit indirectly.

"We'll get Buddy into the appropriate hands. We have to make sure that the vet we work with understands that regardless the severity of the wounds, every effort must be made to save him. Once we are totally convinced that Buddy is going to make it, we'll figure out our next move."

Kate settled into the back seat. She was smiling because she had heard what she wanted to hear. Jack then carefully handed Buddy through to her, doing his best to keep Buddy's broken leg away from hard surfaces.

But as soon as Jack pulled away to get into the driver's seat, Buddy made a frantic effort to escape Kate's grasp. In so doing, his broken leg struck the back of the seat, and when it did, he leveraged himself enough to twist his body around to a standing position, with Kate beneath him. Immediately he lifted his splinted broken leg, so as not to put pressure on it.

"Hey, Buddy," Kate said, realizing that she had lost control. "Are you sure this is how you want it?"

Buddy was happy to be standing, even if only on three good legs. He ran across the seat to get a better look out of the window. And then he started to whine.

"He's looking for Red," Jack said. "As long as he doesn't put much weight on that bad leg, he should be fine. Obviously he is feeling better."

"Look at his neck," Kate said. "I think it's safe to say that this dog has never been fitted for a collar. He's always been just as free as Red. I wonder how he's going to handle the vet, and the dog hospital."

"The way he's perked up, I'm betting that we won't have to find out about the hospital part," Jack said. "If the vet can put a real splint on that leg and give him a shot, or whatever vets do for open wounds like this, I'm thinking that Buddy can go with us to rescue Red."

"I like that idea," Kate said. "We'd better make sure that Buddy has all of his shots before we take him into Canada. Don't need any problems like that."

"Deputy Restin?" Jack said, after dialing his cell phone. "I'm looking for a vet to take a look at a dog. Do you have one you'd recommend?"

Chapter 45—Buddy meets "Dr. Save My Pet"

"Injury or illness?" Deputy Restin asked.

"Injury—broken leg."

"If it were me, I'd take a dog with a broken leg to Dr. Rex. He has an office in his house, just south of the Soo. He advertises that he is a "Large Animal Vet," but he's the best around. And he will take care of your dog if I call him and give him a heads up. How long before you can be there?"

"Not sure. Depends where the vet is."

"Where are you right now?"

"Kate and I are on Sugar Island, headed for the ferry."

"Sugar Island?"

"Right."

Deputy Restin paused for a long moment and then said, "Let me guess—you've got Red's dog. Am I right?"

"I'd rather not answer that."

"I don't even want you to tell me how you came by that animal. If Lamar catches wind of this, your vacation will be over. Just turn left when you get off the ferry. Catch the first right, and Dr. Rex will be on the right side of the road, maybe half a mile down."

"Does this doctor know how to keep his mouth shut?"

"He's old school. I've heard he's even treated some of the locals from time to time. As long as you pay him with cash, he will be discreet."

Deputy Restin paused for a moment, and then chuckled, "Of course, if you don't pay him with cash, you might need a doctor yourself."

"Turn left, then right?"

"Yeah. Should be no more than ten minutes, once you get off the ferry. What's up with the kid? Red?"

"Don't know anything about that. All we know is that we found this nice dog along the side of the road with what looks to be a broken leg. And we want to get him to a vet. I really appreciate your help."

"Happy to be of service. If you hear anything about the kid, let me know. Okay?"

"Kate and I will keep you in mind if we learn anything."

"I'll give the good doctor a call right now. *Dr. Save My Pet.* That's what some people call him around here. If an animal can be saved, Dr. Rex will do it."

"Much appreciated. … We're just getting on the ferry," Jack said, disconnecting the call.

"Has he got it figured out?" Kate asked. "Does he know we've got Red's dog?"

"Yes, but he's not eager to share that info with the FBI. Or so he suggests"

"That figures, don't you think? I doubt that he's particularly fond of Lamar."

"But it is his responsibility to keep the FBI apprised of all pertinent information. And if he suspects we have Red's dog, he should be calling Lamar right now."

"But he isn't making that call. Right?"

"I don't think so. He does want us to keep him up to speed regarding Red, but I get the feeling that he will not be sharing that sort of stuff with

Lamar. Could be competition, I suppose. Or something else."

"We're not in the big city anymore. They just have a different way of doing things up here."

"You could be right. … The sheriff had the same attitude. He gave the appearance of cooperation but was more about doing his own thing. I imagine it's difficult for the local authorities to submit to outsiders— even to the FBI."

"*Especially* to the FBI," Kate said. "No agency likes surrendering the lead to the FBI. They don't play well with anyone. Certainly not with people like the sheriff. The FBI hogs all the toys."

Both Jack and Kate sat silently for several moments, as Jack approached and drove onto the ferry.

"That's Red's dog," the attendant said as he motioned their vehicle into row three. "How'd you come by him?"

"Red?" Jack replied. "Who's Red?"

"He's a young fellow who lives on the island. And that's his dog."

"Could be," Jack replied. "But he needs a vet. He's got a broken leg. If you run into this young man, Red, you can tell him that we are taking his dog to Dr. Rex. You know who that is?"

"Dr. Save My Pet, everyone knows him. Good choice. If anyone can help you, he can. He likes to get paid in cash. Just remember that."

"So I've heard."

"What happened to the dog?"

"Can't be certain. Just know he has a broken leg."

"Nice splint," the attendant said with a smile.

"It'll do."

"You know how to get to the doc's house?"

"Pretty sure," Jack replied. "I turn left outta here. Take the first right after that, and the doctor is just up the road."

"That's right. Can't miss it. He knows you're coming?"

"He does."

"Well, good luck," the attendant said, stepping back to check for remaining vehicles.

As soon as he had completed that task, he removed the mooring line and secured the ramp. He then turned his back to Jack's vehicle and dialed a number on his cell phone.

"Wonder who *he's* calling?" Jack muttered.

"Don't you get the feeling that nothing goes unnoticed on this island?" Kate said.

"One thing for sure," Jack chuckled. "He's not calling Red."

"My bet is he's calling the doctor, just to verify that you were telling him the truth."

"That's what I think," Jack agreed. "According to Restin this Dr. Rex also treats humans from time to time—"

"Humans with cash, I'd bet."

"Exactly. Humans with gunshot wounds and cash."

"You know, Dad. I've been thinking. If I were wanting to hide out, If I wanted to lie low for a while, I think that Sugar Island would be a great place to do that."

"Everyone knows everyone here. But if you had a little cash, and a cottage on the island—you could live here forever, and no one would really care."

"I think what they say is true, that there is no law enforcement on the island," Kate said. "They've got Homeland Security running around ostensibly looking for terrorists in wetsuits. But, at the same time, they allow that black helicopter to move in and out with virtual impunity. If I owned a little cottage in the woods, I believe I could hide out there without a problem, for as long as I wanted."

"A little like Red?"

"Right. Red has moved about freely for years. Technically, he should be in school."

"Until now," Jack added. "I don't think you could say he's free anymore. The more I think about it, the more certain I become that the boy must have something the guys in the black helicopter want."

"Well, after we get Buddy fixed up we'll get to the bottom of this."

Once the boat docked, Jack followed Deputy Restin's simple directions. He turned left, and then right. Within minutes, he spotted Dr. Rex's sign: "Dr. Rex Brown—Large Animal Veterinarian."

"Looks like he's here—there's a van in the garage," Kate observed as they drove all the way up the long driveway.

"Not likely his. It's too long for the garage, and it's not four-wheel."

Jack had noticed that the garage door was lowered to the point that it struck the rear bumper.

"Nice house," Kate observed, as they drove in. "Must be his cash business is doing just fine."

Before they had even parked, Dr. Rex met them with a syringe.

"Ah," he said, opening the rear door. "I've got just what this fine fellow needs—a little shot of happy juice."

Kate's jaw dropped as she looked at her father.

Chapter 46—Buddy's injury "no big deal"

"You do the gift wrap?" Dr. Rex asked, sarcastically. "Looks pretty good. Hope you're not after my job."

Neither Jack nor Kate acknowledged his comment.

"You're Jack?"

"I'm Jack."

"Why don't you be a good gentleman and help your daughter get this lovely fellow into my office so I can take a better look at him. I'd carry him, but I've got a bad back."

Again they did not verbally acknowledge the doctor. Jack, who was already headed around to assist Kate with Buddy, simply allowed the doctor time to inject the tranquilizer and then proceeded to lift Buddy from his daughter's lap.

Jack could not figure out what it was, but there was something about Dr. Rex that did not sit well with him. At first he thought that the doctor came off unprofessional. But it quickly became obvious that Dr. Rex did know his trade. Jack then concluded that two of the main reasons he didn't care for the doctor was his cocky cavalier air, along with a poorly disguised New England accent.

Plus, the doctor looked out of place for the Soo—especially with the way he dressed.

Dr. Rex was wearing a pair of well-polished brown loafers, tan pressed trousers, and a short-sleeve brown and green flowered shirt—in

November.

Top all that off with his freshly manicured nails, and perfectly groomed short hair. Jack's first inclination was to slap him silly. Kate sensed her father's frustration but did not try to mediate.

"I assume you're paying with cash."

"That would be true," Jack replied.

"Just follow me in. I'll show you where to lay him."

Once Jack had picked up the dog, Kate then squeezed out of the vehicle and followed him in.

"Right over there," Dr. Rex said, pointing to a stainless steel treatment table.

Buddy was already beginning to doze off.

"How was the leg broken? I'm assuming that the leg is broken—with the splint and all."

"Not sure about that," Jack said.

"Let me take a closer look," the doctor said, peeling off the gauze and exposing the injury.

"That's a bullet wound. Sure enough—this dog's been shot. With a high-powered rifle. At least, that would be my guess."

"Really?" Kate said.

"Really. And my guess would also be that the same rifle that broke this poor fellow's leg was the one that was used to crease your noggin."

Again neither Kate nor Jack acknowledged the doctor's comment.

Jack thought about what the doctor said for a moment and then asked, "What's this going to cost me—just how much cash am I going to need?"

"Well, it looks like a pretty clean break. There's actually some bone left intact—not much, but enough. Lucky it didn't pop out. Then we'd have problems. I'm going to put a cast on it, and it should heal okay. I would like to see him next week, ten days at most—just to check it out. We can determine later when we'll want to remove the cast. If you get concerned about something, you can come back sooner. But I don't see the need for surgery."

"So what's today going to cost?"

"You know I'm supposed to report bullet wounds?"

"You're not treating my daughter—you're treating this dog."

"Well, unless there is a hunting season on dogs, then this is an illegal bullet wound—actually two bullet wounds. That crease high on the dog's neck was also caused by a bullet."

"Are you telling me that you are going to call in the cops on this?" Jack asked, getting a bit irritated.

"I said that I was *supposed* to report all bullet wounds. I didn't say that I was going to."

"I would say that two hundred dollars in cash will cover today. If all goes okay, when I see him next, it will be a standard seventy-five dollar office visit. And then another hundred when we remove the cast."

"Fine," Jack said. "And could you give him his shots—whatever he needs to get us into Canada?"

"That would be seventy-five dollars. I shouldn't really give him his shots today, given his injury."

"But you could, right?"

"Sure. I can get him fixed up. And how about you, hon? Let me take a quick look at your scratch. And you don't have to worry. I've treated a few two-legged animals in my time. Let's see now. Just as I suspected, that's not serious at all. Infection's all that you have to worry about. But half an inch over, and it would be a totally different story. Just let me swab a little of this on it, and it will heal up just fine."

"About the cast on the dog, Doc—how will he react to it when he wakes up?" Jack asked.

"He's not going to like it much. Do you have a muzzle? 'Cuz he's going to want to get rid of it."

"No muzzle. Like I said, we've just sort of adopted him—temporarily."

"You know who he reminds me of—that kid's dog—Red's dog. They call him Red ... because he has red hair, and freckles. I've seen him with a dog that looked a lot like this one."

"Do you have a muzzle you can sell me?"

"I don't stock stuff like that," Dr. Rex said, as he was just applying plaster on Buddy's cast.

"But I might have something in the back. I'll check when I get this done."

After a few minutes, Dr. Rex stood erect, signaling he was finished with the cast. He placed his hands on the pit of his back and stretched. He then disappeared into a rear storage area. A short time later he re-emerged carrying two devices.

"These oughta fit your dog. I used them on my 'Pal' a few years back. I know they're free from any diseases. ... And they should fit. Pal was about the same size as your dog."

Dr. Rex put an E-collar on Buddy.

"This might do the trick. It could keep him from chewing the cast off. But if it doesn't, then try the muzzle. Or, you could apply some of this to the cast. It's called *Bitter Apple.* Sometimes it will discourage a dog's chewing on a dressing, or a cast."

Before Dr. Rex turned his attention to the graze wound on Buddy's upper neck, he applied a small amount of the Bitter Apple to the cast.

"Matching wounds," he said chuckling. "His and hers. Another half inch and he'd be a goner. Just like you, darlin'."

"Okay, we should be all set here."

"Shots?" Jack reminded the doctor.

"Right, shots," the doctor said, walking over to a drawer and removing a sealed sterile package. Using a pair of stainless steel scissors, he cut the top off and removed a syringe. After filling the needle, he returned to Buddy and unceremoniously rolled him over, and poked him in the muscle of his good hind leg.

"You're going to need some documentation on this," Dr. Rex advised.

He scribbled out a vaccination history and signed it.

"This should do it," he said.

"They don't like you to bring some breeds into Canada, but you should have no problem with a golden retriever. Do you have any papers on him?"

"No."

Dr. Rex sat down at his computer and wrote the following on his letterhead.

"This pure bred golden retriever is four years old, and has been duly vaccinated for rabies. Aside from a slight fracture of its leg, which I have successfully treated, it is in perfect health. Signed: Dr. Rex Brown, Veterinarian."

And he dated it.

He then prepared and signed a "Breed Certification," formally substantiating the age and breed of Buddy.

"Now you should be all set. They will have no problem with your dog."

"How long will he be out?" Kate asked.

"Actually he should be starting to wake up about now. I'm a little surprised he didn't flinch when I just poked him.

"He's not going to think much about this cast," the doctor said, tapping on it to test it. "It's very fast drying. In fact, it's hard already. You can't do much to keep a dog down. But he's not going to be able to use that leg, so he will carry it. He will quickly figure out how to get around a little—not enough to satisfy him, but enough. There are plenty of three-legged dogs, you know. Your dog will do just fine once he gets a little used to it."

"Then we're all set here?" Jack said, peeling off four one-hundred dollar bills and handing them to the doctor. "This should cover everything for today?"

"We're good—very good," the doc said with a smile.

As Jack shook hands with Dr. Rex, he reminded him that he greatly valued his discretion.

"I also appreciate the loan of the collar and the muzzle, Doc, and I'll be sure you get them back when we return."

"Happy to help."

Kate also thanked the doctor, as they prepared to leave.

By the time Jack had placed Buddy in the back seat with Kate, the dog had begun to wake up.

At first he struggled to stand, but Kate subdued him by hugging him around the neck.

"It's okay, Buddy, the doc has got you all fixed up."

Buddy liked the soothing sound of Kate's voice. He was not used to hearing the voice of a human being directed at him, much less that of a female.

Buddy's eyes, still dilated from the drug, darted back and forth. And he persisted in his effort to gain footing, but Kate prevailed, initially.

"Dad, what do you suppose would happen if I released Buddy?"

"You're going to have to eventually. With that cast on his leg, he's not going to further damage it. Might as well let him get the learning process started."

With that, Kate immediately released her grip, and Buddy sprang up to a standing position—but not a terribly steady one.

He made his best effort to hop over to the side window, but came up a little short. Half lying down, he reached his head back to sniff the new cast. Were he not wearing the device Doc Rex provided, he would probably have chewed it off right then.

Instead, he just whined, and looked back at Kate.

Then he struggled back to his feet, and looked out of the window.

"What are we going to do with Buddy?" Kate asked. "Our hotel has a no-dog policy."

"We're going to pick up what we need, and then head to Canada," Jack said. "I thought we discussed this."

Kate looked surprised.

"Yeah, I knew we talked about rescuing Red, but I didn't realize we would be heading north so soon. We don't know where to look."

"We will in a few minutes," Jack said, picking up his cell phone.

Chapter 47—Jack calls on an old friend

"Roger. I need some help. ... Is this a bad time?"

"Never a bad time for you, old friend."

Roger Minsk was more like a business associate than a close friend to Jack. But they did trust each other implicitly and worked together on occasion. The reason Jack called Roger on this day was that, as a senior agent in the Secret Service, Roger might be able to provide Jack with helpful information.

"Would you check this out for me? Earlier today. Ten hundred hours—give or take twenty minutes. Interested in the destination of a helicopter leaving Sugar Island, in Michigan's Upper Peninsula, and landing somewhere in Canada—suspect not terribly deep. At least I don't think it went deep. It's a Bell 429, and it has hopped back and forth a few times recently."

"This sounds like an international issue, Jack. Whatcha got yourself into?"

"It's nothing like what you might think. Kate and I are trying to track down a kid—we think he was kidnapped and hustled out on a chopper shortly after ten this morning. In fact, you might find that same chopper making a similar run last evening, about twenty-two hundred hours. If you can get me the Canadian coordinates, it could be most helpful in retrieving the boy. Time is short."

"I'll see what I can do—how soon do you need the location?"

"Half an hour would be great. But whatever you can do would be appreciated. We will be crossing over within the hour. From what I have observed, the bird stayed low, and to the northeast. Good chance they won't put it up anymore in the near future—those things make a terrible racket."

"How would something like that escape the scrutiny of Homeland Security, or the Canadian Border Patrol?"

"Great questions. I have no idea. There's no such thing as a stealth chopper, so that's why I'm calling you … to see if your people have any info on it."

"I'll see what I can do."

"Whoa, Buddy," Kate said, trying to subdue their now fully awake passenger. "He doesn't really seem that concerned with his leg. But that E-collar—that's a different story."

"We're going to need some dog food, water, a bowl—two bowls."

"And a leash," Kate added. "I doubt that Buddy has ever seen one of those. But we should have one anyway. And a collar.

"By the way, are we taking firearms across the border?"

"Too risky. We're going to have to depend on my guile, and your good looks."

"Don't forget about Buddy—he's our secret weapon, you know."

"We'll run over to that Walmart," Jack said. "Buddy and I will dispose of the guns, and you pick up the supplies."

"Anything else you want?"

"Toothbrush and razor for me—and whatever else. Non-spoiling food would be good. Who knows what we're getting into … or for how long."

Just as Jack dropped Kate off at the store, Roger called.

"There were no corresponding flight plans filed—not here and not in Canada. This thing must have literally flown under the radar."

"That's what I suspected," Jack said. "Each time I saw it, it barely cleared the tops of the trees. It does seem strange, at least to me, that it could operate with total impunity like that."

"I wouldn't read anything into it," Roger said. "Most likely you won't see it again. I'm sure the Canadians are looking for it. I do have one thing that might prove useful. I can find only one privately registered Bell 429 in that area. It belongs to a charter service operating out of Montréal. I checked further, and according to its owner, their chopper was rented to a private party. But they're not certain exactly where the bird is right now—it appears the GPS locator has been disabled. I've requested a copy of the rental agreement. My guess is that it has been phoneyed up. I really should be turning this over to DHS—"

"I'm sure you should. But give me a few days. I'll keep you informed."

"Please don't," Roger replied. His terse response signaled the end of the conversation.

After Jack wiped the two handguns clean, he put them in Ziploc bags and tossed them over a fence at a junkyard.

With a little luck, he reasoned, *I can pick these up later.*

He then pulled up next to a Federal Express storefront that he had spotted earlier. Retrieving the bloody bandages he had removed from Red's hiding place, Jack placed the Ziploc containing them in a large paper envelope and entered the store.

"I need this expedited," Jack told the clerk. He scribbled an address on an overnight envelope, paid for the service and returned to his vehicle.

Jack had no more than shifted into 'drive' when his phone rang again.

Chapter 48—Jack learns the possible location of Red's abductors

"Jack—not sure how much this will help you, but this is what I found out."

"That was fast."

"Fast maybe—but that's not always good. This time it means there's not much to find out. But here's what I've got. There are apparently not many Bell 429s in that area. That's the good part.

"While there were no flights recorded by a Bell 429 in that time frame, we do show one chartered for the past month to a group of fishermen who seem to be located near Hamilton. The chopper is based at John C. Munro Hamilton International Airport in Hamilton. That's about five hundred miles from the Soo. But the man who has chartered the chopper operates an elite fishing lodge near Sudbury, which is only about three hours east of the Soo—driving, that is. A Bell ought to make that trip in less than an hour from Sugar Island.

"But, the interesting thing is that this developer, Mitch Martin, has been looking for investors for a similar club closer to the Soo. He has purchased an option to lease a parcel equal to about two thousand acres between Matinenda Provincial Park and Eliot Lake. That would be only fifty miles or so from Sugar Island—maybe a little less. The best land route to that location would, of course, be Highway 17.

"You and I know that all the info I just gave you might be useless—it might not get you anything but lost. But, if I were in your shoes right now, unless something more concrete comes up, this seems like your best bet."

"I would agree," Jack said. "How much trouble would it be to run him, this Mitch Martin, and see what comes up?"

"Already got it in the works. I'll call you with whatever I learn—good or bad."

"Much appreciated, Roger. I'd tell you that I owe you one, but we'd both know that'd be a lie. I owe you much more than that."

"Trust me, my friend, I'll call in your tab one of these days."

"I'm sure you will," Jack said, disconnecting the call.

"How's my puppy doing?" Kate asked as she squeezed in beside Buddy. He was now fully awake and growing even more concerned with his protective collar.

"You know what, Dad, I don't think Buddy is that worried about his cast. His issue is with this stupid collar. What would you say to removing the collar, and see if he can be taught to leave his cast alone?"

"I'd give it a shot. If it works, then we can try the collar only at night. Besides, Buddy might have a real aversion to that stuff the doc put on the cast—that Bitter Apple."

"I think it's worth a try," Kate agreed. "It's bad enough that poor Buddy is going to have to hobble around on three legs. It just doesn't seem fair that he would have to wear that lampshade around his neck as well."

"Fair's got nothing to do with it. We need this dog performing at his best. He's the one who is going to have to lead us to Red. A bad leg is disconcerting enough—without that lampshade, as you called it."

As soon as Kate removed the E-collar, Buddy began shaking his whole body as if to say "thank you."

"There you are. He sniffed the cast once, and that's it."

"We'll see how it goes. We can put a little more of the stinky stuff on it tonight. But I think he's going to ignore the cast—for now."

"So, where're we headed?"

"I got word from Roger, my friend in the Secret Service, that the only Bell 429 in this area might just be east of here—an hour or so driving. Up Highway 17."

"So that's where we're headed?"

"Let's roll."

Chapter 49—Red holds out

"Look, kid," said the balding man with the tan jacket, "all you have to do is tell us where you hid that gun, and you get to go home and see your dog. That's all we want from you. We don't want to hurt you."

"I don't think the kid can understand you," interrupted his tall, skinny accomplice. "He's got something wrong with him. He doesn't talk."

"He might not talk, but he hears okay. And he understands *everything* we say."

"Red. Right? That's what they call you? Red, don't you want to make sure your dog is okay? He's gotta be getting hungry. He needs you to take care of him. We will take you home to him, and back to your precious Sugar Island, but first you have to show us where you hid that gun. It's evidence in a murder we're investigating. You know who I mean—that resort owner. We're not accusing you of stealing it. We know you just borrowed it. But we're the police. It's only right that you give it to us. And if you ever want to go home, that's what you're gonna have to do."

The two men holding Red had secured him to a heavy wooden chair with duct tape—his hands taped behind him. Each of his ankles was taped to one of the legs of the chair, exposing his bare feet, and three layers of tape over his chest secured his torso to the chair.

"Look, kid, you've only got one good foot left. And now you've got your right leg bunged up. If you ever want to walk again, you'd better start telling us what we want to hear."

"He's not gonna *tell* us anything. He can't talk."

"He knows how to communicate, you idiot. So just shut up. He can shake his head. Here, let me show you."

With that the man who was doing most of the talking struck the top of Red's good foot with a three-foot length of chain. The blow struck higher on the foot than the abductor had intended. The pain was excruciating, causing Red to cry out in a grotesque scream.

"Did that hurt, kid? I'm really sorry to have to do this stuff to you. If it hurt you, just nod your head and let me know. Or I'm gonna do it again, only harder. Let me know if you felt it, son."

Slowly Red nodded his head. Tears were running down both cheeks.

"See there, the kid can communicate."

"Okay, Red. Now that we've established that you can hear me, and that you understand what I am saying to you, let's get this over with. Do you understand what a gun is?"

This time Red did not answer. So his abductor drew a simple line drawing of a handgun on a piece of paper and stuck it in his face.

"This is a gun. Do you understand me? Do you know what a gun is now?"

Red nodded his head affirmatively.

"Okay, great. Now we're getting somewhere. Did you know Alex, the owner of the resort on Sugar Island?"

Red nodded his head again.

"Well, this nice man was shot with a gun like this. And we're investigating that murder—what a shame. We understand he was a friend of yours. Well, now, we need that gun for evidence. We know you didn't have anything to do the crime itself. But you were there. There's a witness who puts you there at the time of the murder. He's in custody. He's a suspect. But he told us that you swooped in and grabbed the gun while he wasn't looking. Do you remember this? If you don't help us with this, the killer might get off scot-free. You don't want that. Now, I'm gonna ask you again—do you remember the night Mr. Garos got shot?"

Red didn't answer at first.

"I asked you a question, kid," Jacket Man said, preparing to strike Red's foot again with the chain. "Do you remember the night Mr. Garos was murdered?"

Red acquiesced to the questioning with a quick nod to acknowledge that he did recall the event. It was obvious that Red was frightened and hurting.

"Great. Did you get a good look at the killer?"

Red reluctantly nodded his head yes.

"That's wonderful, we might want to call you as a witness," Jacket Man said, grinning as he looked at his partner. "But for right now, we need to locate that gun. You put it somewhere, right?"

Red again responded affirmatively.

"Well, then all we need to do to get you home to your dog is to have you tell us where you put it."

"He can't talk. He can't tell us where he hid it."

"But he can show us, you idiot."

"And how, exactly, is that gonna work? Once he gets on his own turf, he'll be impossible to deal with."

"Not necessarily so. Red, here, wants to get back to his dog. Right? We can help with that. That's what you want, Red, to get back to your dog?"

Red quickly nodded his head in agreement.

"Well, then, let's figure out how we can help you with that," Jacket Man said. "Your dog's gotta be getting hungry."

Jacket Man unfolded a map in front of Red and said, "So, show me where you hid the gun."

Red looked up at Jacket Man and made a noise the men had not heard before.

"Cut the tape from his right hand," Jacket Man ordered. "But make sure his left hand is still fastened to the chair behind him. Give him one hand free."

"Okay, kid, point it out," Jacket Man said, putting a felt marker into Red's hand. "Tell … rather, *show* me where you hid that gun."

Red sat motionless, staring at the map.

"Maybe he's never seen a map of Sugar Island before," Skinny Man said.

"Shut up and let him think. He can't talk, but he's a smart kid. And deep down, he wants to help the police catch and convict the killer. And he wants to see his dog again. Give him a minute."

Red studied the map carefully, and then touched the marker to it. But instead of indicating a single location, he drew a circle.

"The gun is inside that circle?" Jacket Man asked. "Answer me."

Red signaled affirmatively.

"Good job. Now let's try to refine it a bit. That's a lot of real estate—probably an acre or more. We could spend a whole day searching for it—maybe more. Can you be more specific?"

Chapter 50—Jack and Kate close in

It took the three of them—Jack, Kate and Buddy—only about an hour and a half to drive from the Canadian border to the area that Roger had suggested.

"By the way, Dad, you wouldn't be kidding me about our not being armed?"

"We're armed," Jack responded with a chuckle. "But only if you consider Buddy's canines as being armed."

Kate then wrapped her right arm around Buddy's neck and lifted his upper lip exposing the dog's substantial ivories.

"That ought to be just about all we need. Right, Buddy?"

Buddy fixed his big brown eyes on Kate's face and whined wistfully.

Kate then hugged Buddy with both arms and said, "It's gonna be okay, Buddy. Together we're gonna save Red. Don't you worry about him."

Every time Kate spoke to Buddy, he acted as though he fully understood her.

"You know, Dad, I think that Buddy gets what we're doing. It's almost like he's got a sixth sense."

"I'm not so sure that the sixth sense analogy actually can apply to a dog. But I would agree that Buddy is smart. And very well trained. Red did a great job with him."

"I'll bet that this Red is a very cool kid once you get to know him."

"Has to have a lot going for him to survive the way he has."

"Exactly what do we know about him?" Kate asked. "Aside from the fact that he has lived on his own for all these years."

"He was the son of a woman who worked at your uncle's resort."

"Seriously?"

"That was in the report Sheriff Northrup gave me. Red's mother practically ran the resort back then."

"And the father? Who was the father?"

"The mother was married to a Native American."

"Where'd he come up with that head full of curly red hair?"

"Red's mother was Irish."

"So, Red must have spent a lot of time hanging around the resort?"

"He did. In fact, Red worked for Alex—unofficially, doing odd jobs. The two of them struck up a pretty good relationship."

"I take it that Red's family lived on Sugar Island?" Kate asked.

"They did."

"That explains why he is so good at hiding out there. He must know every tree and stream."

"It gets even better than that. Red's father owned a large parcel of land on Sugar Island, and he operated a hunting lodge there. Up until he died, which was several years ago, he had been grooming Red to take over. So Red had some great training."

"What happened? How'd the father die?"

"Unfortunately, both the mother and the father were killed in a tragic house fire."

"And Red survived? How did that happen?"

"Red and Buddy were at your uncle's resort when the explosion occurred. Red was scrubbing down the resort's fishing boats."

"Explosion?"

"Yeah, apparently there was a gas leak, and it led to an explosion—killing both of Red's parents instantly."

"Dad, that sounds suspicious. Gas explosions don't usually occur when people are home. They put that stinky stuff in the gas for that very purpose—so that people can tell when there's a gas leak. Whenever we run into that in New York, forensics always suspect arson. Did this get investigated as anything other than an accident? Who was in charge of that investigation?"

"It appears Sheriff Northrup investigated it. And there was nothing in the report to suggest anything other than an accident."

"What do you think?"

"It got my attention. I would agree that, at least on the surface, it looks suspicious. But the cause of the explosion was actually dismissed with only three lines on the report."

"How traumatic that had to have been for Red."

"I understand that Alex tried to coax the boy to move into the resort, but child welfare wouldn't allow it, plus Red preferred to be on his own."

"Did Red continue to work for Uncle Alex?"

"Nothing formal. But during the summers Red did continue to take care of the resort's fishing equipment. And he even worked for tips as a fishing guide. But the boy was never on the payroll. Alex just made sure Red had food to eat—and warm clothes."

"That was all in the report?"

"It was."

Jack then pulled into a bait/party store.

"They ought to know where this proposed new hunting club is located. That is where Roger thinks they might be holding Red. Actually, I'd bet that this new lodge is what all the people around here are talking about."

When Jack got out of his vehicle, Buddy tried balancing himself on his one hind leg in order to hop over the center console. But instead, when he tried to jump his rear end landed on the floor of the back seat.

"I'll be right back."

After grabbing three bottles of bottled water, Jack asked the cashier if he knew the location of the new hunting club.

The diminutive middle-aged clerk took Jack's Canadian currency and replied, "You mean *proposed* hunting club—it hasn't happened yet. You're there—or almost there. You see this road," he continued, pointing his left hand out of the window at the end of the counter, "if you turn left on that road, and drive four kilometers you will see a dirt road leading off to the right. It's the only one showing traffic lately. The proposed sportsmen club is down that drive about half a kilometer."

"Is it marked? … Any signs?"

"No, but you can hardly miss it. It's exactly four kilometers. The only drive off to the right. You can't miss it."

"Much appreciated," Jack said as he received his change. He put the coins in his pocket, peeled off a Canadian five-dollar bill, and handed it to the clerk.

"Have you met the man in charge? I think his name is Mitch?"

The clerk took the money from Jack and looked at it. "I think I know who that might be. But the fellow we've had in here on several occasions—his name is not Mitch. And I don't think he's the owner, either."

"Could you describe him?"

"He doesn't talk much. Maybe a little overweight. Bald. About my age. And he usually wears a tan jacket—a windbreaker. Even when it's hot. Pretty sure he's not from this area, or even from Canada, for that matter. I'd guess he's from the US. Probably from the New England area.

I don't know much about geography, but my wife and I drove down from Maine to the Appalachian Mountains two years ago. Beautiful country. Reminded us of some parts of Ontario. Well, we noted that the residents of New England had a distinctive accent. This fellow talks like that. He doesn't really talk much, but he's pleasant enough."

"Have you seen him lately?"

"As a matter of fact, he was in here only an hour ago—maybe closer to two hours. Bought some milk."

"Milk?"

"Right. Whole milk. First time he ever did that."

"Interesting," Jack said, preparing to leave.

As he reached the door, he turned and asked another question, "Oh, by the way. Have you heard that helicopter? I understand the developers use a large helicopter. Do you know anything about that?"

"Now you've touched a nerve. A number of us have complained about it, but guess it's all legal. At least no one wants to help us. It's been especially noisy lately. It's like they're deliberately trying to irritate us."

"How's that?"

"Barnstorming. I don't know if that's the right word. But they're flying in and out at treetop level. Used to be that they'd come in at a decent altitude, and then land. But now it's ridiculous. They're actually stirring up the dust out front when they come over. But no one seems to want to do anything. Just let it get tangled up and crash. Then they'll be wondering what happened. Let it start a fire and burn us all out."

"Thanks," Jack said, as he left the store and headed back to Kate and Buddy.

"Right down that road."

"Got a specific plan in mind?"

"We've got about five minutes to come up with something. I've got a feeling that they're gonna make me as soon as they see me. From the description the clerk provided, the guy holding Red sounds a lot like a fellow I ran into just before Donna got murdered. We might have to send you in first."

"Me and Buddy?"

"They're gonna recognize Buddy too. This could be very interesting."

Jack, who had driven very conservatively on his mission to save Red, now shoved his foot fully into the gas pedal.

"Whoa, Dad, not worried about getting stopped?"

"Maybe we could use a little bit of that sort of attention.

"There, that's our drive," Jack declared, slamming on his brakes and skidding onto the drive leading toward the new hunting club.

"Do you hear that?" Kate asked.

"I do. That sound is becoming altogether too familiar."

Chapter 51—Up, up and away

Jack steered his vehicle off the drive and under the thick cover of a large evergreen tree, and slammed on the brakes.

"If they haven't spotted us, no use tipping them off now."

It took only a few seconds for the Bell 429 to disappear, again barely clearing the treetops of the hilly terrain.

"Okay, let's hit it!" Jack proclaimed. "Great chance that they've got what they want out of Red and cleared out."

"Did they spot us?" Kate asked.

"Doubt it—we ducked under cover too quickly … and they weren't looking for us."

As soon as the helicopter had totally disappeared, Jack backed onto the drive and pulled up to the front entrance of the small cottage.

"Take Buddy and position yourselves in the rear. We're gonna have to take our chances—element of surprise."

Jack ran up the steps and immediately drove his foot into the door, splintering the jamb and throwing it wide open.

Less than twenty seconds later, Kate and Buddy entered through a back door.

Even before Kate appeared, Jack's eyes located a very welcome sight—an AK-47 lying across a small rustic coffee table. He grabbed it and disengaged the safety. But before he had time to check if it was loaded, a bedroom door opened.

"What's going on out here?"

Jack spotted a Glock 10mm hanging from the hand of a tall skinny man. Holding the AK-47 at his waist, he stiffened his left arm to brace against the recoil. He was not sure if the assault weapon was fully automatic. He soon found out. With one pull on the trigger he fired three rounds—all striking the man holding the Glock.

Kate took cover behind a couch. Buddy barked—he did not appreciate the noise.

The blasts from the rifle knocked the wounded man back into the bedroom. Launching himself into that room as the man was falling, Jack stepped on the writhing man's wrist and removed the Glock.

Emerging a few seconds later, Jack handed the Glock to Kate on his way out of the back door. He was looking for anyone trying to escape.

Not encountering additional threats, Jack walked back into the cabin through the open rear door.

"Dad, check this out," Kate said, pointing to the drawing of the handgun, which was lying on a table. "And this, it's a map of Sugar Island. See what's circled? It looks a lot like that area around the resort—maybe a mile or so to the northeast."

"We're getting close—very close."

Buddy went nuts. He had already caught Red's scent. Doing his best to make do with a single hind leg, he hopped around the room, looking for new evidence of Red's recent presence. Perhaps if he tried harder he might find his friend.

The skinny man that Jack shot would be dead soon. But for right now, he was still in the process. One of the rounds had splintered his spine, so even though still breathing he was unable to move.

"We gonna get him help?" Kate asked.

"No point—none at all. He took three to the midsection. We've gotta take what we need and get outta here. Nothing can be done to help him, and no amount of explaining would get us cleared. Best we can hope for is that when these fellows return, they will bury their friend somewhere on the back forty.

"They can't be much excited with having the authorities brought in either. We just need to act swiftly and get outta here."

"I'll gather up the map. Why do you suppose they left that here, anyway?" Kate asked.

"Odds are they've searched there already—but without success," Jack offered. "They determined that they would need Red to find what they're looking for. And on the basis of the drawing, my guess is that they're looking for a handgun."

"We don't have much time, do we? As soon as they get what they want from Red, they'll kill him."

"Exactly how I see it," Jack agreed. "Five minutes earlier, and we'd saved him. Now, the odds are really against our success."

"Massachusetts!" Kate declared, after pulling the dying man's wallet from his pocket and removing his driver's license.

"A US citizen, from New England," she said. "I'll bet that doesn't surprise you though, right?"

"It fits with everything else we've been hearing."

"What's the deal with the gun?"

"I would guess that Red found and hid that gun. In fact, there's a good chance that Red witnessed a shooting with that gun—quite possibly the murder of your uncle. We've gotta move quickly. Let's sanitize this place and get going."

"This guy should have a cell phone. Let me check the bedroom."

Kate disappeared into the bedroom for only a moment before she called to her father.

"Dad, you're gonna want to see this."

Jack hustled into the room to see what she had discovered.

"This look like anything to you?" Kate asked, sliding a cell phone into her pocket while pointing to an assortment of various electronic and chemical components neatly spread out on one of the twin beds. The materials had been covered with two bath towels.

"This is where the explosive devices were constructed. And this skinny fellow was probably the bomb maker."

Jack opened the top of a black plastic construction quality trash bag that was sitting beside the bed, and dumped the contents onto the other bed.

"He's unwrapped a significant amount of chemicals and timers— more than we've seen so far. Isn't there one more bedroom? From the outside, it looks like there might be another bedroom. Let's check that out before we go."

"I think that is a bedroom off the other side of the big room," Kate said, as she hurried out of the bomb room, stepping over the now-dead explosives expert.

"It's locked," she said, just before she kicked open the door. Jack had stopped to pick up some additional ammunition for the dead man's Glock, but was now right behind her, with Buddy closely following.

"This room's been used, all right," Kate observed. "And check this out. These shoes—they look to be size twelve, or even thirteen. They belong to a pretty big man."

Jack examined the excessive wear on the shoe sole closely and then tossed one of them back on the floor.

"Who wears string-tied black wingtips anymore?" Jack asked rhetorically. "And who would wear them into this condition? Stick one of these in a bag, and let's get going."

Kate had walked over to the closet and found several extra-large shirts hanging neatly, along with another pair of wingtips—same size, only brown.

"Our big man has been here a while, or at least plans to stay a while—there is a significant amount of his clothes in the closet," Kate said.

Jack took one last moment to examine the contents of a wastebasket. He reached in and removed a one-liter plastic bottle.

"Unless I'm wrong," he said, "this has been used to transport blood. And there are two more here just like it. This whole thing just keeps getting weirder and weirder."

Jack tossed the empty bottle into the trash bag with the shoe and headed toward the door. He did, however, scoop up three boxes of Russian-made ammo for the assault rifle on his way out. Kate and Buddy were right behind.

Just as Jack tossed the trash bag into the back of his SUV, his eyes were drawn to an orange glow inside the cabin.

"Oh my God!" Jack exclaimed. "Someone has set the place on fire!"

"And there he goes," Kate said, pointing at a large figure on an all-terrain vehicle speeding through the woods behind the cabin.

"This place is going to explode—we've gotta get outta here."

Chapter 52— Buddy comes through

Boom!

Before they reached the road the cabin virtually exploded into violent flames.

"So much for our having left evidence," Kate quipped. "Where do you suppose the big guy was while we were in the cabin?"

"I suspect he went out the bedroom window about the time you came in the back door."

Kate thought for a few moments, and then said, "You've got a plan, right?"

"Sort of," Jack replied. "But I'm open for suggestions."

"We've got virtually no time. … I don't think there is anyone we can trust to save Red. Besides, if we engage law enforcement, we will have a lot of explaining to do about *this* business. Our best bet is to get back onto Sugar Island before Red is forced to produce that pistol."

"And, we need to arrive on the island armed."

"Can't bring this hardware over the bridge—so, we'll have to find an alternative method of entry," Kate said.

"The North Channel out of Lake George is very narrow, and shallow. Didn't Deputy Restin tell us that Red and Buddy might have been crossing over into Canada from time to time—using that channel?

"We need Buddy to help us out with this. He's going to know where and how to get across."

"I remember reading that the DHS watches for crossing attempts. I guess the channel has grown so shallow that a person with waders could virtually walk across it."

"That could be by Squirrel Island. I think that Red and Buddy probably crossed a little east of there. I don't think Red would want to be isolated on that island."

Jack zeroed in his GPS. "We're going to get off 17, and onto 17B. And then take a look along Wigwaus Street. My guess is that we will find where they have been crossing somewhere in that area. Even if I'm wrong about that, we will still have to find a way to get across—and that area looks to be the best."

Kate took the next few minutes to make sure both the Glock and the assault rifle were fully loaded and ready for action.

Even though Jack was concerned about getting stopped for speeding, he restarted his radar detector to be sure it was working and hit the gas.

"We will need to find a boat to get across—we can't have Buddy swimming. It would ruin his cast."

"Gemah Street," Jack barked, slamming on his brakes as he turned. "Stick the rifle in the trash bag, and hand the pistol to me. We're going to find the first place we can to hide this vehicle, and see if Buddy can get us across."

Jack reached over his shoulder, and Kate placed the fully loaded Glock in his hand.

"Round in the chamber," Kate informed him.

"Okay, Buddy, it's time to rock and roll," Jack said after he had driven his SUV into a group of trees close to the channel.

Buddy was the first to hit the ground. It was as though he knew exactly what his job was, and why. If a dog can be motivated—Buddy was motivated.

"Look at that, Dad. He's been here before."

"It's a good thing he's got a bad wheel, or we'd never keep up."

Buddy ran as fast as a three-legged dog could be expected to run. He passed up several aluminum boats, all of which were secured with chains. With his nose glued to the ground, he ran between two older boats and found a small wooden Jon boat. It was turned upside-down but was not secured. He stood beside it, looked up at Kate, and whined.

"That's it," Kate said. "That must be one of the boats he and Red have been using. But we're gonna need some oars."

"Let's check under it," Jack said, flipping the boat over.

Underneath the boat were two aluminum oars.

"Good job, Buddy!" Kate said, dropping to her knees and hugging her new best friend.

Jack yanked the nylon rope that was attached to the front of the flat-bottomed boat and headed for the water. Before he had a chance to launch it, Buddy had already hopped in, followed closely by Kate.

"No time to waste—we've got to move quickly," Jack declared, pushing the boat into the water and jumping in.

Buddy sat in the front. And like a good helmsman, stared intently at their destination—Sugar Island.

"What's the worst that could happen?" Kate asked.

"The boat could have a hole," Jack quipped. "But the water is so shallow we could wade across."

"Okay for us, but not so good for Buddy."

"We need to make it across before DHS discovers us," Jack said.

"When we reach land we need to make a dart for the first vehicle that looks like it will start."

"Car theft? When we finish here I'm gonna have some real explaining to do to my boss."

"I don't think we will talk about this for many years," Jack chuckled.

"That Red's a pretty sharp kid," Kate said. "I'll bet he understands the situation better than they think. I'm sure he has no idea we're coming after him, but I think he will stall it as long as he can."

"That's what we're counting on," Jack agreed. "I can't help but think that DHS is getting pretty sick of that helicopter. Every time it flies over, I'm sure that they get a call. Chances are that they have sent out a vehicle or two to try to find it—again."

"I'd bet you're right," Kate said. "We made it so far. … And I see a Jeep—late model. It's just sitting there waiting for us."

Jack jumped into the water as the boat neared land, and pulled it up on the dry bank.

"Must take our time here," Kate advised. "Can't appear to be in a rush. Someone could be watching us."

"Exactly right," Jack agreed.

Just as they turned toward the waiting Jeep, a white DHS Tahoe sped past. Both Jack and Kate saw it appear and disappear, but were not certain if the two of them had been spotted.

"Stay," Kate commanded Buddy, pressing on the dog's forehead as she hopped out.

Jack and Kate then dragged the boat up the bank and into a patch of bushes. As soon as the boat hit dry land, Buddy jumped out as well.

"Let's hide this thing—we just might need it again," Jack said. "Technically, we're still in Canada. …This could get very complicated."

"Already is," Kate retorted.

By the time she and Buddy had reached the Jeep, Jack had started the engine and was waiting.

"You've not lost your touch," Kate said after Buddy had crawled down the center console and made himself comfortable on the rear seat.

"The key was hidden over the visor. Not too sophisticated."

"How long will this take—to reach Red?"

"Ten minutes," Jack replied. "That is, if we are even able to find him."

"GPS says we head down Eastshore to Sugar Island Road, west to Brassar Road. That should get us into the vicinity. How do you propose we go about this?"

"We'll have to take it as it comes. The only known here is that we have very little time. Our only objective must be to save Red."

"I think if we get close, we should let Buddy take the lead," Kate said.

"Exactly. It's a given that Buddy was with Red when he hid the gun. We get close, Buddy will take us in."

"According to the GPS, we need to turn in here," Kate said. "We *are* in four-wheel drive?"

"We are," Jack confirmed. "Does it appear that the terrain is tricky?"

"Sure does look dicey. Perfect place to hide something."

"We might have a bit of an advantage here," Jack said. "They had to have landed that bird in an established location—probably someplace where they have a thermal cover available to hide it.

"The chopper would have got them to the island faster. But once down, the advantage shifts to us. … Hopefully, it took them some time to hide the chopper, and then hike through this brush."

"Five hundred yards straight ahead—does that look right to you?" Kate asked as the three of them jumped out of the Jeep.

"Once we crest this hill, we might be able to get a look at them," Jack said, dropping to all fours in his effort to slide under some low-hanging brush.

Buddy was no longer satisfied to follow. Clumsy and exhausted, he still pushed past Kate, and then overtook Jack just as he reached the top of the hill.

Not slowing her pace, Kate still managed to pull the assault rifle out of the trash bag and prepare it for use.

"Go get 'em, Buddy," Jack said, encouraging the dog's determined three-legged effort.

Chapter 53—Buddy Finds Red

With powerful determination, Buddy plunged his body down the hill. Jack still was unable to see Red, but Buddy's passion seemed a clear sign that the boy was just ahead.

With a woeful bark, followed by another and another, Buddy broke into a run that shocked both Jack and Kate.

Perhaps the slope aided his effort, or maybe it was just a super-K-9 shot of adrenalin, but for the moment it appeared that Buddy was running unencumbered.

"There they are!" Kate declared, falling on her stomach to stabilize her aim. She switched the AK-47 to single shot action.

"Take out the one guarding Red!" Jack ordered. "Do you have a clear shot?"

Before he had completed that sentence, Kate's shot rang out, and the top of the balding head of Jacket Man blew off. She then shifted her attention to the second man. Brandishing the Glock they had swiped from the cottage, Jack broke into a full-speed run toward the boy.

Unfortunately, after Kate's first round, the other abductor fell to the ground in a defensive posture behind a tree.

Initially, Buddy had broken for Red. But when he saw the second attacker peering out from behind the tree, he recognized the ploy and zeroed in for his attack.

Tragically, before Kate could take the second man out, he managed to get off three rounds from his semi-automatic 10mm. Two rounds struck Buddy.

Red, who had been forced to dig around searching for the hidden gun, let out a blood-curdling scream and ran full speed toward his fallen friend. The noises he emitted did not sound human.

Jack, now approaching Glock range, began raining rounds in the direction of the second attacker. Even though he did not have a clear shot, he wanted to make certain that the man did not have the opportunity to kill Red.

And his efforts were rewarded—he not only forced the second shooter to take cover and cease shooting at Red, some of Jack's rounds hit their mark.

Kate was now also running down the hill toward the scene of the action.

By the time she reached the bottom, Jack was standing over the dead body of Buddy's killer. A bullet from Jack's Glock had caught the man in the neck, severing his brain stem. He died instantly.

With both men clearly dead, Jack and Kate turned their attention to Red, who had lain down beside his fallen friend and was holding his body against Buddy's.

Kate dropped the rifle and laid herself down behind the sobbing boy. She reached over his convulsing body and placed her hand on his, which was entangled in Buddy's bloody coat. She then pushed her face into Red's matted hair and wept with him.

Long after it was obvious that Buddy had left them, she remained on the ground with the boy, both expressing their shared love for this magnificent friend.

Jack knew better than to interrupt. Instead, he walked over to the area where Red had been forced to dig. Observing that Red had dug three holes, Jack at first suspected that the boy was trying to stall. It was possible that Red had forgotten where he had buried the gun, but Jack didn't think that was the case.

Jack then noticed there was a major disparity in the three holes. Two of them were nearly thirty inches deep, while the third was just over eighteen inches.

Looks to me, he figured, *that Red intentionally stopped digging in the shallow hole because he knew that the gun was buried deeper.*

So Jack picked up the short shovel that Red had been using and began to dig in the shallow hole.

The third time he put the blade into the soil, it struck something metallic. Dropping to his knees, he dug the loose fill off with his hands until he was able to see a buried object.

"This is it, I'd bet," Jack said aloud. "This is the gun that killed Alex."

Placing latex gloves on both hands, he carefully pulled a white plastic bag out of the hole, and opened it.

A twenty-two with a suppressor, Jack silently observed. *Could have been a professional. … Could have been the same guy who shot the sheriff.*

Jack sat down on the edge of the hole to think. He remained there for about one minute. He then stood to his feet and walked over to where Buddy had fallen, and there knelt down.

Placing one hand on Kate's shoulder, and the other on Red, he softly said, "Red, you do understand me, don't you?"

Red waited a few seconds and then nodded his head affirmatively.

"Son," Jack said, himself beginning to tear up, "I am so sorry that you lost your friend. Kate and I got to know him a little bit, and I have to tell you that he won our hearts over too. He was determined to save you, absolutely determined … and he did it. If it weren't for your dog, this *wonderful* dog, you would not be alive right now."

Red, who had been convulsively sobbing to this point, stopped and listened intently to what Jack was saying.

"Kate and I both loved your dog. We called him Buddy. Do you know what the name 'Buddy' means?"

This time Red did not acknowledge Jack's question.

"A buddy is a friend who will do absolutely anything for you. A buddy is a partner in life—a companion.

"Well, your friend Buddy loved you more than he loved himself. He was very happy to lay his life down to save yours. Not many people have a friend like that. You are a very, very lucky young man to have had a companion like Buddy. ... Do you know what I mean?"

This time Red acknowledged Jack's question by closing both eyes and slowly nodding "yes."

"Now, son, Kate and I have some work to do."

Kate took the cue and lifted Red up to a sitting position. Still hugging the boy, she took his hands in hers and pressed her cheek against the side of his face.

Jack sat in front of them, taking care not to violate their space.

"Son, I need to ask you a few questions. If we're going to punish all the men who are responsible for hurting Buddy, and you, then we're going to need your help. Will you help us?"

"Yes," Red nodded enthusiastically.

"First," Jack asked, holding up the gun for Red to see, "is this what these men wanted?"

Red nodded.

"Is this the gun that shot the resort owner—Alex?"

Red again began to weep uncontrollably, as he responded affirmatively.

"Alex was your friend, wasn't he?"

Red continued to sob, nodding his head.

"You saw who hurt Alex, didn't you?"

Again, Red responded with a nod.

"Were *these* the men you saw hurt Alex?"

This time Red shook his head no.

"Would you recognize the man who hurt Alex if you saw him again?"

Red responded with an enthusiastic nod.

The boy's exuberance surprised Jack.

"Had you ever seen the killer before? Before he killed Alex?"

Red nodded. He then pulled his hands free from Kate's and formed a circle on his chest just above his heart.

Jack thought for a moment and then asked, "Was the man who hurt your friend Alex—was he a police officer?"

Obviously terrified, Red slowly nodded his head yes again, but this time failing to make eye contact with Jack.

Just then three vehicles, all with red and blue lights flashing, appeared on the horizon.

Chapter 54— Planning can be
a waste of time

"We've gotta get the kid outta here," Kate said. "If the killer is a cop, we can't know who all might be involved."

"Red," Jack said, scrutinizing the extensive bruising and blood on Red's injured foot. "Are you able to walk?"

The boy jumped to his feet, clearly signaling that he was.

"Tough kid!" Kate said.

Handing the two firearms to his daughter, Jack told her to wipe the assault rifle down and to ditch it. But to hang on to the Glock.

Jack then scooped up Buddy and motioned that they should make their escape by climbing the same hill from which they had come.

Red, however, grabbed Jack's arm and pulled him in a different direction.

Not sure what Red was suggesting, Jack still complied with his wishes.

"Okay, son. You take the lead," Jack said.

Instead of heading back to where Jack and Kate had ditched their commandeered Jeep, they followed Red along a path that appeared to lead northwest toward the upper part of Lake Nicolet.

Within fifteen minutes they came upon the mysterious helicopter.

"Well, what do you know—*der Hubschrauberlandeplatz*. No wonder they never found the chopper," Jack said. "It would be totally invisible from the air."

Draped over the Bell 429 was a thick camouflage thermal cover. It was suspended at the top by ropes pulled taut between the tops of several tall trees. The edges of the thermal cover were secured with a series of industrial-grade bungee cords.

Red had intentionally guided the group past the helicopter, even though that was not the shortest route to his ultimate destination.

Almost a quarter mile past the landing site, Red led Jack and Kate toward a large thicket. At first Kate hesitated. But Jack seemed confident that Red knew exactly what he was doing.

Just as Kate reached the thicket, Red pulled on a rope that was looped over a low limb on a tree. When he did, it compressed a large group of pricker-laden branches and tugged them to the side. This exposed an opening barely large enough for an adult to squeeze through.

Once the group had cleared the opening, Red erased the tracks of their approach using a rustic broom he had constructed for that purpose. Then, with another rope located within the encampment, Red re-engaged the limbs of the pricker bushes. This blocked the approach, essentially closing the door into Red's hideaway.

"Ingenious," Kate declared, looking back at the totally concealed entry.

"Dad. Have you ever seen anything like this before?"

"No. It's quite amazing. Obviously the boy has cultivated these bushes to suit his purpose. It's no wonder law enforcement was never able to catch him."

"It's a compound," Kate said. "Red has created a compound for himself."

Even though his foot was now badly swollen where he was beaten with the chain earlier that day, Red approached Jack without a limp and indicated that he would like to take Buddy from his arms. Jack complied, carefully passing the dog's limp body into Red's waiting arms. Once Jack was confident that Red would be able to support Buddy's weight, he released him.

Red had no problem carrying the heavy corpse of his beloved friend. With his now tear-filled eyes fixed on Buddy's face, Red turned and carried the body around a plywood shed, about twenty feet from the entrance. There he carefully set Buddy down and returned to the shed to retrieve a shovel.

"He's going to bury Buddy," Kate said.

"First things first," Jack added. "The kid is going to honor his friend."

Looking inside the same makeshift shed Jack saw another shovel. Even though it had a broken handle, Jack removed it and started digging alongside Red. While the boy did not acknowledge Jack's presence, he didn't object.

The soil was soft and moist. So after a relatively short time, the grave was complete. Red motioned for Kate to join them.

There the three of them knelt around Buddy, paying their last respects.

"Hang on for a bit," Jack said, looking over to where they had left the plastic bag containing the pistol used to kill Alex. He wrapped it tightly, and tossed it in the grave.

Jack then emptied the pockets of his black leather jacket and took it off.

"Help me slide this under Buddy," he said, laying it down beside the body.

Just as Red and Jack started to grip the jacket to lower Buddy into the grave, Kate stopped them. She knelt over the dog one last time, and gently stroked the side of his bloodied head.

Then, without looking at the other two, she gripped a corner of the jacket, and together the three of them lowered Buddy into the shallow grave.

Red then removed his shirt and laid it over Buddy's eyes.

Jack and Red then took turns shoveling the fresh soil into the grave. Red's tears mixed with blood and dirt, creating long streaks down his face, and then dripped from his chin into Buddy's grave. After every few shovels full of soil, Red wiped his face with the back of his hand.

Once the task was completed, Kate looked around and found a sizable rock and placed it as a marker at one end of the grave.

Red wiped his hands on his pants, cleaning them as best he could, and then he walked over to Kate. She stood about five feet seven inches. Red was a few inches shorter. So when he wrapped his arms around her, his head fell on her chest just below her shoulder. She could feel his body convulsing in sorrow.

After a very long moment, she pressed her face into his long red curls, and kissed him. This caused him to hug her more earnestly.

Finally, Jack broke the silence.

"Red. Kate and I have some unfinished business to take care of."

With that, Red slowly released his grasp on Kate.

As they separated, Kate placed one hand on each side of Red's face, and kissed him on the forehead.

For another extended moment, Kate and Red looked deeply into each other's eyes, and an inexplicable bonding took place.

"We'll be back, Red," Kate told him. "We've got some things to take care of—and then we'll come back."

"Can you help us get out of here?" Jack requested.

But Red held up his hands, indicating that he needed to do something first.

Even with all his injuries, he easily managed to climb his lookout tree.

After making certain that it was safe to leave, Red came back down and opened the pricker bush gate.

Jack patted Red on the head.

"See you later, kid."

Kate gave Red one more hug, before joining her father on the other side of Red's compound. As they hurried off, Red broomed out their tracks, retreated into his compound and then released the rope that restrained the gate.

Both Jack and Kate turned to marvel once more at Red's resourcefulness.

"We're only half done with this episode, my daughter," Jack said. "Officially, we are still in Canada."

"I've got an idea," Kate said, smiling at her father.

"I know exactly what you are thinking. ... And it just might work."

Chapter 55— *Flying is a piece of cake*

"Have you ever flown a helicopter before?" Kate asked.

"Not exactly," Jack replied.

"Do you think we could take the boat back—is that a viable option?"

"We could, but what are the chances that the DHS won't be watching that boat right now, waiting for us? Right now, as we speak?"

"Yeah. That's what I'm thinking," Jack agreed. "That option's off the table. We've got to use the chopper. If I'm right about this, the bird's owner will have a printed checklist," Jack said. "I've rented planes, and that's how it worked with them.

"A helicopter is a much more complicated machine. But they've probably become computerized like everything else. I guess we will soon find out."

Jack and Kate retraced their steps until they arrived at the secluded makeshift hanger.

"Here, take these," Jack said, handing Kate a pair of latex gloves, "Let's pop off these bungee cords and see what we've got."

They started together and worked themselves around the cover in opposite directions.

"That's the last one," Jack said. "You give a pull on this rope, and I'll get the other one."

Once the helicopter was totally exposed, Jack glanced into Kate's eyes, almost as though he was reading her mind. For a brief moment, father and daughter connected on the highest of levels—both understood that this just might be the end of their last adventure. And then the two of them climbed into it.

"Time to ditch the Glock," Jack said, wiping it down and tossing it on the ground.

"Is this what you were talking about?" Kate asked, sliding a bound notebook out of a slot below the control console.

Jack took the book from Kate, as he buckled himself into the cockpit. Thumbing through it, he began nodding his head.

"This just might do it," he said.

After studying the notebook for a few moments, Jack started engaging switches.

"The thing is, all of these birds are a little different," he said. "If a company wants to rent theirs out, they will usually provide a very detailed cheat-sheet manual giving step-by-step procedures for taking off and landing—one that's specific to a particular machine. It explains everything you really have to know to it get up, and then to get it down. Flying it is not the tricky part—it's taking off and landing."

"Do you know where we're going?" Kate asked.

"That's your job."

Kate took a look at her father and smiled.

She then studied the GPS on the console and said, "I think I'd prefer using my iPad, but this looks manageable."

"I intend to scrape the treetops all the way back to Canada. But orientation can sometimes be a bit of a challenge. Just plug in Sault Ste. Marie, Canada—and then follow 17 to Wigwaus Street. That's where we left the truck. If we have to take some evasive action, it could be handy to be able to zero back in on our target."

"Got it."

"All we have to figure out is how to get this bird in the air, and everything else should be a piece of cake ... until it comes time to land it."

"I thought these things were next to impossible to fly without training."

"They used to be. Actually, they still are plenty hard. But, like I said, when a company creates a business out of renting their chopper out, they have to make it as easy as possible."

"Well, the rotor seems to be working," Kate said, shouting as loudly as she could in order to be heard over the enormous din of the rotors.

"The gauges match up with the manual—that's always useful. Let's see if we can get it off the ground."

Kate was nodding her head affirmatively, even though she did not understand a word. She began fumbling around with a headset but realized that her father was not wearing one, so gave up on the idea.

Jack realized that it was critical to make his ascent as vertical as possible, to avoid nearby trees. Yet, he did not want to explode off the ground. The manual did not detail very much about taking off. So he throttled it up to maximum, with a rotor speed of 395 RPMs.

"Here we go!" he declared, pulling the stick back.

Initially, it started to lurch forward. So he eased off to settle it back down. An experienced helicopter pilot would not have had a problem with that, but this part of the process was not covered in his abridged manual.

"Let me take another look at that," he said, grabbing the manual back from Kate.

After flipping from page to page for a few more moments, he handed it back to her and said, "I think I'm going to have to figure it out on my own."

This time he opted for a very rapid ascent. The Bell 429 shot up, and forward. Plus it also started going in circles. He soon stabilized the chopper and turned it toward Canada.

"Great ... we're up. Please don't tell me you haven't done this before," Kate said, laughing out loud.

Even though Jack could not hear her, he did see she was laughing.

"The closest I ever got to flying one of these is riding around with my buddies in a traffic chopper in Chicago. ... I'm afraid getting down is not as easy as getting up. If you think that was bad, just wait until I try to set it down. I hope the owner has it well insured."

Once the helicopter cleared the taller trees, Jack pointed it toward the Canadian border at close to its top speed.

"What happened to the Garmin?" Kate asked. "It doesn't look right to me."

"I don't think we need it," Jack said.

"You're headed in the right direction," Kate said, looking out through the side window. "We should be crossing the channel soon, and Wigwaus is directly on the other side. Just hold a straight line."

"I'm going to start taking it in—this could be very interesting. The bank was not very level. I'm going to shoot for the soccer field just past that growth of trees.

"We should be good, but remember to keep your head down when you get out."

"Power lines on the other side of the field ... do you see them?" Kate shouted and pointed at the same time.

Jack nodded and put on his headset.

Kate did the same, and then repeated her warning about the power lines.

"Shouldn't be a problem, if I can stabilize it in the middle of the field."

"Easy does it," Kate said, encouraging her father to take it in slow.

"Not so easy to do. I think we're going to come down a little too …"

"Holy cow—I think you just drove my spine through my head," Kate complained, as the helicopter literally bounced back up into the air. She was no longer laughing.

"Let's try this again," Jack said, this time coming down a little more gingerly. "Good thing these Bells are put together well."

As soon as the gear hit the field the second time, it again bounced, but not quite as hard as the first time.

The third time worked better. So as soon as the gear touched ground that time, Jack cut the engines and unhooked his belt.

"Let's bolt. And remember to keep your head down."

Kate followed Jack off the helicopter. And she did crouch down, even though she observed that there was ample space to walk upright.

"We should get moving before the authorities show up," Jack advised. "I don't think I can come up with a good excuse for what we just did."

Jack and Kate had no more than backed their truck out of the brush, when they spotted two patrol cars driving across the soccer field to inspect the helicopter.

Jack slammed on the brakes.

"We can't get caught. If we do, you're done as a detective in New York—or anywhere else. … Check the GPS—see if there's another way outta here."

"Head west … all the way to the end. Then just follow it north back to the highway."

Instead of heading back to the highway the way they came, Jack drove west on Wigwaus Street, and then north on Greenski Avenue.

When they reached 17B they had to wait for a fire truck. The driver of the truck appeared to be looking for smoke, or a particular street. It slowed as it passed Greenski Avenue and then turned south on Shingwauk Street. Jack patiently waited until the fire truck was safely past before entering the highway.

"No real need to rush now," Jack said, removing and storing his radar detector. "These can get you in trouble in Canada."

"How are they going to handle the fact that we are reentering without Buddy?" Kate asked, after they had driven several minutes.

"Good question—maybe we simply should just tell the truth," Jack suggested. "Our golden retriever was shot and killed by a guy with a Glock semi-auto. …That oughta work, don't you think?"

"I have an idea," Kate countered.

"And what would that be?"

"We could *deflect* their attention."

"By doing what?"

"A major shopping spree."

"I wonder why that doesn't surprise me. And how exactly would that work?"

"If I buy over two hundred dollars' worth of clothes here in Canada, we would establish the purpose of our trip and where we were, plus we would be eligible for a seven percent Goods and Services Tax Rebate on the Canadian side.

"Of course, we would have to declare it on the US side, and possibly owe up to ten percent. But, they could waive that if they choose, because we have not been in Canada for the required forty-eight hours. As long as it doesn't amount to more than a thousand dollars, they just might let it slide."

"But you think that it might provide a distraction?"

"That's what I'm thinking. There is a minimum on the Canadian side—I think it is two hundred Canadian dollars."

"It's worth a try, I suppose. ... But we're still going to need a story to explain the absence of Buddy."

"Let's stop over at the police station in Sault Ste. Marie, on the Canadian side, and report that Buddy is missing—file a report, or whatever one does when one's dog runs away."

"Hold the presses," Kate interjected. "I've got another plan—you're gonna love this one!"

Kate was correct—Jack did like her *revised* plan. Together they implemented it, and they made it out of Canada and back into the US without a problem.

* * *

"Why are we stopping here?" Kate asked as Jack pulled up to the fence at the junkyard.

"You will soon see," he said, jumping out of his truck, lifting the chain link fence and retrieving the firearms he had stashed there before their Canadian interlude.

"I'm pretty sure these are going to come in handy."

Before Kate had a chance to respond, Jack's phone began to vibrate. He looked at it to see who was calling. It was Roger.

"Well, that was fast."

Jack listened intently to what Roger had to say for over a minute. And then he said, "But nothing was ever proven? And no arrests were made? Very interesting. ... And someday we can talk about the last info you gave me. I'm sure you'll get a kick out of the adventure you sent us on. ... But it's not something we can discuss now. And certainly not over a phone. I would say this—if this new information is half as helpful as what you gave me earlier, it will clarify much of what's been happening up here. Thanks again, my friend. I will be in touch."

Chapter 56— Tracking down the culprits

"Hello. Special Agent Lamar?" Jack asked. "Thank you for taking my call. Earlier you had requested to interview me. Just wondering when you would like to do that? ... Tomorrow morning—nine-thirty. I'll be there. ... Good to talk to you too."

"Doesn't that make you a little nervous?" Kate asked.

"You've heard that it's wise to keep your friends close, and your enemies closer? Well, in the case of the Feds—close is not enough. You should climb inside their skin whenever possible. Besides, I have the feeling that if I don't meet with him soon, he'll be coming after me."

"Yeah. I see your point," Kate agreed. "I still don't trust him. I would like to know where he's going with Uncle Alex's case, and why he's so eager to talk to us ... "

"Hang on a minute. Didn't you notice what I just told him? I said *I* would be there tomorrow—not *us*. And he did not stipulate that you had to be there. That means I just drew you a get outta jail free card."

"Oh, don't you think you're slick?"

"Actually, I need you around to keep an eye out for an email from a Chicago buddy of mine. He's a detective. I asked him to expedite some tests for me."

"You had it sent to my address?" Kate asked.

"Right."

"And you've got a good reason for that?"

"I do."

"Concerned yours might be compromised?"

"Not so much. … I just know you check your emails better than I do mine—especially if this business with Lamar turns out to be very time consuming. And this might be significant. Probably won't mean a thing, but everything we can eliminate gets us closer to catching your uncle's killer, and getting a conviction."

"I'm all for that," Kate said. "Care to share with me what you're looking for?"

"I sent some of Red's blood to him, requesting him to have forensics do an expedited DNA. That's all."

"You retired detectives—you never quite retire, do you? … Just like in New York. My captain keeps sending memos down about how much these unauthorized tests cost the city."

"Do his memos do any good?"

"Never. We have a half dozen retired detectives that lean heavily on their buddies to help them out. And they do—usually. One retired detective kept requesting paternity testing. That didn't cut it. But, a couple times cases have been solved with the help of a retired detective who worked in private security. So, I don't think the captain is too adamant with his objections. He has to put up a stink, just in case the city finds out what the guys are doing. He just likes to know the whos and the whats, so if he ever needs to call in some favors.

"… And what could that prove—Red's DNA? That he's related to Tom Sawyer? I thought we already knew that."

"I really have no concrete ideas. I just got to thinking, after my lengthy conversation with Donna at our hotel—just before she was killed. And the sheriff's report. It just struck me that here we have a boy with matted red curls. Granted, his mother was Irish. But I'm fascinated by his fine features—and all that red hair."

"What do we specifically know about the father?"

"Just that he was Native American. And a tribal leader."

"No kidding. And, you said he operated a hunting lodge?"

"Hunting and fishing. And he also worked as a guide—a very much in demand guide."

"And that certainly helps explain Red's ability to fend for himself in the wild."

"After the fire, Alex not only wanted Red to move into the resort, he actually tried to adopt Red. But Social Services blocked both efforts. Apparently he had a reputation for drinking too much—Alex, not Red, obviously. And, of course, they served alcohol at the resort. So Red was placed in a series of foster homes. You know the rest of *that* story."

"The explosion, the one that killed Red's parents, I'm still very troubled about that," Kate said.

"So was I, but fires like that do happen—pilot lights go out, thermocouples fail. I know it's not the norm, but genuine accidents do happen."

"You know, Dad, nothing we have experienced here over the past few days has been normal. Think about it—in your whole life, how many times have you been forced to steal a helicopter, and then fly that helicopter into a foreign country … to avoid arrest for killing two people, no less. Forget about commandeering a boat, and secretly crossing that same border, to save a red-headed kid—one who couldn't talk, no less.

"The more I hang around with you the less sure I become about the meaning of *normal.*

"I have worked as a detective in New York City for over ten years. Now, most people would not consider that a boring job. Yet, I have experienced more excitement with you, particularly over the past few days, than I have during the decade in New York.

"It just seems that whenever you and I get together, crazy things start happening. … Don't get me wrong. I love the adventures."

Kate remained silent for a moment, and then said, "What got me going on that tangent? … Oh! Yeah. As soon as I hear about someone dying up here, particularly on Sugar Island, I immediately think murder. Go figure.

"Which brings me back to my original question: is it safe to assume that Red's parents died in a regular old house fire? Or should I be trying to read more into it? … Because, I would rather not try to wrap my head around any more murder cases—at least not until we get Alex's behind us."

"Of course, there could be more to it," Jack chuckled. "But Donna, the clerk at our hotel, she filled me in on some of Red's background. … Her father is a retired sheriff, and he apparently talked to her a lot about his work. She said that the fire occurred shortly after her father retired."

"Oh my God!" Kate responded. "Is he still alive? Donna's father."

"He is still alive. … But, getting back to your other question, according to Donna, there was no evidence of arson in the explosion and fire that killed Red's parents. The fire inspector wrote the deaths off as accidental, and the authorities accepted the inspector's report."

"Maybe we should talk to him—Donna's father," Kate said.

"After Donna's mother passed, he moved to Florida."

"He'll be up for the funeral?"

"I would assume so," Jack said. "She has other family in the area, so someone should be able to contact her father."

"… Let me guess," Kate said, hearing her father's cell vibrate.

Jack looked down at his phone, and smiled.

Chapter 57—Deputy Restin with a new wrinkle

"Restin, this is a surprise."

After listening to Deputy Restin for a short time, Jack interrupted.

"Dr. Rex was very helpful. In fact, he did a great job. But, unfortunately, the dog didn't make it. I think the shock might have been too much. Or maybe internal injuries. Unfortunately, dogs cannot tell you where they hurt. But the doctor was great. I'm sure the dog's death is no reflection on his work."

Again Jack remained silent, intently listening to Deputy Restin do what he did best—talk.

Finally, Jack responded.

"Kate's fine. I'm not sure where the good doctor got the idea that anyone had been shot. Kate caught a limb in the face while we were walking in the woods. It was my fault. … But I do appreciate your concern. Kate's fine. I'm fine. But the poor dog—he's moved on to a better place."

After another moment, Jack decided to change the topic.

"How's it going with Special Agent Lamar? Is he still bugging you? That's good. … I'm meeting with him in the morning. … I'm happy to hear that, I'm looking forward to talking to him as well."

After disconnecting the call, Jack sat silently for a long time. His conversation with Deputy Restin troubled him.

They are altogether too close, Jack thought, *Restin and the vet.*

Deputy Restin had asked about Kate's gunshot wound.

Why, he wondered, w*ould the doc ever share that with a law enforcement officer?*

His expectation was that the doc should have observed at least a minimal level of confidentiality. Jack knew, of course, that Dr. Rex actually had nothing concrete that could harm him or his daughter. In fact, the doc had more to lose than they did. After all, he had no business treating a human gunshot wound—he could lose his license for that.

And Jack knew that he and Kate had plausible deniability working in their favor. They could simply deny that she was shot, and the doc would not be able to prove a thing.

But the part that Jack found most troubling was the fact that the doc would even consider discussing the matter with a law enforcement officer, no matter how good a friend Restin was. It made Jack wonder just what the nature of that relationship really might be.

"How big a hurry are you in?" Kate asked, after pondering her father's silence.

"Not in a hurry—what's on your mind?"

"This coffee shop. I'd like to stop in and see what's happening."

"Used to be that if you wanted to find out what people are thinking you stopped into the local pub—now it's the local coffee shop."

"Bars are still a good source of information," Kate said. "But the upwardly mobile, particularly the younger ones, spend more time drinking lattes than martinis."

"How'd you find out about it?"

"Actually we drove by it earlier—on our way to Walmart. It's the one Restin was talking about."

"Joey's—isn't that what he said it's called?"

"I think so. I just know that it's not a Starbucks—that's how Restin described it."

"Good."

"Why is that good? I thought you liked Starbucks."

"I do," Jack replied. "But chain operations usually employ young people—kids more interested in who's dating who, or who has cheap tickets for the next concert."

"It's called *hooking up*—not dating. So how's a locally-owned coffee shop different?"

"For the most part, coffee shops operate on a small margin. So, with a locally-owned shop, usually you will find the owner himself waiting on customers. Owners will have been around longer, and have a better feel for their environment. And, generally they are smarter—at least more likely to be privy to the latest *adult* gossip."

"Of course," Kate chimed in, "if they aren't interested in sharing that information, then you would be better off talking to a loose-lipped kid."

"Well, let's find out who we've got to deal with here," Jack said as they entered the coffee shop.

Chapter 58—Joey the coffee guy

"Hello there, young people. Welcome to my little coffee shop. My name is Joey. What can I get for you?"

"Hi, Joey," Jack replied, looking around to determine where he wanted to sit. Under most circumstances, he would choose a table in the rear, with his back to the wall. But this time, he was most interested in talking to the owner.

Jack took a long look at the drink selection posted on a blackboard behind the bar.

"Let's just sit at the counter," he said to Kate.

"You know," Jack then said. "You've got so many interesting selections listed on that board, I think I'm going to have to study it for a minute. Do you know what you would like, Kate?"

"Let me see. Oh, yeah. What is that 'Steamer'?"

"Different kinds. My most popular is foamed milk, shot of espresso, and chocolate."

"The chocolate part sounds pretty good—I'll try one."

"With a little whipped cream? Most young ladies like some whipped cream on it."

"Yeah—that sounds perfect."

"And you, sir?"

"Jack, my name is Jack. And I'll have a tall dark roast, with a shot of espresso—make that two shots."

"I'll whip them right up for you."

Jack took a look around the shop as he and Kate seated themselves.

There were three other customers seated with them—a twenty-something couple sharing drinks at a table underneath a television tuned to FOX News, and a fit-looking thirty-year-old four seats down at the counter. Even though that fellow did not look directly at them, Jack sensed his eyes following his and Kate's reflection in a small tinted mirror on the wall behind the counter. Jack surmised he was an off-duty cop. Jack then studied Joey more closely.

Five eight. One sixty-five, Jack's mind raced. Looks forty-five, but is more likely in his early to mid-fifties. Retired something—probably military. Too young to be retired from any of the local employers. Single or soon to be. He used his retirement to open his business. Wanted to meet young ladies, and what better way than a coffee shop. Most likely he's looking for a woman in her late twenties or early thirties. That would explain the fact that he's working alone ... and sports a store-bought tan.

Jack glanced to his right. Out of the window he observed a car pull past the front, followed by a second, and soon after, a third.

"Your regular, hon?" Joey said into an intercom located beside a drive-up window.

"This guy can multi-task," Jack said to Kate, as he watched Joey run the espresso machine and prepare three orders simultaneously.

Before he returned to Jack and Kate with their drinks, he bent down to make eye contact with the girl in the first car and said, "Here ya go, darlin'. See you tomorrow."

Jack did not get a good look at the driver, but from what he could make out as she drove off, she appeared to be in her mid-twenties and very good-looking. He did catch a short glimpse of her at that time because she made it a point to maintain eye contact with Joey as she pulled away.

Joey definitely has an eye for the girls, Jack surmised.

Joey then quickly scooped up their two drinks and carried them over to them.

"One of my special Steamers for the young lady, and a Shot in the Dark for you. Hope you like them. Whoa. And yes—I did remember to put two shots in that Shot in the Dark."

"Perfect," Jack said.

Jack started calculating in his mind just how much money Joey's shop could be bringing in. *Three customers in here right now. Pretty good drive-through business. Looks like about twenty cars per hour—at most. He saves money by working the shop by himself. Bet he has short hours.*

"How late are you open?" Jack asked.

"Close at five—open at six thirty. On weekends, I open at nine."

Jack surmised that his rent would be between a thousand and fourteen hundred. *He could be making a decent living at this, but he's not getting rich. ... I wonder what he does if he gets sick? Might have a sister, daughter, or a girlfriend who can step in.*

"How long have you been doing this?" Jack asked.

"This is my fifth year. Before I opened the shop I worked for the US Postal Service—twenty-five years."

"Really. Are you originally from this area?"

"No. I moved here almost twenty years ago from Massachusetts."

"What was the attraction?"

"I like to fish—lots of great fishing around here. And lakefront property wasn't as expensive as it was out East. My money goes farther here. It's really a pretty cool place to live."

"Do you have family in the area?"

"No. I got a divorce nine years ago, and looked for a change of vocation. ... Have not regretted it—not for a second," Joey replied, inserting a lengthy pause between each of his last words.

"Well," Jack continued, "this is certainly a great coffee shop. I wish I had one like it where I live."

"You could buy this one, and move to the UP."

"Are you selling?"

"Not officially. But I'd consider it. It's hard to make a go of it. I love the business, and the people are great. ... So, I don't know. I am pushing sixty, from the wrong side. Maybe if I had a partner—someone who could take some of the hours. Maybe you and your girlfriend would like to go into partnership with me?"

"If you did sell, what would you do?"

"Most likely move back East. I don't know. ... I presume you're not from the Soo. Right? Where are you from?"

"Chicago. I'm retired. By the way, this is my *daughter,* Kate. She lives in New York."

"Chicago, and New York. Wow! ... Vacationing?"

"Not exactly. Alex Garos, from Sugar Island, the one who died a short time ago—murdered—he was my brother-in-law."

"Yeah. The guy who owned the resort on Sugar Island. My condolences to you. What a tough thing that was."

"Did you know him?"

"Actually, I did," Joey replied. "We weren't friends or anything like that. But a couple of times I had buddies visit from New England, and I'd put them up at his resort. It provided more of a relaxed atmosphere than any of the hotels or lodges in the Soo. Alex was a very accommodating gentleman. He always made my friends feel comfortable. And the bar at the resort—outstanding. Better than anything else between the two bridges."

"Did you get to know a young red-headed kid who worked there?"

Kate asked.

"I did. Everyone simply referred to him as Red. I think he was deaf."

"He isn't deaf," Kate corrected him. "He just doesn't talk very well. He has a physical condition."

It was obvious that Kate and Red had formed a relationship. So much so that Kate felt the need to come to Red's defense.

"I didn't know that," Joey apologized. "I just assumed he was deaf and dumb. How's he doing—now that he's not working at the resort?"

"I don't know," Jack answered quickly, noticing that Kate had bristled at the "deaf and dumb" reference. He did not want to have Kate get into a full-blown defensive dialog about Red.

"Have they made any arrests yet?" Joey asked.

"Not yet," Jack said. "I am not sure that they even have any suspects."

"That's such a tragedy."

"I wouldn't expect something like that to happen up here," Jack said. "I've heard that most of the residents of Sugar Island don't even lock their doors at night."

"You might be surprised at what goes on over there—on Sugar Island," the man at the end of the counter interjected. "For all its quaintness, Sugar Island is basically a lawless community."

"What do you mean by that?" Jack asked.

"There's no permanent police presence on the island. If anyone needs a cop, they have to call for help to the sheriff's office in the Soo. And then the responding officer has to get in line and take the ferry—just like everybody else. They might not always lock their doors, but every resident owns a gun, and knows how to use it."

"Well, if anyone would know, Bill here would," Joey said. "He's a deputy—off duty right now."

"For instance, we got a call a month ago. Old Jasper Niles got drunk and was slapping his wife around ... again—for the umpteenth time. I drew the short straw. I waited ten minutes to get on the ferry. But even before it shoved off, everyone on the island knew a marked car was on its way.

"They have a network. One person calls a couple residents, who in turn calls a couple more, and within minutes everyone has been alerted.

"The DHS always has a vehicle on the island, but they don't make arrests. If someone on the Canadian side fishes too close, they might hassle him. But that's about it. The residents know Homeland Security's limitations, and take full advantage of it."

"I'm sorry to hear about your boss. That must have been quite a shock," Jack said to the deputy.

"Yeah. We've had quite a few shocking things happen around here lately. You're that retired detective, aren't you? And you're his daughter—the big-city detective—New York. Right?"

"That's right," Jack replied. "Kate's on leave from her job in New York, and I'm retired out of Chicago. Have you got any leads on the sheriff's death?"

"FBI has taken that over too. They feel that his murder is somehow related to your relative's murder. We're pretty much left outta the loop—and the loop just keeps getting bigger. The only way they would involve us is if we happen to stumble across a fresh body. I think if they could write speeding tickets, they'd send us all home—just to get us outta their hair. I'll be glad when everything gets back to normal."

The deputy stared into his second double espresso for a moment, and then said with a chuckle in his voice, "Actually wouldn't be so bad if the FBI would write citations, and run on the nuisance calls, like Jasper Niles. Then I could go fishing."

"Bill here didn't always see eye-to-eye with his boss," Joey said. "Right,

Bill?"

"The sheriff's okay … was okay. Don't mean to speak ill of the dead, but it's just that he and I never really hit it off. I was born, raised, and went to college in the Soo—LSSU. Sheriff Northrup was an outsider. He just had his own ideas, and his own way of doing things. But I wouldn't say that there was any bad blood. In fact, if he were still alive, and running again, I would probably vote for him."

"He was retiring?" Jack asked.

"That was the rumor. Don't know anything for sure. But he did put his house up for sale—in fact I think he might have just closed on it. From what I heard, he got just enough to cover the mortgage—maybe not even. Don't know what that was all about. He was pretty well liked in the community. Some of us suspected that he was sick—maybe had cancer. But he didn't act like anything physical was wrong. It's very weird. Sells his house, gets ready to retire, and then gets himself murdered."

"Did he buy another house—what were his plans?"

"I don't have any idea. At least, he never talked to me about any plans—he was a very private guy. In fact, Joey here was one of the sheriff's good friends." Bill then looked over at Joey and asked, "Did he tell you what he planned to do?"

Chapter 59—Joey sheds some light

"We weren't good friends, or anything like that," Joey replied. "We both liked to fish, and we both hailed from New England. And, we were both relatively new to the area. So, one thing followed another, and we sometimes went fishing in Canada together."

With a tinge of jealousy in his voice, Deputy Bill jumped in, "Along with your buddies from out East. You'd all get together at that resort on Sugar Island—you, the sheriff, the vet, and sometimes Restin, ... and your friends from New England."

"So Sheriff Northrup was a fishing buddy?" Jack asked.

"We went fishing together a few times, early on. But not in the past couple years—maybe once, a year ago. Like Bill says, the sheriff was a private fellow—he liked to keep to himself."

"Did the sheriff frequent your coffee shop?" Kate asked.

"Occasionally. But, again, that was early on, when I first opened it. I think he felt sorry for me. I didn't have many customers, and he'd sometimes stop in on his way to work. He wasn't much of the gourmet coffee type. He'd sit down and order a large coffee to go, and then sit here at the counter and drink the whole thing. I think he wanted to be ready to run outta here if he had an emergency. He'd then stand up and say, 'Warm this up for me, Joey.' And after I did he'd take off.

"Every time he was here, he'd read my coffee menu, and chuckle. 'What the hell is *espresso*? And *la tees*? Who drinks that stuff, anyway?'

"Or he'd want me to explain how I make a latte. That, in essence, was Sheriff Northrup."

"Were you acquainted with him before you moved to the Soo?" Kate asked.

"No. I'm not exactly sure where he was from. We just both moved here at about the same time."

"And the vet—Dr. Rex—he's one of your fishing buddies?" Jack asked. "I think he moved here at about the same time. And from New England. Is that right?"

"It was all Restin's doing," Joey said, as he took care of another customer at the drive through. "He's quite the talker, you know. When I opened this shop, he would stop in and tell me about all his fishing adventures. Since I didn't know anyone around here, he offered to take me fishing with him.

"I assume he made the same offer to the sheriff, and to Doc Rex. So we would get together at the resort a couple times a year, and then head over to Canada."

"Where'd you fish in Canada?" Jack asked. "I've fished near Dryden. Is there a better place within driving distance?"

"Nothing wrong with Dryden—I've not dropped a line there, but I've heard good things. We fish near Sudbury. Almost directly east of here. I consider it a comfortable drive."

Kate stared into her drink, even though she felt like looking at her father.

"Or you could charter a chopper," Bill quipped.

"Who's got that kind of money?" Joey asked rhetorically.

"I don't know. But from what I've heard, both the DHS and the FBI would like to know. Someone's been flying between Sugar Island and somewhere in Canada for the past couple of days, but up until now they were never able to catch up with them."

"Up until now? Something happened today?" Joey asked.

"Sure did," Bill said. "You haven't heard about it?"

"What happened today?"

"First of all, the chopper landed on the island—again. DHS got the call, or else they spotted it. But they couldn't tell exactly where it landed. It was on the ground, somewhere on the island for over an hour, and then it took back off. And just like all the other times, it headed straight for Canada. Only this time it was different. It came down just off 17, and the Canadian authorities pounced on it. I heard it came down pretty hard this time. In fact, they're calling it a crash."

"Did they make any arrests?" Joey asked.

"I don't know any of the details, but I suspect that if they had apprehended someone, I would have heard about it. My guess is that the chopper was empty by the time they reached it."

"Man," Joey said, "this is sure an exciting place to live these days."

"That's not all," Bill continued. "I talked to Restin a little earlier. He said that just before the chopper lifted off Sugar Island, residents heard a dozen or more gunshots fired in the general area. The assumption is that it was somehow related to the chopper."

"Gunshots?" Jack asked. "Anyone hit?"

"The FBI swarmed on the scene immediately—and they don't talk to us. But the way they've got the place taped off, I'd have to think that they've got something … something big. They called two medical emergency vehicles to the island. And they haven't returned to a hospital, at least as far as I know. So, if they've got some victims, then the likelihood is that they're deceased."

"I can't wait to get home to good old safe and sound New York City," Kate chuckled. "This is way more dangerous than what I'm used to."

"Bill," Joey said, leaning over the counter. "I've gotta use the can. Would you mind the store for a minute? If someone comes in, just tell them I'll be right back."

Less than a minute later Joey reappeared and assumed his position behind the counter. He had a look of concern on his face.

"Somethin' wrong, boss?" Bill asked.

"No. I just think I got hold of some bad smoked fish last night. Not feeling up to par today."

"I thought you smoked your own."

"I do when I catch 'em. Like I said—I haven't been fishing for a long time."

"That ain't no good," Bill said. "Maybe you and I should go. I've got a buddy with a boat up on Whitefish Bay."

"That's a great idea," Joey said. "And maybe Jack and his daughter would like to join us. How about it, Jack—would you like to catch some whitefish?"

"I thought the Native Americans controlled that market."

"They do. Bill here is Native American. The boat he's talking about is one of those fishing tugs. They use nets. Can literally catch a ton on one trip. Those whitefish smoke up nice."

"I can't speak for my daughter, but I'd love to go out. But first I have some business to attend to."

"Solving Alex's murder?" Bill asked.

"Sort of. I can't actually do anything about it myself. But seeing Alex's killer get caught has to be on the top of my agenda."

"I wish I could help. Why don't you give me your number, and if I hear something that might interest you, I'll give you a call."

"Won't that get you in trouble with the FBI?"

"Screw 'em. All they're letting me do is write speeding tickets and deal with drunks. Officially I have no responsibilities with this case. So, if I hear anything, it will be something considered general knowledge. … I'll tell you if I hear anything."

"That would be great," Jack said, writing his number and Kate's on a napkin, and sliding it down the bar to Bill.

"You've already been very helpful. Do you think I could have your number?

"If I come up with something, I might like to run it by you."

"Sure," Bill replied, handing Jack a business card after he had written his cell number on the back of it.

"You should try my cell first. But if you can't reach me, you can hit a voice mail by calling my work."

"That was great coffee, Joey," Jack said, as he prepared to leave. "What do we owe you?"

"Five bucks—for both. How's that sound?"

"Like you're not going to make any money on me today."

Jack laid a five-dollar bill on the counter and stuck another one in the beer money jar.

"Think about my offer—you buying into my business," Joey said. Then pointing toward the Jack's tip, continued, "That could be your down payment. … We could have a great time working together.

"And you, and Kate of course, could have all the free coffee you can drink."

"I'll think about it. The free coffee part sounds pretty good. But I'd probably scare off all those cute girls. That wouldn't be so good for you."

"Maybe you and your daughter should just buy me out. Then you could go fishing any time you want."

"We'll see you again," Jack said as he slid down from his stool. "Bill, nice to meet you. I'm sure we'll talk again, too."

"Take care," Bill said, offering a friendly wave with his left hand. He had been cradling his coffee with both hands. His smile, while less than exuberant, was sincere.

"We've got to run an errand—an *important* errand," Jack whispered to Kate as they hurried toward his SUV.

Chapter 60—Two plus two begins to add up

"And what would that be? Kate asked, closing her door. Jack had already started the engine and performed a head check.

"We've got to return the muzzles the doc loaned us."

"Right now?"

"I think so. I would like to have as much as possible resolved in my mind before I talk to the FBI—and right now I still have questions about that vet."

As they pulled up Dr. Rex's drive, both Jack and Kate noticed that the over-sized van, which had been parked inside the partially closed garage, was no longer sticking out. But neither mentioned it.

"Wonder if the doc is even here," Kate said.

"We'll soon find out," Jack replied, as he bounded up the four steps to the door and pounded heavily on it.

"Do you smell that?" he said, as he knocked even harder.

"It's coming from around back," Kate said, as she turned and headed toward the source of the odor. Jack tried the door again, but then gave up and followed his daughter.

"Looks like the doctor was burning some trash," she said, picking up a broken rake handle that had been used to stir the fire. "What do you make of this?"

"For one thing, I smell kerosene. So the doc wasn't roasting hot dogs."

"The coals beneath it look like he started out with some dry wood, but the ashes on top are quite different. Too uniform to be household trash. It's like he was trying to destroy something. What do you think?"

"Exactly," Jack agreed. "Watch my back, I'm going to scoop up some of these ashes and see what he's been burning out here."

Jack then pulled a plastic Ziploc bag from his pocket and pushed a couple of the larger, and cooler, pieces of the ash into it with a pen.

"That ought to be enough for the lab to test," he said, standing to his feet and turning his attention to the rear of the house.

"I wonder if the doc left the back door unlocked," he said, winking at his daughter.

"Wouldn't be surprised—people often do that," she replied sarcastically.

When they got to the back door, Jack tried the doorknob and found it to be unlocked, but he did not open it.

"Well, that's not what I was expecting. Wonder what the deal is. … Don't touch this for a minute—I need to check something out."

Jack then walked around to a window on the side of the house. This put him in a position to view the inside of the unlocked door. He observed that a keypad for the burglar alarm system, which was located beside the door, indicated that the system was armed.

"That doesn't make sense. Why would he leave a door unlocked, but turn the alarm on?"

After only a few seconds, Jack backed away from the window and said, "Time to go, daughter."

Kate recognized the tone. It told her that her father had just discovered a coiled rattlesnake, angry bull, or some equally ominous threat.

She immediately backed away and joined him in a brisk walk toward his SUV.

"What's up?" she asked.

"The alarm was on, and the cover had been removed from the siren."

"And? ..."

"I couldn't see much more than that, except for a wire hanging down from the siren. It terminated inside a drawer with a second wire leading out of that same drawer, leading toward the front of the house."

"A bomb?"

"A bomb—maybe. But the second wire suggests two or more incendiary devices—wouldn't need two wires for a bomb. Whatever's going on, I wouldn't want to be the one who opened that door—my hair's already too thin."

"Or climbed in a window. No doubt there are motion sensors as well."

Jack did not take the time to turn around. He shoved the shifter into reverse and sped backward to the road.

Handing Kate the deputy's card, Jack said, "Dial this guy's cell phone and tell him what we've found."

"Kate Handler here. We've just pulled out of the vet's driveway—Dr. Rex. It looks to us like you need to get a bomb squad out here. We think that one or more incendiary devices are wired into the alarm system. We just stopped by to pay a visit. It appeared no one was home, so Dad looked in a window."

"What'd he say?" Jack asked.

"He wondered what we were doing there. I'm sure he'll get right on it."

Less than fifteen seconds later Jack exclaimed, "Oh my God!"

Chapter 61—Fireworks

Jack immediately pulled to the side of the road and made a U-turn.

As soon as he did, Kate was able to see what he had observed in his rearview mirror—a large plume of black smoke shooting into the sky. It looked like the mushroom cloud after a nuclear explosion.

"So much for finding evidence at the doc's house," Kate declared.

"Call the deputy back and tell him to roll the fire trucks," Jack said.

Jack pulled up and stopped when they reached the driveway.

"Let's check that out," Jack said, getting out of the vehicle.

"Whoa," she said. "The tracks say the doc was here after all just hiding—he pulled out right behind us. And he turned in the other direction."

"He would have been in the far garage—he left the door up after he pulled out," Jack said, pointing at the manually operated garage door just to the left of the one where the van had been parked when they visited Doctor Rex with Buddy.

"Looks like he pulled up and abruptly stopped at the end of the drive, and then pulled out on the road. When he took off, he spun his tire. Undoubtedly opting to head south because we had turned north.

"My guess is that he used a remote activator—probably an audible panic button—to set off the alarm.

"And that detonated the incendiary. When he stopped here," Jack said, pointing at the tracks, "he hit the transmitter—he knew that he was far enough away to be safe."

By that time, the farmhouse was fully engulfed. Fire was shooting out of the upper-level windows, and the asphalt shingles on the roof were smoking. It would be only a matter of minutes before the house collapsed into its own basement.

"I'd like to take a look in that garage before the fire department arrives," Jack said.

"Give me a second, and I'll get some shots of that tread," Kate said, kneeling over a particularly clear impression of the non-spinning left rear.

"Let me check out the front impressions as well. Should be able to get a look at them when he turned onto the road."

Jack walked along behind her as she captured images with her cell phone.

"Just as we thought—rear wheel drive—standard differential," he observed. "Only one rear tire spun. That van was not from this area.

"What do you recall about it? All we saw was the rear bumper when we were here before.

"And, how did they get the garage door closed this time? When we pulled up earlier, all the garage doors were closed."

Neither of them spoke for a moment, and then Kate concluded, "General Motors Cargo Van. White. Probably around 2000. It was definitely older.

"I don't remember there being any dents or dings on the rear bumper—at least none that we could see the first time. Probably not driven in a city much."

Jack took a look up the road and said, "If you're done shooting, let's get out of the driveway—the fire trucks are going to be here shortly. I can hear them coming down Portage."

Kate and Jack jumped back in their SUV and shot up the driveway. They parked on the far side of the garage, as far from the flames as possible.

"The vinyl siding is smoking from the heat," Kate said, looking at the siding on the garage. "We might not have long before it bursts into flame."

"Let's take a look inside while we still can," Jack added.

Chapter 62—The garage floor provides a clue

As they entered the garage, they could see a whole parade of emergency vehicles headed down the road toward them.

"I don't see anything in here," Jack said.

"Except that they nearly knocked the back wall of the garage out," Kate observed. "Looks like they just drove the van into the studs, pushing the wall right off the foundation. ... That would explain how they managed to get the door closed this time."

"Let's take a look in the other stall," Jack suggested.

As they entered the garage where they had first spotted the van, the first fire truck leading the procession was already turning in.

"What's this?" Kate queried. "Looks like chips of gold paint—and there's quite a lot of it."

As is typical of outbuildings in the UP, the garage had a dirt floor, much of which had recently been disturbed.

"They did a lot of messing around right here," Jack said. "Those deep marks in the dirt—looks like they used an ax on something."

"That something is probably what they were burning out back," Kate quickly added.

Jack removed another plastic bag from his pocket. And, finding a small gardening tool, began scraping chips of gold painted wood into it.

"Here comes the deputy," Kate said. "Maybe it'd be best to get out of here before he questions what we're doing."

"Is it Restin, or Bill, the fellow from the coffee shop?"

"Not tall enough to be Restin—must be Bill … or a different deputy. I'll guarantee you that the fire department will want us to vacate quickly. Besides, I can see this garage catching fire very soon unless they cool it down."

"Let's go before we become a distraction," Jack suggested. "We've got what we came for."

"Jack—fire department wants you to pull back to the road."

Jack recognized his voice—it was Bill.

"Will do," Jack responded.

He and Kate jumped in his SUV, swung around and headed toward the road. The route Jack chose for his departure was through a patch of berries.

"I'm going to park on the road. But I have a question for Bill," Jack said.

"It has to do with that alarm system, doesn't it?"

"You got that right."

"Hey, Bill. I have a favor to ask," Jack said, jumping out of his vehicle and running back toward the deputy.

"I just met you, and already you're asking favors?"

"It's not so much a favor, as a suggestion. I think you will agree it's a good idea. This is what I'm thinking. I'm pretty sure that explosion was initiated by using the remote activator on the alarm system."

"You're suggesting arson?"

"At least!" Jack said. "It could have been *murder*—had I or Kate opened that unlocked door. It would have killed us.

"Hell, could have been *you*. Had you arrived and checked it out."

"Anyway, I'm betting you can use your pull with the alarm company to get a report for that alarm event. It should indicate that it was generated by a remote audible panic button—a radio transmitter.

"The alarm communicator is probably in the basement, so there would have been time for it to have communicated before the fire got to it. With the info the alarm company gives you, you can determine which alarm transmitter was used to detonate the incendiary—all transmitters have serial numbers. When you make your arrest, you will probably find that alarm transmitter on the suspect's keychain—would be excellent evidence. The *favor* part of it would simply be for you to let me know what you find, if anything."

"Sounds like a great idea—I'll get right on it. I might be able to get some info if I do it before the FBI takes this fire over."

"That's what I was thinking."

"Did you find anything in the garage?"

"No, not really. Just some paint chips. You might want to check them out before that building burns down too."

The fire burst through the roof of the house. And when it did, the intense heat virtually exploded the asphalt shingles, sending bits of burning tar nearly a hundred feet into the air. Many of them were still on fire when they landed on the garage's steel roof.

"I'll get on it," Deputy Bill said, getting back in his car and pulling up closer to the garage.

"I need to take a look in the garage," he yelled in the direction of the firefighters. "Put a little water over here to cool it down, especially on the outside walls—I'll only be a minute."

"I think we can get going," Jack said to Kate. "No one really wants us around here anyway. Besides, I'm sure that Special Agent Lamar will bring this up tomorrow."

"How long before you can get the results back on the materials you gathered?" Kate asked.

"If I overnight them, and have forensics expedite the tests, they can probably email me preliminary results within hours after they receive them."

"How do you get that type of service? It would take days if not weeks for me to run that through our lab."

"Daughter. We're talking Chicago. I've got enough dirt on some of those guys to put them in jail until their kids get gray. They either help me, or kill me. So far they've chosen the former. Besides, I don't take advantage."

As they drove off, Kate asked, "What do you think we found on that floor? If you had to guess, what would you say it was?"

Jack pondered her question, but did not respond.

Chapter 63—Jack finally meets with Special Agent Lamar

The next morning Jack prepared to meet with the FBI.

"You're sure you don't want me to go with you?" Kate asked.

"Positive. Your presence was not explicitly requested. I think that we would do well to minimize exposure. When he's done with me, you and I will go over the questions he asked—and my answers. He's not going to entertain my questions. At least I doubt that he will. But I'm not certain just how formal a meeting this is going to be. This is what I would like you to do. Call a taxi, and go shopping. You should not hang around the hotel in case Lamar decides you need to be at the interview, and sends a car for you.

"After an hour, take a taxi back. Then you should hang around the hotel. And keep my cell phone with you—I am expecting some important calls. Now, don't answer your cell. Not unless you get three calls in a row, with no voice messages. That will probably be me.

"When I get there, if Lamar wants to interview you today as well— to see if our stories match—if he makes that request, I'll use his phone to call you once, and I'll leave a message. Just disregard *that* message. If I actually need to talk to you—I'll call you repeatedly. But do be sure to frequently check your email."

"You don't think he views us as suspects, do you?"

"Not that so much. But I'm not a hundred percent sure about what his intentions actually are.

"Both you and I know that if Lamar really thought we were suspects in a crime, he would have dragged us in and questioned us. Or worse.

"I think that Lamar does not regard you or me as suspects," Jack continued. "But he does not want to get careless, either. In my view, Lamar is under considerable pressure. People just keep dying around him. And he's the one responsible for putting an end to it. This is not a nice position to be in.

"More than anything, I expect him to pick *my* brain—to see what *I* know."

"Do you think he's discovered the bodies of the two fellows we had to kill to save Red?" Kate asked.

"That's a good question. If his people were the ones who were in the woods, I think it likely he would have pulled us in immediately and tested us for GSR. Makes me wonder who it was out there."

"And what they did with the bodies."

"Exactly."

* * *

"Mr. Handler," Special Agent Lamar said, as Jack was escorted into his office. "I'd like to keep this interview as informal as possible. I'd hoped you'd have brought your daughter with you."

Jack did not respond to the comment regarding Kate's absence, but he was pleased that Lamar had opted not to conduct the meeting in an interrogation room. While he had no doubt that every word that came out of his mouth was being recorded, and possibly monitored by a battery of investigators in real time, he still felt more at ease answering questions while seated in a comfortable chair.

"You do understand that anything you say can and will be used against you should any formal charges be brought against you in any of these matters? You have a right to remain silent. You have a right to have an attorney present during this interview. Do you wish to waive your right to an attorney at this time?"

"For now. I don't think I will need an attorney to talk to you about my brother-in-law. Do you?"

"And you do know that it is a federal crime to provide wrong or misleading information to an agent of the FBI?"

"I am aware of that. I will tell the truth."

"Great. Now that we've got that out of the way, I want to express my sincere condolences to you with regard to the loss of your brother-in-law."

"Thank you."

"Of course, you are aware that it has become my job to solve his murder. And that's why I wanted to have this conversation with you this morning. I'm just sorry that it has taken so long for us to get together.

"What can you tell me about the car bombing at your hotel?"

"The girl whose car caught on fire was named Donna. I had been talking to her earlier, while she was working. And then, after I returned to my room, I heard the explosion."

"What did you discuss with her?"

"We talked about Alex's murder. It seems she had overheard a conversation right after Alex was killed. She suspected it might have been related to his murder. She actually met with Sheriff Northrup and told him everything she knew, or suspected."

"I've listened to the tape of that interview. Is there anything that stood out about your conversation with her?"

"Two things. First of all, she thought that she detected a Saudi accent. I suspect that she might have alluded to that in her interview with the sheriff.

"The second thing that stands out is that I think my conversation with her was eavesdropped."

Jack's comment caught Special Agent Lamar by surprise, "And what makes you think that?"

"When I walked away, I glanced over to a chair just the other side of the lobby entrance—probably only fifteen feet from where we had stood. There was an artificial tree separating us from that area. Seated behind that tree was a middle-aged man. He looked suspicious to me."

"How would you describe him?"

"He was seated. But I would estimate his weight to be about a hundred and seventy-five to eighty-five. He was a little chunky. Balding. About fifty—perhaps a year or two older. Glasses. He was wearing a tan windbreaker."

"What makes you think he was eavesdropping?"

"He was holding a rolled up newspaper. Not very practiced at that sort of thing. It's impossible to read a newspaper like that. When I stopped to take a better look, he glanced up at me nervously. If they have cameras in the hotel lobby, you might want to check him out."

"They don't have cameras. That is, they don't have a working system in the lobby."

"That's too bad."

"Have you ever seen this man before, or after, that time?"

"Can't be certain about that. While I did get a pretty good look at him, he was very average looking. Remove his glasses, give him a Tigers' cap, and he could pass right by me unnoticed. I don't know one way or the other. I think that if I had talked to the fellow, or got him to make extended eye contact with me, I might have been able to provide a positive ID. But as it stands, I could not."

"You were out on Sugar Island the night that Sheriff Northrup was allegedly murdered. Would you tell me why that was?"

"A strange set of occurrences. I had just talked to Deputy Restin, at the site of the hotel car bombing, and he requested that I go downtown right then to meet with you. On my way there I received a call from Sheriff Northrup. He requested that I come out to the Sugar Island resort—that he had some new evidence regarding Alex's murder. While I was on the phone with him, I heard what sounded like three rounds from a suppressed .22 revolver. And that was followed by what sounded like the sheriff reacting to his being shot. I flagged down Deputy Restin, and we headed out to the island."

"Did the sheriff provide any hints as to what that new evidence might be?"

"None."

"And you were also there when the emergency vehicle transporting the sheriff's body was blown up. It seems as though there has been a lot of disaster following you around. Care to explain that to me?"

"I have no idea why that was. I can't say that it was pure coincidence, but I have not been able to string the numbers together. Maybe you can tell me if there is anything to what Donna suggested—that there might be a Saudi connection?"

"That's the only Middle East reference I'm aware of."

"Is that what attracted the DHS to this whole matter?"

"I can't speak for them. I can only tell you, as a courtesy, that Donna's comment about the Saudi gentleman stands alone—aside from video images shot at the resort. And they really don't mean anything. That's it.

"But, we really don't have anything else, either. I'm not suggesting unequivocally that there is not a terrorism component—goodness knows that there is enough of that going around these days. But aside from Donna's comment, we have not seen anything concrete to suggest that."

"The sheriff did show me some video," Jack said. "Surveillance tapes from Alex's resort. They showed a number of customers that appeared to be Middle Eastern. And it looked to me, judging by the date stamps, that some of these gentlemen might have gained some substantial frequent flyer bonus points."

"Initially, they looked interesting to us as well. But they all checked out. One group of the men were IT specialists from Traverse City. They came up here periodically to service equipment for a local company. The owner of the company knew your brother-in-law, and liked to stay at his resort. One or more of them made half a dozen such trips over the past two years—three such visits were documented on the tapes.

"Regarding the two other cases—we cannot demonstrate any terrorist connection."

"So, you have no additional suspects? Or theories?"

"If we were close to making an arrest, I still wouldn't talk to you about it. But that is just not the case. There are several leads that we are following up on, but there has not been a break in the case."

"Is there anything to tie Donna's death to the explosion out on Sugar Island—the one that blew up the emergency vehicle that was transporting the sheriff's body?"

"Are you suggesting there's a connection?"

"From my experience in Chicago, both explosions appeared to be fairly sophisticated."

"Is that how you would characterize them? As the work of a professional?"

"Well, they weren't rags in gas cans," Jack quipped. "Donna's car seemed to have been rigged with an incendiary device, while the emergency vehicle looked to be a combination, with either a timed or remote activator. I think it obvious that whoever built the devices knew what he was doing."

"I would agree."

"I have to tell you something, Special Agent. Yesterday I stopped in to visit Doctor Rex—he's a vet. I heard at a local coffee shop that he liked to go fishing with a group of friends who frequented Alex's resort. When I got there he was apparently gone. When I took a peek in the back window, it looked to me like his alarm system had possibly been rigged to trigger an explosive device when activated. I called Deputy Bill—don't recall his last name. I had met him earlier at the same coffee shop. I do have his card.

"Anyway, while I was on the phone with the deputy, the house was blown up. I suspect that Deputy Bill is about to inform you about it—if he hasn't already."

"He has contacted me with his suspicions. You think this house fire is also somehow related to your brother-in-law's murder?"

"I can deal with a certain level of coincidence, but the threshold of credulity has been crossed—at least in my mind it has. Too many explosions, too many people killed. My gut tells me there's likely a link. "

"We have taken that fire over as well. I don't know how it relates to the rest, but I also suspect it might.

"I'm pleased that you told me what you knew about it. I just hope you're being equally candid about everything else."

"Am I a suspect?"

"Certainly not in the death of your brother-in-law."

"But am I a suspect in any of these other so-called related crimes?"

"Should you be?"

"No, of course not. But if you're thinking that I am somehow involved in any of this, then this conversation is finished—and I would want a lawyer. I'm just saying, I would like to tell you what I know, and what I'm thinking, but not if you're considering me a person of interest in any of this."

"Well, you certainly are an interesting person, Jack Handler. But I do not consider you a suspect."

"That's refreshing," Jack said. "Now I have a question for you. What do you know about a boy they call 'Red'?"

"He keeps popping up, doesn't he?"

"Both literally and figuratively. But what do you know about him? As far as your case is concerned?"

"Well, first of all, the boy can't talk. I have requested the local authorities to pick him up, but so far they've come up dry. It's almost as though they would like to avoid the issue."

"Do you think he had something to do with the murder? Or any of the murders?"

"No, I doubt that. I want to bring him in for questioning, he might have seen something. Although I'm not so sure about how that would work out. I'll have to find a way to communicate with him. What do you know about the boy?"

"I have met him. He's seems to me to be above average intelligence. Has a problem talking, but that's strictly a physical issue. From what I've been told, the boy has had a tough life—tragically lost his parents several years ago. I've heard he spent a lot of time with Alex. Deputy Restin told me that in times past, they have tried to bring the boy in, but he always escapes. That was back when they were trying to place him in foster care—the boy wanted nothing to do with that. My gut tells me that he knows something about the murder. But if the wrong people get to him, he would be in danger."

"And who would those wrong people be?"

"That, Special Agent, would be the sixty-four-thousand-dollar question."

"Is there someone who looks good to you?"

"Not really. I have worked scores of homicides in Chicago. Never have I seen a case with so many unknowns, so many twists and turns. We don't even have a motive yet—much less a suspect. At least that's what you're telling me. If I had some notion as to why Alex was murdered, then I could start eliminating people. You suggest that it is not likely to be terror related. But how about drugs, or other contraband?

"The one thing that makes this location unique is its proximity to the Canadian border. Maybe that means something—maybe not. But right now, I haven't crossed any names off my list."

"That's right where we are on it as well. I've only had the case for a couple days. But before he was killed, Sheriff Northrup seemed to be leaning toward a Middle East connection. He gave me nothing beyond that. But the DHS, as I said, has now virtually ruled that out—at least as far as there being any *demonstrable* terrorism component.

"Of course, there could be a smuggling angle. But there is no evidence to suggest that either.

"I do have another question for you," Special Agent Lamar said, adjusting his posture a bit, and looking even more intently into Jack's eyes. "What do you know about a chopper that's been seen in and around Sugar Island lately?"

Chapter 64—Jack dodges inside fastball

Jack carefully weighed his words.

If this guy had any evidence about my involvement with that chopper, Jack reasoned, *he'd have picked me up immediately. He doesn't suspect that I actually was the guy that flew it to Canada. Still, I must be careful here. I really don't know how much he knows.*

"I did see a helicopter a couple of times—heard what I think was it on one or two other occasions. One of those times was on the pier with Deputy Restin the night the sheriff was killed—right before you arrived."

"That's what he said. Do you have any theories about it?"

"I've done some checking. You might look into a group of fishing enthusiasts who are trying to open a sports club in Canada. They leased a Bell 429 from a company based in Hamilton."

"That's exactly what it was—a Bell 429. It was crash landed on the Canadian side recently."

Jack looked directly into the Special Agent's eyes, affecting surprise. He did not want to appear as though this made him nervous.

"Any arrests?"

"No. Whoever crashed it got away. And it was based out of Hamilton—just as you suspected. We've not been able to round up the fellow who leased it."

"Any reason to suspect his involvement with the murder of Alex?"

"Sounds to me like you might have more information about this guy than I do—who is your contact? Where're you getting your info?"

"Just a buddy who used to work for the federal government—like you. He'd get in trouble if anyone found out he was helping me. I just had him do a search for Bell 429s in the area, and he came up with the one based out of Hamilton. That's all I know."

"What made you think it was a Bell 429?"

"The sound—twin jet engines. No other chopper sounds quite like that. Besides, the Bell 429 is the most popular helicopter that size."

"Well, that's exactly what it turned out to be. Canadian Border Patrol is going over it with a fine-tooth comb as we speak—if there's anything to be found, they'll get it."

"How'd they manage to elude Canadian and US Border Patrols? I know I saw it cross the border at least twice."

"Flew very low. I guess that's their secret. Also, they must have had some way to conceal it on Sugar Island. I'm not sure how they managed that either. But we won't be seeing it anymore. The Canadians have taken care of that."

Jack did not want to talk about the helicopter anymore. So he sought to change the direction of their conversation.

"As I understand it, most murders involve money, sex, and sometimes politics. So far, I have not been able to come up with a viable motive—regarding Alex's murder."

"I agree. If we had a motive nailed down, it would certainly help. But I don't think we're there yet. And until we figure that out—why someone would want him dead—we're sort of stuck on figuring out the who. ... Unless we get lucky."

Jack carefully weighed his next words.

"What if?" he asked. "What if there were to be several members of this community who were working together, for whatever reason? That is, what if Alex just happened to get in their way? Maybe he found out something he shouldn't have."

"Sounds like you have a theory."

"I wouldn't characterize it like that. I don't have a *theory*. But, I don't think I have ever known a man who was as honest and hardworking as my brother-in-law. He didn't think much of me, but that wasn't his fault. I had given him ample reason to hate me—at least in his mind. But a straighter arrow I have never known. I do not believe that he was involved in anything dishonest."

"How about a crime of passion? Did your brother-in-law have an eye for the ladies—perhaps the married ones?"

"That's possible. He never got married. I'm not sure why. He probably had his reasons. Back when my wife, his sister, and I were spending time at his resort, he was seeing someone. He didn't talk much about it. And he never introduced us. But from time to time he would say something that suggested he had a lady friend. What do you know about that? Did he have someone he was seeing?"

"We can't find anyone. The only person he was close to seemed to be that kid—Red."

"You're not suggesting that it was an unwholesome relationship, I hope."

"No. Certainly nothing like that," Special Agent Lamar said.

"You've probably already heard this," Jack said. "But after the boy's parents died, Alex pretty much treated him like his son. The kid spent every day doing something at the resort—usually having to do with the fishing boats in the summer, and the snow machines in the winter."

"I knew the boy worked there, but I was not aware of the significance of the relationship. Did Red move in? Did he live there, at the resort?"

"No," Jack replied. "From what I've been told, for some time the boy stayed at his parents' place, living in the barn—and sometimes in the woods nearby. But Children's Services removed him and placed him in foster care. And we all know how that worked out—he kept running away."

"What was Alex's involvement, at that time? Or did he get involved at all?"

"According to Restin, and Donna, Alex tried to adopt the boy, but he was not permitted to. When his attempt was rejected, he tried to be the boy's foster parent. Social workers didn't like that idea. It was nasty. Red just kept running away from the court-appointed homes the county found for him.

"Finally, Social Services just gave up on him and left him to fend for himself. While Red didn't actually live at the resort, apparently he stayed somewhere nearby. That made it possible for him to work with Alex."

"So, in a *de facto* sort of way, Alex did become Red's foster parent?"

"You could say that."

"I'd sure like to talk to that kid. Do you have any way of getting hold of him?"

"The kid's like a ghost. He comes and goes in the night, and he trusts no one. I think that he had a bit of a relationship with Donna. At least she used to put food out for him. In fact, I'm not if sure you are aware of this, but he was at the hotel the night Donna was killed."

"Really? Could he have witnessed the bombing?"

"Might have—he sure enough was in the area."

"You seem to have a lot of information about the boy. Why is that?"

"We discovered that someone had broken into our vehicle—just before Donna was killed. I thought it strange at the time that all that was missing was some junk food. So when I was talking to Donna, I asked her if she had any ideas. She suggested that it could have been this kid—Red. She thought it sounded like him—food only, and no damage done to the vehicle."

"If you wanted to talk to Red, where would you start looking?"

"Have you tried Sugar Island?"

"Tried it? We've combed the entire island—fifty square miles of it. But turned up nothing."

"Well, I think I would concentrate on the island. But like I said. The kid is like a ghost. He can avoid detection with the best of them."

"In most cases, there is family. And eventually a fugitive will seek out a familiar face. But the kid has no family. Just that dog of his."

Jack sat silently for a moment, and then asked, "What if I told you that the kid does have family?"

Chapter 65—Jack drops a bombshell

"If Red had family in the area, I think we would have found them. What makes you think you have better information than we do?"

"Just a theory, Special Agent, but I think that there is a fair chance that Alex was actually Red's biological father."

For the first time during the entire interview, Special Agent Lamar had heard something that surprised him, "Why do you think that?"

"I did a check, and his blood type matches Alex's. So, I sent in a sample of the kid's blood for an expedited DNA—my buddies at the department should let me know soon. But, my detective's intuition strongly suggests that is the case."

"So, that would make you family?"

"Actually my daughter Kate would be Red's blood cousin—that is, if I'm right."

"You're suggesting that Alex had an extramarital affair with his desk clerk. If that were the case, why'd he keep quiet about it—when he was trying to adopt the boy?"

"Don't know exactly why Alex handled it the way he did. But my guess is that he was trying to save the reputation of the boy's supposed father—the mother's husband. If he were to have spelled it out, then it would have cast the boy's Native American heritage in a bad light. Alex was a piece of work—strong old-country values. I know he would have done what he could to preserve Red's reputation, and the reputation of the boy's family.

"Another possibility for his secrecy might have been to protect himself from retribution. Or to protect his resort from bad publicity. I never was able to follow Alex's rationale in other matters either. I think he intended to do what he could to raise and train the boy, and then, eventually, bring him into the company. That way he would not have to adopt him, or declare that he was the real father.

"And that would help explain why he left his entire estate to Kate—knowing that she and I would eventually figure it out, and make sure the boy was protected."

"If you are correct, Red would be your nephew."

"Right. Please understand, I have not yet told Kate about this. I'm waiting on the DNA. But I'm telling you now, anticipating your discretion. I will let you know the results of the DNA testing—one way or the other."

"That's an interesting theory—Alex naming your daughter in the will and all, anticipating that somehow you two would figure out that Red was his son, and end up ensuring his ongoing care. It would seem that he would be leaving too much to chance. What's to say that your daughter won't sell the resort?"

"Of course, that was always a possibility. But the way Alex set it up—by putting the resort in a trust, with his attorney as the trustee, Kate will have no inheritance tax. He apparently had good management in place. Theoretically, Kate could oversee the business from New York, and leave the day-to-day operation in the hands of those on site—which eventually would involve Red. At least, that's how I'm beginning to see it. And, if I'm correct, Alex will have left more information regarding Red, perhaps in his private papers. Can't be sure about it at this point. But I do think it's an angle worth following up.

"Of course, nothing would suggest that Alex anticipated his own death. I am quite certain about that—Alex's murder came as a surprise to him."

"Does this business with the boy lead to motive—in your mind?" Special Agent Lamar asked.

"I don't see how. To this point, the family of the mother's husband has been virtually non-existent. They have either chosen not to participate in Red's life, or there are no close relatives residing in this area. From what I can surmise, the latter is the case."

"Well, one thing for sure, you've got my attention with your theory—or, story. Now I *really* want to talk to the boy."

"Good luck with that," Jack chuckled.

Kate had finished shopping and had returned to the hotel. She was seated in the eating area having coffee, and anxiously awaiting the return of her father. She had both her cell phone, and Jack's. Her father's phone was the first to vibrate.

"Hello. This is Kate, Jack's daughter. My father is tied up right now —he asked me to take his calls."

The voice at the other end identified himself as an old friend of her father's and told her he had some information that Jack had requested.

"Really?" Kate responded, as the voice at the other end explained. "And how long ago did that take place? And no arrests were ever made? Is this something that Dad suspected?"

When the caller said that as far as he knew, this was a possibility that Jack had considered, but for which he was seeking confirmation. She thanked him and then asked if there was anything else."

"Not yet," the man said, "but I will call back when and if I have more information."

Kate set her coffee down on the table and stared blankly into space.

Chapter 66—Kate receives a text message

As Kate sat there thinking about what the caller had told her on her father's phone, her own phone began to vibrate, indicating a new text message—from an unknown texter. She did not recognize the 603 area code, much less the rest of the phone number. So, she almost didn't view it.

But then she remembered that she had given Red the cell phone she had picked up at the fishing lodge in Canada. And she taught Red how to text her in an emergency.

"Kate you there?"

"Red! RUOK?"

"At resort."

"Y?"

"Found Gabby on phone. Man shoot Alex arrest me before. Never shut up. So text him to meet at resort. He did with a man."

"Can you stay hidden, omw"

"Think so."

"who is w him?"

"Don't know. But friends."

"Describe Gabby"

"Name tag Restin."

"how'd you get in? Front door?"

"Window. They came in back door."

"How should I get in?"

"Use back door be careful they are bad."

"Omw. Take battery out of phone"

"ok"

Kate could not tell, but Red's last response was delivered through tears. Not since his mother died had anyone treated him in such a tender, loving way. While he never doubted that Alex cared for him, the old Greek emigrant was by nature a gruff man. As he popped open the cell phone he nearly dropped it, because his hands were slick from the deluge of snot and tears he had wiped from his freckled face.

And even though Kate was by now a seasoned big-city homicide detective, she, too, was fighting back tears.

"Hang on, darlin'. Be very careful. I'll get there as quickly as I can!" This she said aloud, for her own benefit.

Now, this is going to be a challenge, she thought, as she prepared for her rescue mission to Sugar Island.

Her father had their vehicle, and she had his cell phone. She quickly pulled out Special Agent Lamar's card, and dialed the number.

"Kate Handler here. My father Jack Handler is meeting with Special Agent Lamar—this is an emergency. Could you get my father on the phone?"

Reluctantly the agent answering the call put her through to Special Agent Lamar.

"Your father is here with me, but we are busy."

"This is an emergency. I need to talk to him immediately."

Special Agent Lamar sneered, but did hand the phone to Jack. It took only a very few seconds for Kate to make her point.

Jack terminated the call and handed the phone back to Lamar, "I'm sorry, but my daughter has a personal emergency. I need to pick her up right away. I hope you can appreciate my haste. You've made it clear that you are not going to hold me. You will be the first person I talk to if something comes up."

"We're not finished here! Sit back down."

"You'll have to arrest me then. But I've got personal business to attend to. I promise I'll be in touch."

"Don't leave town," Special Agent Lamar insisted, as Jack left the building.

"Not about to—thanks for your understanding."

While their conversation was brief, Kate made it clear that she was headed to Sugar Island for an important matter, and that Jack should pick her up on the way. They had both grown familiar enough with the city to know that if Kate made it to the bottom of the hill, and headed east on Easterday toward Ashmun, that it would take her father only few extra seconds at most to pick her up. And if she ran, she could even make it all the way to Ashmun—that would even save more time.

She ran. Not only did she make it to Ashmun before her father, she sprinted an additional two blocks before spotting his speeding SUV approaching from the south.

Jack slammed on his brakes and skidded to the curb.

"What's going on?" Jack asked, as Kate jumped in.

"Red is at the resort. And so is Restin, and another man. Red ID'd Restin as the shooter, in Alex's murder. They are in Uncle Alex's office on the island right now."

"How'd he manage that?"

"I don't know all the details, but Red managed to entice Restin out using the cell phone I gave him. One of the stored numbers on the phone was called "Gabby." Red recalled that the killer talked a lot, so he texted him to go to the resort. That's where we come in."

"Who's he got with him? At the resort?"

"Don't know. But I would not be surprised if it were the doc. He's without a house right now, and it sure smells like he's involved."

"The kid's in a lot of trouble. Restin is an experienced officer. Chances are that Restin will quickly conclude that it's a setup. And given enough time, he'll figure out that he's got unwanted company."

"Red did not tell me he brought the murder weapon with him. So once Restin figures out that it was Red who lured him there, he'll find the kid. He'll then force Red to give it up—make him take them to it. And once they get their hands on it, they'll have no need to keep Red alive. We've gotta hurry."

Jack swung his vehicle around and headed full speed toward Sugar Island. He and Kate sat silently for over a minute. Finally, Kate broke the silence, "I've got an idea."

Chapter 67—Kate's plan

Deputy Restin walked over to the rear sliding glass door and motioned with his head that Doc Rex should move in close to him.

"Doc. Don't you think it's a bit odd that Slim insisted I meet him here, and then he don't show?" Restin whispered.

The doctor looked up at Restin and nodded. Restin was at least six inches the taller of the two.

"I'm thinking this could be a setup," Restin said.

"By who?"

"Good question. We haven't heard from Slim since he went after that kid—Red. And we know that the Handlers have been hanging around the kid.

"Could be Slim loaded my number in his cell, and then lost it. Slim's such an idiot. I told all of you not to load numbers. But he's a fool. He has to do things his own stupid way."

"Who do you think has it? Handler?"

"Possibly. Could even be the kid. And if so, then he's probably here right now—maybe waiting for help."

"Hiding?"

"Yup. And if help is coming, we need to find him and do it quickly."

"Can we call Slim and listen for the ring?"

"That could work, but he probably turned it off. I think I have another way. Let's do this. Follow my lead."

Restin took a step to the side and checked his watch.

"We've waited long enough," he said loudly. "Something must have happened to Slim. Let's get outta here."

"Maybe we'll pass him on the way out."

With that, both men left the resort through the slider, and closed it behind them. They then turned left and headed around the building toward where they had parked the patrol car.

Once out of sight, Restin said, "Let's give him a few seconds to power back up. He'll want to alert whoever he's been calling."

Carefully Restin peered through a side window.

"There he is—hiding under the bar. I can see the reflection of the cell in the mirror. Let's go get him."

* * *

"What are you thinking?" Jack asked Kate.

"It's gonna take us a bit to get to the resort," Kate said. "Pretty good chance that Restin will have captured Red. We could split up—you take the resort, and I'll wait for them at Red's hideout. Restin's gonna want that gun, and if we're late, that's where they'll be headed."

Just then Kate's cell signaled an incoming text message. All she received, however, was, "They're le—"

"Hey, kid, good to see you again," Restin said, snatching the phone from Red, and smashing it on the floor beneath his size thirteen boot.

* * *

Jack thought for a moment, then looked over at his daughter.

"I'll drop you off on the road close to Red's hideout—you're going to have to cover a lot of real estate. And keep in mind, Restin is a very dangerous man."

"I totally realize that."

Chapter 68—Red captured

"You've got something that belongs to me, and now you're gonna give it back. I know you live around here, someplace. And I'll bet that's where you've got it. I'm gonna make it easy for you. All you have to do is take us to it, and we will let your friends live. Otherwise, we will kill them. Get me the gun, and they live. Do you understand me?"

Red nodded affirmatively. Restin had pushed the right button this time. Red would not relinquish the gun to save himself, but would do anything to save his friends—especially Kate.

"It's at your place, isn't it?" Restin asked, securing Red's hands behind him with a zip tie. He squashed it tightly on Red's wrists, cutting off the blood, and nearly forcing his right wrist out of its socket.

Red struggled to loosen the zip tie, but without success. He then nodded his head yes.

Restin then grabbed a fistful of Red's hair and commanded, "Then let's go get it done."

He lifted Red off the floor by his hair and swung him around the corner of the bar, shoving him across the room toward the slider. Red fell on his face, opening a wide cut on his freckled left cheek. Restin lifted him to his feet, again by the hair. Blood was dripping from Red's chin by the time they reached the door.

"We can walk from here, right?" Restin asked. "I don't want you bleeding in my car."

Red again nodded his head yes. While it was true that Restin did not want any of Red's DNA in his car, he also wanted to avoid being seen driving around with the boy.

"Okay, kid, you lead the way."

Red knew it was over—Restin exuded an aura of confidence the others lacked. Red was ready to turn over the gun. He knew he would be killed once he did, but he believed Restin would kill Kate if he did not.

"You were texting Kate, weren't you?" Restin asked.

Red shook his head no.

"Liar! All I can say is that if you don't get me that gun, right now, your precious Kate is going to die a very nasty death. You want to save her, don't you?"

This time Red responded with an enthusiastic nod.

"Good boy. Then you lead the way—and quickly."

* * *

Jack and Kate reached the ferry just before it pulled out. Neither Jack nor Kate spoke again until they reached Kate's drop off point. All Jack was able to think about was the day Kate's mother was killed—by bullets intended for him. He had lived with that guilt for nearly thirty years. Now he was placing his daughter in danger. Sure, she was a seasoned detective. But Jack knew that when bullets started flying, people often died—even the best of detectives.

"Have you got it from here?"

"Sure do."

"What are you carrying?"

"Glock 10mm."

"How many clips?"

"Two."

"Backup?" Jack asked, pretty sure that Kate did not have one.

"No."

"Take this," Jack said, handing his puzzled daughter a fully-loaded five-shot Airweight.

"I'll come in from behind, if it shakes out like you think. Sooner if I hear anything. So try to find a safe position. Remember, this guy, Restin, while he comes off like a Barney Fife, he's a stone-cold killer, with all the skills of a veteran cop."

"I'm good on that. My focus is saving Red—just like you."

Jack pulled to the side, and Kate jumped out. Their eyes met briefly, but no smiles or additional words were exchanged. They each etched in their memory what they understood might be the last time they would see each other alive.

Her door barely closed before Jack sped away.

Kate immediately burst into a sprint, much like a runner at the end of a 5K. She figured that Red would be leading Restin in from nearly the opposite direction, so she did not have to concern herself with detection, at least until she neared Red's hideout.

Even though it was Kate's idea to split up, Jack was uneasy about having her head alone directly into Red's hideout. Because that was Restin's presumed destination, her task was fraught with more danger than was his. *But it was* her *plan,* he reasoned. *And she is very good at what she does.*

By the time Jack arrived at the resort, it was clear that Kate had been right—Restin and the doc had already cleared out. The blood on the floor, and on the deck outside the slider, did not escape Jack's attention.

"Cinch that's Red's blood. Not a good sign."

Jack knew exactly what to do. He double checked his Glock, and confirmed that his Walther .380 was ready—safety on.

He then headed in haste toward Red's hideout.

A few drops of fresh blood on the front parking lot confirmed that he was in hot pursuit.

"I've got to catch up with them before they reach Kate," he said aloud.

While he did move quickly through the brush, he had to exercise caution not to come up behind them too quickly, as that would surrender the element of surprise.

Kate reached the hideout entrance, and then took a few seconds to survey the site. It was impossible to discern whether or not Restin had arrived before she did.

Kate could be confident only that Restin was not approaching the hideout right then, but it was possible that he was already inside.

She scrutinized the approach and determined that there were no fresh tracks leading into Red's hideout.

It was at that point that Kate made her first mistake. She reasoned that *Red would not take the time to brush out the tracks this time—therefore they must not have arrived yet.*

But she couldn't gamble on waiting outside. "What if they did beat me here—as soon as Restin gets his hands on that gun, Red's dead—simple as that."

So, she pulled on the rope that opened the entrance. She took a long look inside, and decided to proceed.

She then lowered the gate to its natural position, and quietly made her way toward the spot where Red had buried the gun.

But before she reached it, she felt a crushing blow on the back of her head. And then everything went dark.

Doc Rex had stuffed a rag into Red's mouth to keep him silent, and Deputy Restin had hammered her over the head with a shovel.

Kate was stunned, but not entirely out.

Her whole body tingled.

She landed face down on the ground, her head in the hole where Red had buried Buddy. Restin had arrived at the hideout before she did, and he was savvy enough to wipe out his tracks.

Her Glock had gone flying when she was clubbed on the back of the head. She felt a tug on her midsection—that signaled she was also losing her backup weapon—the Smith and Wesson Airweight. The pressure of her body pushing on her stomach, and the obvious concussion, made her want to throw up. She fought it.

"Look, kid. That's your dog. I want my gun. I know you have it. You see what can happen when I don't get what I want. Take your precious girlfriend here. Not very pretty now, is she?"

Restin then grabbed Red by the upper arm, and made him look closely at Kate.

"There, get a good look."

The blood from the back of her head was now streaming down her face, and dripping off her nose.

"Don't worry, kid. She ain't dead—at least not yet. It's up to you—she doesn't *have* to die. … And neither do you. Not if you give me what's mine."

Then, pushing Red to his knees, and shoving his face down to within inches of Kate, he told the boy, "Check it out. Right now she's gonna have one horrible headache. But unless you quit messing with me, I'm gonna have to hurt her worse—much worse. And it will all be your fault. It doesn't have to end like this."

Red was sobbing. He placed his right hand on Kate's back. She could feel it.

"Ain't nothing gonna convince you I mean business?" Restin shouted at Red. "What do I have to do to her to make you think I'm serious?"

He then lifted Red up by his arm, and flung him back away from the hole.

"Maybe if I cut a few of her fingers off, then maybe you'll find the gun for me," Restin said, walking over to pick up the shovel.

This is my chance, Kate thought.

Knowing Restin had turned his back on her, she forced her hand into the soft earth beneath Buddy's partially exposed body until she touched the plastic bag containing the .22 caliber pistol.

This has to work perfectly, or we're both dead, she thought.

Restin was still walking toward the shovel and had not yet detected her movement.

She slid the bag out from under the dog, felt around for the grip and trigger.

No time to remove it from the bag, she concluded. *Got to get a round off through the bag.*

She could not be sure that there was even a round left in the cylinder. She did know that her father would not have tampered with the gun when he buried it, so if there were bullets in it when Red gave it to him, they would still be there.

Restin had just picked up the shovel and was walking back over to where Kate was lying. He was not expecting to see her moving, so when she looked over her shoulder at him, he was caught by surprise.

"Well, I'll be damned! I guess you're begging to taste my shovel again!"

Kate was holding the bagged pistol in her left hand, and she was right-handed. But she knew that she had no time to switch it.

Forcing her shaking finger against the plastic, she struggled to pierce the bag with her index finger to engage the trigger. But the strength of her off hand was not sufficient to do the job.

She spun around to her back. This maneuver provided a little more space between her and Restin, and it allowed her to use her right index finger.

Still, she could not force her finger through the plastic.

"Well, what do ya know. The bloody princess is waking up. And, do you believe this? I'll bet that's my gun in the bag. Right, honey? I guess it was there all the time. … Now, just hand it over to me, and I'll be on my way."

Kate continued to force her fingernail against the tough plastic while at the same time extending her arm out as though to hand the gun to Restin.

Just as he reached down to accept it, her nail knifed through the plastic, and she squeezed the trigger.

But nothing happened when the hammer came down. It either misfired, or it was on an empty chamber.

Chapter 69—The final battle begins

"You tried to shoot me! You just had your last chance!"

Restin took one step toward Kate, raised the shovel over his head, and prepared to crush her skull.

Red saw his opportunity. He shot forward. With all of his might, he buried his shoulder as deeply as he could into the big man's back.

The blow was sufficient to dislodge the shovel, and knock Restin to his knees right in front of Kate.

The hundreds of thousands of miles in a patrol car had taken its toll on Restin's back. For years, Restin had tried to conceal his condition. He did his best to hide it so he could retire with full pension. But Red's surprise attack, right in the pit of his back, clearly hurt him.

"Enough of this!" Restin shouted, pulling his service revolver out of his holster and pointing it at Red, who was sprawled face down right behind him.

As Restin turned to shoot Red, Kate gave the .22 one more try. This time it fired. The round struck Restin in the bicep of his shooting arm, paralyzing his hand and forcing him to drop his weapon.

As he turned in shock to face Kate, her next round struck him squarely in the center of his forehead, killing him instantly.

She then turned her attention to Dr. Rex. Up to this point, he had been content to remain silent.

"Drop the gun, Kate," he said from his position to her left. She looked over at him and saw that he was pointing the S&W Airweight at her. Even though the gun had only a two-inch barrel, she knew he would not miss her at that distance. Besides, she was not sure that she had any more rounds left in the .22.

"Give me the gun," he demanded. "Actually, just drop it where you are. No point making this more messy than it already is."

"Doc, how ya doin'?"

It was Jack. He had just arrived from the resort and had taken a position directly behind Doc Rex.

"Don't be stupid, doc. Right now you haven't killed anyone. You will only do a little time—especially if you help us out. I need you to drop that gun right now. If your finger twitches at all on the trigger—you're dead. I'm going to shoot you through the shoulder, then in the gut. And I'll let you bleed out. No mercy. You've got three seconds—one, two, …"

Dr. Rex knew just how painful those wounds would be, and he wanted no part of facing that sort of death. He immediately dropped the Airweight on the ground, turning toward Jack as he did.

"Please don't shoot me. I didn't want any of this. It just got out of hand. I'll tell you everything I know. But please don't kill me."

Jack smiled at him, and then nailed him with a stiff left cross, instantly knocking him unconscious. Jack then picked up the gun and blew the sand out of it.

"You okay, Kitty?"

"I'm fine. I am a little surprised that you didn't shoot him."

"He barely even had the gun pointed at you. And I'd bet he's never fired one before. Besides, the Airweight is a *double* action. It requires a full draw on the trigger. Had his finger even moved I'd have nailed him."

Kate glared at her father, feigning an exaggerated sardonic smile.

"It did feel pretty good to lay him out—I will admit that. Red, you okay, too?"

The boy looked up at Jack, smiled, and nodded his head.

"We've had a big day," Kate said, going over to Red and scooping him up in her arms.

"You, my little darling, saved my life," she said, pulling the boy to her and holding him.

Red took a deep breath, stared straight ahead, but did not move.

Jack bent over the doc, rolled him onto his stomach, and with his own belt secured his hands behind him.

"I can't wait to start explaining all this to Lamar," Jack quipped.

"Do you think this is it?" Kate asked. "Have we got them all?"

"One thing for sure, Restin is the one who shot Alex. And he's dead. There are some loose ends. I think we may have at least one or two more major players left."

"Besides the doc?"

"I'm pretty certain of it."

"Who do you suspect?"

"I think there were four of them—initially. Doc here, Restin, and Joey, the fellow from the coffee shop."

"You said four—who would the fourth one be?"

"I think your father is referring to me, darlin'," said another tall man who had just entered Red's courtyard—in his latex-covered left hand he held a Smith and Wesson .357 service revolver, which he pointed at Jack.

Chapter 70—The visitor no one expected

"Sheriff!" Kate exclaimed. "We thought you were dead!"

"Well, as you can see," the sheriff said with a chuckle, "that rumor greatly exaggerates my condition."

The sheriff walked over to Jack, and said, "Lay down on your stomach and extend your arms straight over your head, palms down on the ground. … You know the drill."

The nice sheriff that Jack and Kate had met and liked was now all business.

"I need your guns, Jack."

The sheriff proceeded to reach under Jack, remove his Glock, and then yank his pants leg up, revealing the leg holster where Jack carried his Walther .380. He unsnapped the holster and removed that firearm as well.

"This looks like your jacket," he said to Jack, reaching into the hole and yanking Jack's jacket off Buddy's body. "What's it doing here?"

Once the sheriff had the jacket, he promptly wrapped it around the .380. Kate knew what was about to happen, and she covered Red's eyes with her hand.

Sheriff Northrup placed the jacket-covered pistol to the back of the doc's head, and fired. He then fired a second shot—this one into the back of the dying man, stopping his still-beating heart.

"Only two of you left, now," Jack said. "That will dramatically increase your share."

"So, Mr. Big-City Detective—you've got it all figured out. ... Actually, I'm the *last* one. Poor Joey couldn't handle the pressure. He hanged himself earlier today. Right there in the kitchen of his little coffee shop. Too bad, I liked him."

"What are those paintings valued at, anyway? There can't be that many potential buyers. So, just tell me, how much are you going to sell them for?"

"You really do have it all figured out, don't you?

"Five hundred mil., rounded off. And, we've already made delivery, and the money is deposited. I suppose that would make me the richest man you've ever met."

The sheriff was very proud of the deal he had made. It is always very difficult to find buyers for stolen art, particularly when the works were painted by such notables as Rembrandt, Vermeer, Degas and Manet. Usually, the people putting up the money for such works are actually renting the pieces, because eventually the works end up coming back to the legitimate owners—sometimes decades or even centuries later.

"I actually got more for them than they would have brought at auction," the sheriff boasted.

"Foreign buyer? Is that right?" Jack asked. "Middle Eastern?"

"You guessed it—Dubai, to be specific. You must have been a great detective."

Kate still had Red's eyes covered. She knew that within the minute they would all be dead. Unless something dramatic happened.

"Where's Restin's service revolver?" the sheriff asked. "Only fitting that he gets to be the fall guy. After all, I'm already dead, you know."

Red began to stir. Peeking beneath Kate's hand, with his left foot he hooked the plastic bag containing the .22 that Restin had used to kill

Alex, and that Kate had then used to shoot him.

Slowly and quietly he slid it on the dirt up to where he could reach it with his hand. Kate felt him stirring, and knew he was up to something. Carefully he placed the bag against Kate's left hand.

The sheriff looked around until he spotted Deputy Restin's firearm, and bent over to pick it up.

Kate's mind raced. She knew she had to act decisively. She picked up the bag and again felt around until she found the handgrip. Not immediately locating the trigger hole she had poked in the plastic earlier, she exerted all the strength in her finger until she had stretched the plastic enough to possibly allow her some access through the trigger guard.

"Sheriff, you're gonna probably want this, right?" she said, extending the bag out toward Sheriff Northrup, still with her left hand.

"Well, I'll be. That would be the gun Restin used on your uncle, I'd bet. You can just lay it down on the ground, darlin'. I'll get it a little later. Right now I have some other business to attend to."

Kate had no idea how many rounds remained in the pistol—if any. She knew that Restin had shot her uncle twice and that she had used two rounds on Restin. That should leave two, or even perhaps three if the pistol was a seven shot model.

She also knew that experienced shooters would often rest the hammer on an empty chamber as a safety precaution. That could mean there would only be one round left in the gun—if that.

Knowing that a .22 does not have much knockdown power, she determined that because her first round just might be the only one she would get off, it had to be placed perfectly. So, instead of firing from an awkward position, with her left hand, she released Red entirely and flipped over on her stomach.

Sheriff Northrup knew immediately what she was doing, and he raised Restin's pistol to shoot her.

Even though Jack could not see Kate, he knew what was going down. So he did the only thing he could from his position on the ground.

Spinning around, he kicked the sheriff in the right knee. The impact caused Sheriff Northrup to fire prematurely, missing wildly.

Now gripping the .22 in her right hand, Kate steadied it with her left and began firing as many rounds as she could.

Pop. Pop. Pop.

Her first round caught the sheriff squarely in the middle of his forehead. His gun slipped out of his hand as he began to die.

Her next two rounds struck him in his chest.

Kate continued pulling the trigger as Sheriff Northrup fell to the ground, but no bullets remained in the chamber.

Kate then jumped up, grabbing Red and lifting him to his feet. She did not say a word to him or her father until the two of them were outside Red's compound.

Once safe, and away from the carnage, she sat down on the ground, leaned up against a tree, and drew Red to her again.

"You are safe now, darling Red. I promise. No one can hurt you anymore. I promise you. No one even *wants* to hurt you anymore. And I'm here to protect you ... forever. I promise."

Jack then walked up to them.

"Kitty, I think you should let me mop up. I think it's time to get Lamar in here, and this kid out—he's been through enough.

"Why don't you take him back to our vehicle, and show him his surprise."

"Great idea," Kate said, "Come on, Red. I've got something to show you."

Jack watched them walk away, and then he returned to Red's compound. He glanced over the three dead bodies. "No point of even trying to tidy this mess up—I'll leave that for the Feds."

Jack then entered Red's shack and sat down on Red's sleeping bag. *This is where Red slept the night Alex was murdered.* He pondered that thought for several moments.

After replaying all the events of the past week in his mind, he took out his cell.

"Special Agent Lamar? Jack Handler here. I've got a present for you. I think you're going to like it. Where am I? Well, I'm on Sugar Island. Let's see, maybe I can tell you *exactly* where on the island."

Jack then took out his hand-held Garmin 62 STC, and read the co-ordinates to Special Agent Lamar.

"There, that should do it … and bring some body bags—three of them. Who died? All the bad guys. Red is here with us, and he's okay. And Kate is fine. Just the bad guys have passed on."

Jack then walked out to the entry point of the compound, and released the bush that covered the opening.

There. I guess we'll see just how competent our junior J. Edgar is at using his GPS. … I just can't believe he's calling my perfectly fine chopper landing, a crash landing. I sure hope Kate never hears about that.

Jack smiled broadly as he looked around, *I wonder where Red pees around here …*

But before Jack located an appropriate tree on which to relieve himself, his cell phone vibrated. It was a call from Pam Black, Reg's widow. Reg was short for Reginald—Jack's best friend and most trusted associate. Reg had been shot less than a year earlier during a successful effort to free Kate from a group of rogue international agents.

"Exhume Reg's body! Who's behind that—and why? They can't do that without your permission. Pam, I'm just winding up a case here in

Michigan. I think you should put the brakes on. Let's talk more about this later."

Jack knew that to exhume Reg's body would be to open old wounds. *Why would anyone want to dig poor Reg up?* Jack wondered. *I'll bet Allison has something to do with it.*

Allison was the former First Lady who had hired Reg and Jack to assassinate the sitting president. But, instead of carrying out the plot, they secretly sabotaged it, even though Reg had accepted full payment—one hundred million dollars in gold.

She's got to be very angry to have lost that fortune, Jack surmised. *And she's probably following up on every lead she can, trying to get back her money.*

Jack also had an interest in the gold, because he never received his share of the payment. He had consoled himself with the satisfaction that their efforts saved the life of the President, but Jack never liked to work for free—Reg had told him his share would be at least ten million.

The last time Jack saw his friend was the day he and Reg stormed the hideout of a group of rogue agents in New York—the agents had been holding Kate hostage. During the ensuing melee, all of the kidnappers were killed, and both Kate and Reg were shot.

Roger Minsk, who had been assisting them, declared Reg dead of his wounds, and arranged to have Kate removed to a hospital, where she made a full recovery. Roger also spirited Jack away, to keep him out of trouble.

Jack requested, and received, Reg's clothing. It was in a pocket of that clothing that Jack found a bloody note. Jack had since always carried a copy of that note with him. It appeared to be a coded message. Jack did not attempt to decipher it at the time, as he felt that he really needed to get out of town. But, in the back of his mind, he suspected that Reg had left it for him to find and that its plaintext would somehow eventually point him to where the gold was hidden.

Jack suspected that Allison was now in hot pursuit of that gold, and that she might be behind the proposed exhumation of Reg's body—just what she thought she would discover by so doing, Jack didn't have a clue.

Jack then removed his billfold from his pocket and pulled out an image of the bloodied handwritten puzzle he had found in Reg's pocket. He studied it for a moment, smiled, and then returned it.

"One of these days," he said aloud, "… one of these days I'm going to have to see about that puzzle. I'm sure Reg left it there for me to find."

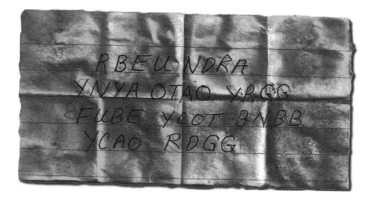

Chapter 71—Red meets a new friend

The two of them, Kate and Red, stood to their feet. While Red's head had quit bleeding, the drying blood had left a brown labyrinth of tracks almost totally covering his freckled face.

Kate wrapped her arm around the boy's shoulder as they headed back to the resort where Jack had parked his vehicle.

"Your foot gonna be good enough for this trip?" Kate asked.

Red nodded.

She knew the boy needed to get away, and that even if his foot was broken he'd somehow tough it out.

Neither of them looked back.

When they drew within sight of the buildings, Red started to lead them toward the river where the boats would normally be tied. But Kate tugged him back to where Jack had parked.

As they walked through the resort's drop-off area, Kate observed Red's inordinate interest in the resort's impressive front entry. So she led the two of them past the yellow ribbons that still cordoned off the area and right up to the locked glass doors.

Red stopped directly in front of them. Pressing his face against the tinted glass, he studied the front desk where his mother had worked. Even though he had never walked through those doors, he recalled his father driving past them close enough so that he could wave to his mother inside.

Kate could see that he was emotionally riveted.

Tears again began flowing down Red's freckled face, making new paths through the blood and dirt. Using his sleeve to wipe his dripping nose, he smeared blood and tears across his right cheek.

As Red stood staring unfocused in the direction of the front desk, Kate gently squeezed his shoulder. She knew something big was going on in his mind, but she did not know what it was.

After what felt like an emotional eternity to Kate, Red unconsciously pulled his right hand out of his pocket and slowly waved at a vision of his mother. When he realized what he was doing, he immediately turned toward Kate and hugged her tightly.

Kate could feel Red's hot face on her chest, the moisture of his tears soaking through to her skin.

She turned her head slightly, and placed her cheek on top of the boy's head. The ferrous scent of Red's blood, freshly released by his tears, moved her deeply.

After a moment, Kate pulled back enough to talk to Red.

"I've got something to show you. I want you to come with me. Okay?"

The boy was ready to move on. He had no idea what was in store for him, but he knew he could trust Kate. Besides, he remained embarrassed by his outburst of emotion.

Maybe they've bought me some clothes, Red was thinking. *I'll pretend that I like them—can't hurt Kate's feelings. But I'm perfectly happy with the clothes I have.*

The closer he got to Jack's SUV, the more he rehearsed his feigned gratitude.

Finally, when the two of them were about ten feet away, Kate said, "This'll do. You wait right here. ... In fact, I want you to turn your back to the car."

Kate then physically turned Red around so that he was facing away from the SUV, which had all the windows open a few inches.

"Stay right there—don't move," she said, as she approached the rear door of the vehicle.

When she got close, a six-month-old golden retriever stood up inside a kennel that filled the whole back seat. The huge puppy stretched and whimpered, as startled puppies do. He had obviously been sleeping.

When Red heard a little yelp, he spun himself around.

With barely two hops, the puppy greeted Red's chest with his front paws. The force of the impact knocked Red back a couple steps.

The love affair had begun between this boy and his new best friend.

Once Red regained his balance, he entangled all ten fingers in the puppy's long mane, and then fell to his knees so he could hug the dog.

"I know that Buddy here will never take the place of *your* Buddy," Kate said. "But I can see that he really likes you."

Red did not respond at first. He was totally engrossed. Even though Buddy was still only a puppy, physically he was nearly full grown.

Red released Buddy from his hug, sat down on the ground and leaned backward on his two outstretched arms.

Buddy went nuts.

First he backed off slightly. But then he began running around Red, barking playfully as he did it.

He then pounced toward Red, stopping only a foot or two from Red's feet. Placing his head between his front paws, he looked up at Red and yelped.

Red understood the language. He knew Buddy was saying, "Hey, kid, aren't you gonna play with me?"

Red lunged forward, slapping his hands palm down on the ground only inches from Buddy's front paws. The dog didn't flinch.

After a few seconds, Buddy jumped back up and scampered about fifteen feet away. Finding a stick, he brought it back and dropped it at Red's feet. But when Red reached for it, Buddy quickly snatched it up and retreated a few feet.

Looking directly into Red's smiling eyes, Buddy then snapped his head in the boy's direction, flinging the stick toward Red.

Buddy then placed his head between his paws again, and whined.

Finally, Red looked over at Kate, who stood motionless nearby. He placed all ten fingers on his chest, and let his pleading eyes ask the question.

"Yes, my cousin, Buddy is *your* puppy now," Kate said.

Red was ecstatic. He ran on all fours over to where Buddy had deposited his makeshift toy, and the fun continued.

Kate watched the two of them play for several moments. Finally, she realized just how strange she must appear.

My smile muscles are getting sore, she thought. *I don't ever recall that happening before.*

Kate bent her knees and dropped to her haunches. Then, allowing gravity to take over, she rolled backward on her rear end and kicked her legs forward until she had stretched out fully on her back.

Placing her hands under her head she stared through the high limbs into the cloudy UP sky.

Kate lay there for several more moments basking in the knowledge that she and her father had solved Alex's murder, saved Red, and that no one would be shooting at them anymore.

Lifting herself to her elbows, but still smiling, she again focused her attention on the boy frolicking with his dog.

Yes, Red, Kate thought, *Buddy will be your best friend forever. And you will be my favorite cousin, forever.*

And then she gleefully proclaimed, "But we are really going to have to do something about your texting skills!"

Chapter 72—How they tricked Border Patrol (Rest of Chapter 54)

When Jack and Kate were driving back into the United States from Canada, after commandeering (stealing), and subsequently crashing the helicopter, they realized that Border Patrol would be concerned about their not having the dog they initially entered Canada with.

That's when Kate came up with her plan:

"We could buy a dog—a four-year-old golden retriever. One that looks just like Buddy."

"You mean no shopping trip?" Jack replied.

"You could say that."

"I think that might be the best solution," Jack said. "But what if we took our time and bought Red a younger replacement for Buddy?"

"That's a great idea!" Kate declared. "You're thinking a puppy?"

"Why not," Jack agreed. "It's not as though they checked Buddy's passport or birth certificate when we entered. We'll just have to make sure the puppy has the necessary shots. We would have to declare him on the US side."

"Perhaps not," Kate said. "We could just use Dr. Rex's letter stating that our golden retriever had his vaccinations. I don't think they will even care on the Canadian side, as long as we're not trying to get a rebate."

"Worth a try," Jack agreed. "It would work best if we could find one nearly full grown—maybe four to six months."

"Exactly. But, I still think that it would be a good idea to buy a few clothes. So we would have something to declare. Maybe two, or three hundred dollars. That way they get their ounce of flesh."

"And that way you get some new clothes," Jack chuckled.

"That's right. But wouldn't you agree that it would be a good thing?"

"Actually I do think it might help—sort of a distraction—a misdirection," Jack said. "I'll drop you off at the store of your choice, and I'll see about finding a dog."

"I don't think so," Kate said, feverishly working her iPad. "I want to help you pick out Buddy's replacement. And I just located the breeder we need to talk to ... turn right at the next light."

Recent news tabloid report

Breaking News:

After more than two decades of virtual silence, new evidence has now emerged regarding one of the largest art heists in history.

An unnamed source within the FBI has informed this reporter that while none of these irreplaceable paintings stolen from a Boston gallery in 1990 have so far been recovered, they may be getting closer to solving the crime.

It appears that immediately after the paintings were stolen, the thieves transported them to a remote resort on Sugar Island, located off Sault Ste. Marie, in Michigan's Upper Peninsula.

There, posing as commercial decorators, the art thieves hid the treasures under the works of local photographers and painters that hung throughout the resort.

And recently, again according to my source, representatives of a foreign buyer were sent to the resort to retrieve the paintings.

It was during this effort that the owner of the resort—and four of the suspects—all met violent deaths. One of the suspects, a convicted Boston burglar who had moved to Sault Ste. Marie shortly after the heist, hanged himself in the coffee shop that he owned. The other three suspects were all shot and killed as law enforcement closed in.

Details of these shootings remain sketchy at this time.

Compounding the tragedy was the murder of Alex Garos, owner of the resort where the art had been hidden. According to what my investigators have learned, he was not involved in the heist. Nor was he even aware that the valuable paintings were hidden right under his nose.

Apparently he was killed when he became suspicious that guests had been tampering with some of the wall hangings at his resort.

My source also tells me that two of the suspects were former Boston police officers, and a third was a popular Boston veterinarian.

The forth alleged thief, the one who hanged himself, had a lengthy criminal record for high-end home invasions in and around the Boston area during the late 1980s.

While it is not known for certain at this time if or when others knowingly became involved in some sort of criminal conspiracy involving the stolen art, my source indicates that the FBI is convinced that only these four suspects were responsible for the original theft and subsequent stashing of the art.

Apparently all four of the suspects had moved to Sault Ste. Marie soon after the heist to be close to the treasures they had hidden. Unfortunately, the death of all four of them could make finding the stolen art much more difficult.

The paintings, which include works by Rembrandt, Vermeer, Degas, Flinck and Edouard Manet, are now estimated to be worth close to half a billion dollars on the international market.

My source did not disclose to me any information regarding the suspected location of the art at the present time. But it does appear that Interpol and various private entities are hot on the trail.

As I indicated at the beginning of this piece, this is a developing story. And it is a big one. So, whatever I learn from my sources over the coming days, weeks and months, I will immediately report to you—you can count on me for this.

Stay tuned!

What people are saying about the Jack Handler books

Top Shelf Murder Mystery—Riveting. Being a Murder-Mystery "JUNKIE" this book is definitely a keeper … can't put it down … read it again type of book … and it is very precise to the lifestyles in Upper Michigan. Very well researched. I am a resident of this area. His attention to detail is great. I have to rate this book in the same class or better than authors Michael Connelly, James Patterson, and Steve Hamilton. — Shelldrakeshores

Being a Michigan native, I was immediately drawn to this book. Michael Carrier is right in step with his contemporaries James Patterson and David Baldacci. I am anxious to read more of his work. I highly recommend this one! — J. Henningsen

A fast and interesting read. Michael ends each chapter with a hook that makes you want to keep reading. The relationship between father and daughter is compelling. Good book for those who like a quick moving detective story where the characters often break the "rules" for the greater good! I'm looking forward to reading the author's next book. — Flower Lady

Move over, Patterson, I now have a new favorite author, Jack and his daughter make a great tag team, great intrigue, and diversions. I have a cabin on Sugar Island and enjoyed the references to the locations. I met the author at Joey's (the real live Joey) coffee shop up on the hill, great writer, good stuff. I don't usually finish a book in the course of a week, but read this one in two sittings so it definitely had my attention. I am looking forward to the next installment. Bravo. — Northland Press

My husband is not a reader—he probably hasn't read a book since his last elementary school book report was due. But ... he took my copy of *Murder on Sugar Island* to deer camp and read the whole thing in two days. After he recommended the book to me, I read it—being the book snob that I am, I thought I had the whole plot figured out within the first few pages, but a few chapters later, I was mystified once again. After that surprise ending, we ordered the other two Getting to Know Jack books. — Erin W.

I enjoyed this book very much. It was very entertaining, and the story unfolded in a believable manner. Jack Handler is a likeable character. But you would not like to be on his wrong side. Handler made that very clear in *Jack and the New York Death Mask*. This book (Murder on Sugar Island) was the first book in the Getting to Know Jack series that I read. After I read *Death Mask*, I discovered just how tough Jack Handler really was.

I heard that Carrier is about to come out with another Jack Handler book—a sequel to *Superior Peril*. I will read it the day it becomes available. And I will undoubtedly finish it before I go to bed. If he could write them faster, I would be happy. — Deborah M.

I thoroughly enjoyed this book. I could not turn the pages fast enough. I am not sure it was plausible but I love the characters. I highly recommend this book and look forward to reading more by Michael Carrier. — Amazon Reader

An intense thrill ride!! — Mario

Michael Carrier has knocked it out of the park. — John

Left on the edge of my seat after the last book, I could not wait for the next chapter to unfold and Michael Carrier did not disappoint! I truly feel I know his characters better with each novel and I especially like the can-do/will-do attitude of Jack. Keep up the fine work, Michael, and may your pen never run dry! — SW

The Handlers are at it again, with the action starting on Sugar Island, I am really starting to enjoy the way the father/daughter and now Red are working through the mind of Michael Carrier. The entire family, plus a few more are becoming the reason for the new sheriff's increased body count and antacid intake. The twists and turns we have come to expect are all there and then some. I'm looking for the next installment already. — Northland Press

Finally, there is a new author who will challenge the likes of Michael Connelly and David Baldacci. — Island Books

If you like James Patterson and Michael Connelly, you'll love Michael Carrier. Carrier has proven that he can hang with the best of them. It has all of the great, edge-of-your-seat action and suspense that you'd expect in a good thriller, and it kept me guessing to the very end. Fantastic read with an awesome detective duo—I couldn't put it down! — Katie

Don't read Carrier at the beach or you are sure to get sunburned. I did. I loved the characters. It was so descriptive you feel like you know everyone. Lots of action—always something happening. I love the surprise twists. All my friends are reading it now because I wouldn't talk to them until I finished it so they knew it was good. Carrier is my new favorite author! — Sue

Thoroughly enjoyed this read—kept me turning page after page! Good character development and captivating plot. Had theories but couldn't quite solve the mystery without reading to the end. Highly recommended for readers of all ages. — Terry

Consider writing an Amazon Review?

If you like my books, please leave a short five-star review on Amazon. I would appreciate it! (Note: it is not necessary to have purchased the book from Amazon, only to have an Amazon account.)

This is how I approach writing reviews: When I consider a book I start with what I know about the author. Does he/she write on topics that are of interest to me? Is the book in a genre I like?

I then look inside the book on Amazon. If not dissuaded after having read a portion of it, I proceed.

Once finished, if I did not like the book well enough to give it at least 3 stars overall (with one 5-star element), then I pass on the whole thing. The reviews I write are always 5-star based on the 5-star element(s).

Why would I write a 5-star review of a book that might not in *every* respect be fully worthy of a Hemingway review? Because, I understand that no author becomes successful without a following, and no author obtains a following on the basis of reviews. All a positive review does is help a good author attract a one-time reader. What the author does with a reader from that point on is totally on his shoulders.

✶ ✶ ✶

Here are all my Jack Handler books:

Jack and the New York Death Mask:	Available on Amazon
Murder on Sugar Island:	Available on Amazon
Superior Peril:	Available on Amazon

Superior Intrigue:	Available on Amazon
Sugar Island Girl Missing in Paris:	Available on Amazon
Wealthy Street Murders:	Available on Amazon
Murders in Strangmoor Bog:	Available on Amazon
Ghosts of Cherry Street, and the	
Cumberbatch Oubliette:	Available on Amazon
Assault on Sugar Island,	
Suicide by Jihad:	Available on Amazon
Dogfight:	Available on Amazon
Murder at Whitefish Point:	Available on Amazon
From Deadwood to Deep State:	Available on Amazon
Sault:	Available on Amazon
To China with Love:	Due Spring/Summer '21

Of course, all are also available through the better bookstores